PRETTY SCARS

CD REISS

PRETTY SCARS

PART I
CARRIE

CHAPTER 1

LOS ANGELES - 1995

*M*y palm was sweating.

The Dorothy Chandler Pavilion was full but not hot. I wasn't getting sick. But there I was, in a sleeveless gown, sweating like a schoolgirl with my damp hand holding Peter's on the armrest.

Adam Brate had just drawn his bow across the strings for the final moan of the first movement of the famous concerto we'd all come to hear. *Ballad of Blades*. I knew the piece, and I knew what was next. But he paused. Lit from behind, face obscured by a shadow perfected over years of staging, he was now and always would be the anonymous genius. His body in silhouette, paired with the instrument between his legs, he dominated the concert hall like a giant. The music had molded the space into its own form, then died.

Someone coughed.

And still, Adam Brate sat in the shadows, legs spread, bow poised. This was his piece. A piece I loved, memorized, played loudly when no one was around. It had made him famous, and yet, he stayed anonymous.

My hand got damper with every second that passed. I pulled it off the armrest and put it in my lap. Peter, never one to take a hint, moved his hand to join mine. He squeezed twice to get my attention, then shifted my diamond ring back and forth twice, as if it was some kind of lever.

I didn't look at my husband. I couldn't. My body belonged to the man on stage. I was in the third row, but I was sure his attention found every last person in the auditorium.

Adam Brate shifted his shoulders forward as if starting the next movement. The orchestra behind him laid the first notes, but Brate snapped his bow vertical. The conductor stopped moving, and twenty-two hundred people held their breath. We knew what came next. My mind played the first measures for him.

"What the hell is he doing?" Peter whispered.

Answering would be a waste of time. If Peter couldn't see that the musician was about to turn this entire thing upside down, no explanation would help him.

Adam Brate drew his bow down to the strings and played a single note.

Then another.

And it wasn't *Ballad of Blades*. Or any orchestral composition. He played a Dolly Parton song that I remembered in the voice of Whitney Houston.

"I Will Always Love You."

That was when my sweat turned to tears.

CHAPTER 2

UNIVERSITY OF SOUTHERN CALIFORNIA - 1993

A car screeched behind us right before a man's voice called, "Hey! Miss! Red Hair! Beautiful!"

I turned around when he called me beautiful because that was when I figured out I was Miss and Red Hair, not because that was what I answered to. Andrea turned with me.

"Hello again, Mr. Stravinsky," she purred.

The man chasing us down was around our age, maybe twenty or twenty-one, in worn jeans and boots. USC hoodie. One hand clutched a violin with the bow pressed against the neck, the other held the case. A heavy bag slung over his shoulder bounced on his hip as he ran toward us. We'd seen him in the parking lot across Jefferson, busking outside the University Village food court. He looked as if he'd grabbed his stuff in a hurry.

"We're going to be late," I said even though I had no intention of moving until I found out what he wanted. Professor Richards had his TA lock the doors one minute after the start of class, and I didn't want Andrea to miss Cognitive because of me.

"We have a minute," she said.

When he got to us, he was so out of breath he bent over, gasping.

"Are you all right?" I asked.

"You... you left this... in the..." He held out the hand with the case. A hundred-dollar bill was folded between two fingers. "The wrong bill." He put down the case and held out the hundred.

When I'd given him the money, I hadn't noticed him. The music shut out everything else. Without it, I could see him. His eyes were warm mahogany, and the waves of his dark, unkempt, shoulder-length hair were tinged with the sun.

"No," I said. "It's the right one."

His face twitched for a moment, as if he had to hide surprise, then he smiled. One of his front teeth had a tiny triangle of a chip, and the hairline scar on his square chin got a little lighter. Imperfections, sure, but they only made him look more perfect.

"It's too much," he said. The wind changed direction, blowing his hair into his face. He shifted his head enough to move it to the side, exposing the lines of his tanned neck and the sharp shadows under his jaw.

Funny how I didn't notice how handsome he was while he was playing.

"I've never heard anyone play like that," I said.

"Like what?" His hand dropped a few inches.

Out of the corner of my eye, I saw Andrea look at her watch. There wasn't enough time to describe his music.

"Like they were about to levitate."

He laughed, and it was almost as melodic as what he drew from his violin. "Really"—he held out the money again—"it's my pleasure. A dollar would have been enough."

"Keep it," I said.

Andrea cleared her throat.

I shifted my bag on my shoulder and turned away. "I have to get to class."

"I'm going to throw it away if you don't take it."

"Like hell." Andrea snapped it from him. "I'll stick it in her bag when she's not looking."

"Thank you." He picked up his violin case.

"If you busk again, I'm putting in another hundred, and I'm going to run away so fast you won't catch me."

"I'll catch you. Don't you worry about that."

"What if I don't want to be chased?"

Andrea pulled me by the elbow. "Great. Thanks. Come on."

"Bye," I said, turning with her.

"What's your name?" he called after me.

"Bye," I shouted over my shoulder.

"I'm Gabriel!"

Maybe it was the fact that he didn't press me but offered a piece of himself that erased my reserve. Turning one last time, I saw he wasn't chasing me as if he was entitled to my time. He stood there with his hair flicking in the spring breeze, and I wanted to tell him my name, but I was cautious.

"Bye, Gabriel!"

I had to get to class. I had to finish school. I wasn't in the mood for a sexy musician who could levitate when he played.

"Bye!" He waved and picked up his violin case, but he didn't run after me.

I liked that so much I wished I could stay and talk.

My best friend and I ran to class and made it just before the TA locked the door. We dropped into the seats Andrea's boyfriend, Lenny, had saved for us. He was six-four, skinny and gangly, all elbows, with a long neck and a walnut for an Adam's apple. They had matching horn-rimmed glasses and shared not only a goofy sense of humor but a weird fascination with me. I didn't mind. They didn't want anything from me but my company. Lenny never looked at me with lust or a need to own me. Andrea didn't fly into a jealous rage when I was alone with him for five minutes.

To them, I was me. Carrie Drazen. A normal person who, through no fault of her own, suffered from Pretty Girl Syndrome. Men tripped over themselves for my attention. Women assumed I was a man-stealing siren. Teachers assumed I'd gotten far because of my looks, then cut me more slack than I deserved.

I didn't wear makeup. Didn't spend too much time on my hair. I dressed for the occasion, but there was no hiding the body underneath. I'd bet on the genetic lottery and won and, like most lottery winners, wound up wondering who I'd be if the numbers had come up different.

Being from a super-rich family didn't help. I couldn't complain. Not out loud. But at night, alone, I wondered if anyone with so little suffering in life could ever be a whole person. No one wanted to suffer. My heart broke when we read case studies of traumatized patients. The abused, the refugees, the forgotten. I could sense their suffering. I'd only experienced hurt in the feeling of being valued for what others could take from me. The status of my presence on a guy's arm. The power of money I hadn't earned. Sometimes I wondered if there was anything inside me or if I was no more than a polished shell reflecting what other people wanted for themselves.

Andrea passed me the hundred-dollar bill during the lecture. It was unfolded, and over Benjamin Franklin's face, written in blue ballpoint, was his name and a number. Gabriel. I collapsed it at the creases and tucked it away.

My friend wrote on the left side of her notebook and pushed it toward me. *Are you going to call him?*

To her, the answer should have been yes. I was single. Gabriel was an appropriate age, good-looking, a wonderful musician, and morally upstanding enough to return money he believed was mistakenly given. She thought I'd be crazy not to call him.

Actually, I had no idea what she thought I should do. But I knew what I thought, and I wrote it on the edge of my notebook.

No. I'm not.

And that was that.

Cognitive Psych wasn't the class for distractions. Professor Gannon looked like a slacker with his arms painted in tattoos, but he called on people randomly and mercilessly to make sure we'd read the materials. In the last moments of the class, he was brutal to Andrea, who knew Miller's law but stumbled on the actual capacity of working memory.

"A fourth grader could remember this, Ms. Devonshire. Ms. Drazen?" he called, pointing at me. "Working memory capacity."

Andrea had already done the hard work, and I was left to fill in the detail. "Seven, plus or minus two."

"Correct. Reading for the week is on the board. Please come prepared."

The small auditorium was filled with the sounds of rustling books and murmuring students.

"Asshole," I whispered toward Andrea.

She shrugged.

"Ms. Drazen!" Gannon yelled over the din.

Had he heard me? I sat straight, glanced at the TA for a clue, and got nothing. "Yes?"

"See me after class." He picked up his folder. "Five minutes."

He went out the door behind the lectern. We filed out the other side of the room into the hall.

"Do you think he heard me?" I asked Andrea.

"Maybe."

Lenny shifted his bag on his shoulder. "Don't worry about it. Pretty Girl Syndrome."

"Shut up."

"He probably wants to raise your grade." Lenny took Andrea's books. He was, above all, a gentleman, even when his girlfriend wasn't having it.

"Or ask you out," Andrea said.

Over an off-campus lunch, my Linguistics 202 prof had offered me a TA position I was unqualified for. When I refused, he mentioned a restaurant he thought I'd like, and when I turned down dinner, he threatened my grade. He wasn't a liar. There was no other reason for me to get a C. My parents threatened to take me out of USC, and I was so upset my shame got out of the way long enough for me to blurt out that I would have gotten an A if I'd had sex with the teacher.

I thought they'd be mad at me for leading him on or getting into a position where I had to refuse him. But something else happened. Dad got really quiet. Mom asked to see all the quizzes and tests leading up to the final. They weren't angry. They went from disappointed parents to avenging angels.

The grade was changed, and by the fall, Linguistics 202 had a new professor.

"Do you want one of us to go with you?" Andrea asked, knowing about the entire episode.

"That would be weird," I said.

"Better than a D in Cognitive," Andrea said.

"I'm going to give him the benefit of the doubt."

"Your trust in human nature is both foolish and inspiring," Lenny said. "Let me know if he makes a fool out of you. I'll talk about beating him up before I let cowardice get the better of me."

"You're a good friend," I said. "See you later."

We said our goodbyes, and I went to Professor Gannon's office.

Kevin Gannon shared an office with another faculty member. The desks faced opposite walls with a single window between them. He was in his mid-forties. His tattoos sat in silent contrast to the conservatively cut sandy hair that was beating a retreat from his forehead, and the casual sneakers, jeans, and polo shirts belied the rigors of his coursework.

"Ms. Drazen, sit please." He held out his hand to a chair. "You can close the door."

The door clicked shut, and I sat with my knees pressed together. He spun his desk chair around to face me.

"So," he said, rubbing his hands together. The palms were so smooth and soft they didn't make a sound. "How are you?"

"Fine, and you?"

"Also fine."

"I have Lit 405 at three."

"I don't want to keep you." He tented his fingertips, looking down at them for a moment. "But I wanted to deliver some good news."

"Yes?"

"I recommended you for a Fischer Prize."

My eyes went so wide with excited surprise I could feel my lashes. It was an unexpected honor. "Really?"

"And the nomination was accepted."

His recommendation meant a lot to me, but the fact that it was accepted was huge. I covered my face. I couldn't believe it. Being recommended was wonderful, but being nominated by a board of people I couldn't see and who had never met me just on the basis of my work? I didn't have words. "Oh, thank you!"

"You earned it," he said. "They announce winners in May. Fingers crossed."

"I can't thank you enough."

"You can. But there's one other thing—I don't want to make inappropriate assumptions."

Crap. His change of tone was like getting whipped around on a teacup ride.

"Okay?"

"I saw you before class. I was at the light, and you were walking across Jefferson with Ms. Devonshire."

"We weren't late."

"No, you weren't, but I almost was. I came close to hitting a man who was chasing you. He was carrying a violin."

That explained the screech of tires behind us.

"I'm sorry. I didn't mean to make you late."

"No, no. It's not..." He leaned against the back of his chair, elbows on the armrest. "I stayed in the car and watched to make sure you were all right."

Normally I'd find that creepy, but there was nothing but cold common sense in his manner and voice.

"I'm fine."

"Are you sure?"

"Yes, why?"

"Because you were being chased. It made *me* uncomfortable."

Professor Gannon was so straightforward, so clear, so utterly devoid of weird creepiness that I thought I'd stepped into an alternate universe. The ability to experience social comfort made me uncomfortable.

"It's not a big deal." I shrugged, looking at the old movie posters on the walls. *Casablanca. Now, Voyager. The Birds*, with the black splash of a crow caught in a woman's blond hair.

"You like it?" he asked. "The poster."

"It's strange."

"Have you seen the movie?"

"No, what's it about?"

"A beautiful, intelligent woman with her own mind stops in a small town. She upsets the balance of nature just by existing."

"Really? It looks like it's about crazy birds."

He smiled, then put his hands on his knees, leaning forward as an intro to changing the subject. "So, listen. I understand there's pressure on women students to stay quiet about harassment. That if you just keep your heads down, maybe it'll go away. Sometimes it does. But I want you to know that if this guy was bothering you, or if he's not hearing you say no, that you don't have to put up with it. You can come to me, or you can go to Student Health."

"Okay."

Was he done? Did I have to say something else?

"Good." He stood with the sigh of an aching back or a bad knee and opened the door. I gathered my things. "Don't forget to do the reading."

"I won't."

It wasn't until I was in the hall that I thought of what I had to say. Holding my books to my chest, I looked at him slouching in the doorway in his neat polo shirt and soft shoes. "Thank you for looking out for me."

"No problem."

Andrea was in the hall, holding a slip of paper the size of the ones the staff left in our mailboxes. Her brows knotted when she saw me, and she held up the paper. Gannon had asked to see her as well.

"Don't ruin it, Carrie," Gannon said from behind me. When I looked at him, he winked.

She must have been up for a Fischer as well.

"It's good news," I whispered to Andrea, giving her a thumbs-up.

I practically skipped to my next class, feeling smart and good and worthy. Everything but a reflective shell.

CHAPTER 3

LOS ANGELES · 1995

*Y*ou could tell the tourists from the Los Angeles natives pouring out of the auditorium. The visitors wore sweaters and light jackets. The natives dressed for Antarctica.

As soon as we got outside, Peter draped his coat over my shoulders. I wasn't even cold, but I let him because it made him happy. He looked more like a Midwesterner, and I looked more like an Angeleno.

"Sol's bringing the car around," he said, rubbing his hands together. He was from Encino, after all. A tall, handsome man with broad shoulders and powerful arms that had thin blood running through them.

"Your gloves are in the pockets," I said, twisting around to reach for the side seams.

"It's fine."

"You look cold."

"And you look really beautiful tonight." His gaze was made of pure aesthetic appreciation. It wasn't an unusual expression, and I knew enough to not confuse it with love or respect. That was a different expression entirely—and rarer.

"Don't you wonder why he hides his face?" I asked. "His name is fake. What's the point of anonymity for a cellist?"

"You're so naïve. It's a gimmick. I have a stop to make. Do you want me to drop you home, or do you want to wait in the car?"

It was almost eleven o'clock at night. What could he possibly need to do?

I knew better than to ask.

"How long will you be?"

"Fifteen minutes."

"I'll wait."

"There's Sol. Come on."

Peter took me by the elbow and guided me toward the Bentley, which was just as well. I had plenty to say about who Adam Brate couldn't possibly be.

***

Peter's stop was deep in Downtown LA, on a line of industrial train tracks that curved between a warehouse and a scrapyard. When we turned the corner, two men I didn't recognize got out of a chrome-hubcapped white Honda.

"I'll be back." He pecked me on the lips. "Sol?"

"Yes, sir?"

"If I'm not back in fifteen, call Vlad, then take Carrie home, in that order."

"No problem."

Without looking at me, he got out and closed the door. He and the men exchanged a few words while getting into the Honda, then they were gone, peeling away in the southward direction of the tracks. They turned when the brake lights were dots.

I sighed and leaned back. Peter had late-night meetings all the time. Strange for a banker but maybe not for a banker who worked for my father.

"Some music, Mrs. Thorne?" Sol asked.

"Sure."

He put on a classical station. Stravinsky.

Anyone who said the universe was a cold, insentient garble of atoms and energies was either blind or had never been in love.

Love had brought me to Stravinsky, and when the love died, classical music had stayed.

Seven minutes later, Sol turned on the ignition and put the car in drive. The Honda appeared from the north, headlights off. It stopped a few feet away. Peter got out alone and opened the door next to me. I slid over to make room as the Honda's headlights went on, blinding me for a moment before it made a sharp turn and disappeared.

Sol took off as soon as Peter's door was closed.

My husband put his hand inside my thigh. A lock of hair was brushed down, creating an imprecise fall over his forehead. A line of something—maybe motor oil—curved along his chin. There was something wild about him. Something untamed and dangerous.

"Ready to scream tonight?" he asked under his breath.

I'd seen him like this before, and I knew what he meant when he said he was going to make me scream.

I looked at his hand where it moved up my thigh. The shirt stayed faithful to his wrist, shifting with it, while the jacket was left behind, exposing the crisp white cuff.

A streak of blood was soaking into the fabric.

CHAPTER 4

LOS ANGELES - 1993

The day after a gorgeous violinist chased me across Jefferson Boulevard. to return a hundred-dollar bill, I went to my parents' house in Malibu for my sister Deirdre's thirteenth birthday. The oldest of us, Margie, was there, as well as Leanne, Theresa, and Jonathan, my precocious ten-year-old brother.

My parents were Catholic. Capital-C Catholic. I had been raised to be one of eight obedient, God-fearing, Rome-compliant, redheaded children. I didn't know people lived any other way until college. Not that that changed my behavior or me. My curiosity about other ways to live didn't extend to my conduct.

Declan Drazen was a powerful man. He moved mountains. Brought monoliths to heel. When my sister Fiona was having trouble at our private school, he protected her from expulsion with little more than a meeting with the head of the school and a donation. We—his children—knew the donation was collateral on whatever he'd said in the meeting.

Fiona, who was thirteen at the time, assumed the worst. Threats. Blackmail. Coercion. I didn't. I argued that the school knew she was a good kid. I was convinced Daddy had simply reminded them, laying out his case with facts and compassion. That was what Mom had told me, and I believed her.

Daddy had been born into money and used it for the best interests of his children. Up until my senior year of college, I lived to make my father proud, to take his guidance and obey his rules. That had crumbled so slowly I didn't notice the deterioration until that party.

The kids were playing, and the staff was cutting slim portions of designer cake. I stood on the back patio overlooking the beach, in a cluster with Mom, Dad, Margie, and family friends Gennie and Harry Sackler.

Margie was three years older than me and fifteen years older than Jonathan. She'd benefitted from untrained parents. They'd left her alone to do whatever she wanted, and she'd spent her adolescence screwing up before going to law school. Unmarried at twenty-three. No prospects. Practically a spinster.

They weren't going to make the same mistake with me apparently. That was their official excuse for setting me up with sons of family friends and hovering over my social decisions.

"The Fischer Fellowship is very prestigious!" Gennie Sackler exclaimed after I told the group. "Congratulations!"

"Thanks."

"Honey," her husband said, "he's throwing sand."

They looked over the rail to a length of beach on our property where the children were playing.

Gennie hissed the name of their new nanny. "Excuse us." She and her husband took off down the wood steps.

"I don't think I'll get it," I added.

My mother sipped her second martini. "Well, it's not like you need help paying for grad school." The cuffs of her Chanel jacket had fringe and big gold buttons that clicked on the plate whenever she reached for her drink. We'd all inherited our parents' recessive gene for red hair, but Mom and I shared the bright candy shade you couldn't really get out of a bottle.

"Never turn down money," my father replied, bright blue eyes scanning the party. Declan Drazen had been a wildly handsome young man who was gradually transforming into a wildly handsome middle-aged man. "Especially not under the circumstances."

"What circumstances?" Margie asked.

He didn't answer.

A caterer brought a tray of fresh martinis. Mom took one.

"Yeah," I pressed, "what circumstances?"

My parents looked at each other. Dad's shrug was almost imperceptible.

"We were just concerned," Mom said in her best faux-casual tone. "What if you met someone before you left?"

"Someone? Like?"

"Someone you were interested in?"

I glanced at Margie. Her tongue was jammed into her cheek as if she wanted to stop it from moving.

"Like, a guy?" I asked.

"It would be a shame to leave something worthwhile behind. Don't you think?"

"For something not worthwhile?" I asked in a dead tone.

Apparently sensing my irritation, Mom put her hand on my arm. "Sweetheart, you're not going to *practice*. And these years are the best time to get married. We just don't want you to end up... you know."

"Like me?" Margie interjected.

"I didn't say that." Mom took her hand away in favor of her drink.

"You know what?" I put my soda on the table. "You guys have some messed up priorities."

"Family is the only priority," my father said, stating the oldest proven Drazen fact as he raised his glass to a guest.

"And I'll start one when I feel like it."

I stormed off, staring at the way my feet moved across the

19

floor in pure annoyance. Margie was right behind me, locking the bathroom door as soon as we were in it.

"Why are you following me?"

"You need to calm down," she said. "You know who they are."

I turned on her. "They let you run around with rock stars. You were a groupie or whatever."

"I know. You're different."

I rubbed a speck of mascara from under my eye. "Did they ever tell you who to marry?"

She leaned on the vanity and looked away as if remembering things a century old. "It's complicated."

"What's that mean?"

"It means…" She sighed. "They've taken control when they thought they needed to."

Control? Things between Margie and my parents had been tense for as long as I could remember, but she was implying there had been an incident. A story she hadn't revealed.

"You need to tell me what happened."

I stood straight and ran my fingers through my hair. I didn't feel like taking any more orders. "Why?"

"Because you want to."

I did. I just didn't want to be bossed about it. Margie always knew how to get me to tell her things I wouldn't tell anyone else.

"So, I get here this morning, and Daddy calls me into his office. Mom's sitting on the couch with her legs crossed like she's… I don't know. Like this is some kind of admissions interview. Daddy closes the door and, like, points to a chair. And he sits behind the desk. I felt like I was having a meeting with the dean. So, he starts telling me that I'm an heiress, a member of a certain societal strata. Those words exactly. And though he's been 'generous'—that was his word—in 'allowing' me to date, it's time to think about the kind of man I should marry."

"What did you say?"

"I said I wanted to finish school first. I thought he'd want to hear that, you know? But he frowns. And I'm like, you don't want me to go to grad school? And he says that's fine. He doesn't mind. *Mind*. Right? You're in law school. Does he mind?"

"It's complicated."

I looked at her, waiting for an explanation.

"Finish," she said.

"So, I'm sitting there with my jaw on the floor, and he lays it out. I have responsibilities to my—how did he put it? My family's position. I shouldn't cast the net too wide, he says. There are men who are an appropriate match, but there are a lot more who aren't. And I said, 'Can you tell me what you mean by "appropriate"?' Which led to him basically saying guys from old money. And not to worry, he'd let me know who was good for me."

"And Mom agreed?"

"Quote, 'It's for your own good, sweetheart,' unquote." Dad was uptight and controlling, but my mother's assent had surprised me. She wasn't involved in the business, and Daddy had been clear that he was being all business.

"Is that it?" Margie asked.

"You need more?"

"Here's what I'm going to say," Margie said, leaning toward the mirror to tie her hair in a bun. "And after I say it, that's all I'm going to say."

"You always promise that."

"Yeah." Bracing herself on the vanity, she picked up one foot to restrap her shoe. "This is for your own good."

"I'm going to grad school. That's what's for my own good."

"Right. Obviously." Her heel hit the tiles with a clack. "I meant me telling you what you should know."

"What?" I scoffed. I didn't believe she had anything new to tell me, but Margie was going to say what she wanted regardless.

She got behind me and met my gaze through the mirror. "Have you noticed that since you turned… twelve or so, they… well, Daddy treats you differently?"

"How?"

"The way he looks at you? The way he introduces you to the people he works with? You're old enough now to notice how all this works. I mean, it could have been me, but it wasn't. I'm cute. I have that going for me. But once you came into your own? I guess I was about fourteen and you were eleven. It was obvious you'd be their prize. They stopped treating my reputation like a commodity that needed protecting." She looked away as if remembering something. "To a point, of course. But up to that point, I was free to get into trouble because of you."

"What's that supposed to mean?" I tried to turn to face her, but she held me by the biceps, forcing me to look in the mirror. There were things she wasn't saying. I could see the calculations in her expression.

"It's the nineties, but this family? We live in a fiefdom, and we're leverage. They didn't know how to handle me, but they wanted to. And when they couldn't, it didn't matter because... you. Look at you."

We took stock of my face in the mirror. I was supposed to get something from what I was seeing. Some secret lay there.

"Is this about Pretty Girl Syndrome?"

Margie laughed. "Is that what you call it?"

"Women hate me. Men want to own me. People do things for me, and they don't know why. Blah blah. I'm just trying to live."

"You have an objectively perfect face."

"Whatever."

"Don't let it go to your head. That doesn't make you a good person or particularly bright, even though you are. I'm not saying you're not. But your stock? Looking like that? Way up. That means you have a value that needs protecting."

"And what about you? Why's it all so complicated?"

She stepped aside and leaned on the counter so we could talk without a mirror between us. "Remember the semester I spent in Ireland? You were twelve or thirteen?"

"Yeah."

"Yeah."

"Yeah, what?"

She blinked, biting the corner of her lower lip. "They wanted me away from… someone."

Hiding my shock wasn't an option. They'd sent her away because they didn't like who she was seeing? If she was right and I was somehow more valuable, what would they do to me?

Margie said, "Did you know our mother was basically married off to our father?"

"I know she was young."

Young was an understatement. They couldn't get married in the state of California.

"Where did the Donnelly money come from?" Margie asked. Donnelly was our mother's maiden name.

"Textile mills in North Carolina. Why?"

"Back in the day, Gramps paid his black workers less than his white workers."

"That's gross."

"When Jim Crow ended, the black workers found out and they struck for a union. Because they were cheaper, they were eighty percent of the workforce. Grandpa fought it. He fought to keep the pay as it was, and he fought the union."

"Okay?" None of that surprised me, but I didn't know what it had to do with me.

"He was hemorrhaging money but going broke as a matter of principle. He thought he could last it out, but the unionizers kept coming up with cash flow. They paid the workers, the lawyers, everyone. Money flowed until the mills went into foreclosure. Everyone lost their jobs. Grandpa was insolvent."

"But they had those mills up until last year."

"Right. But what I'm telling you? It's all there in the microfiche. So, what happened?" The question was rhetorical because Margie continued. "I think… no, I know the union and their lawyers… everything was financed by the Drazens."

I blinked as if closing my eyes for a second would make sense of my father—because Drazen money meant my father and no one else—putting money behind the unionization of black workers. Especially in opposition to his future father in-law. It didn't work. I was still confused.

"How can that be? Grandpa would have hated him, but they get along fine. Always did."

Margie nodded. "I'm not sure Grandma and Grandpa Donnelly know. Or Mom either. I'm not telling them, and neither are you."

"I don't know what this has to do with Mom being 'married off' to Dad."

"Before all this happened, Aunt Rose came out to society. Daddy was there, and she had her eyes on him. His name's on her debut dance card four times. After that, he met the family. From that moment, he wanted her little sister, Eileen. Mom. Of course, she was too young. Legally and morally, neither of which Dad concerns himself with. He did what he had to, I guess."

I couldn't connect the dots. "Destroyed her father?"

"So she could marry into Drazen money, which saved the mills."

My father wasn't a righteous man. Religious, maybe. Pious, definitely. But he'd never let ethical proscription get in the way of a good deal or family necessity. When—in a fit of road rage—our sister Sheila had used a tire iron to bust a guy's windshield so she could get at his face, Daddy acted as if whether or not she spent a night in jail was his choice. And when she came back in the morning, it was seemingly her apology to him that made the problem go away. When I was a freshman in high school and Brice March, who was a senior, cornered me in the supply room, putting his hands up my shirt and his tongue down my throat, Daddy said he'd take care of it. He said not to tell anyone. The following Monday, Brice showed up to assembly with a broken nose. I didn't think anything of it until dinner, when Daddy asked how Brice had looked. Even then, I didn't think much. Brice changed schools midsemester. A year later, I saw him at a volley-ball game. When he saw me in the bleachers, his face went white with fear.

"So, wait," I said. "You're saying Daddy made Grandpa broke, then offered to bail them out if he could marry Mom?"

"Yes. He bought her."

Margie wasn't the imaginative one in the family. She didn't make up stories, and she didn't lie. But she was human, and humans made mistakes and assumptions all the time.

"No," I said. "That's crazy."

"Everything is transactional with him. Everything has a set value to be traded. Even us. Especially us."

I scanned the counter for something to do. An activity to occupy my body while my mind raced. But there wasn't a drop of water to wipe or a single object out of place. I snapped my purse closed and slung it over my shoulder.

"I don't know how you even think you know this," I said, opening the bathroom door. The fresh air of normalcy hit me like a winter blast.

"There are ways of finding things out," Margie said. "It's not hard if you know where to look."

"And have you told him this story? Because there could be an explanation. Like maybe he and Mom were in love and the bank-ruptcy was just life. And he and Mom figured they could get permission to get married if he bailed them out. Why couldn't it be that?"

Margie smiled and took my face in her hands. "Don't get sold, Carrie."

I knocked her hands away. She wasn't who I'd thought she was. Couldn't be. "You're deeply deranged. If that's true, our father's a sociopath."

She laughed and picked up her bag off the counter. "He's a lot of things."

When I turned to leave, I saw Jonathan standing just outside the door.

"What's a sociopath?" he asked.

"Look it up," I said before striding back to the party.

CHAPTER 5

LOS ANGELES - 1995

The living room I shared with Peter was wall-to-wall bookcases, but the only books were a dictionary, photo albums, and bound editions of the *Milken Institute Review.* The rest of the shelves displayed photos, global knickknacks, sculptures, and whatever plants didn't grow past the shelf above.

Peter was upstairs showering. Opening the lower cabinet, I reached past his Princeton yearbooks to find mine from USC. They were burgundy leather with gold stamping. One was for the Thornton School of Music. 1993. Still in my dress, I sat on the Queen Anne chair and opened it, cracking the new spine and releasing the thick smell of ink and glossy paper.

USC was huge, and each school had its own book. My picture wasn't in the yearbook in my hand. I'd acquired the Thornton music school yearbook a year after graduation and tucked it in the cabinet, unopened but not forgotten.

Flicking through departments, I found Classical Composition and saw him right away. He was one of a dozen students with a violin tucked under his chin. Gabriel. My Gabriel. He'd pulled his hair back in a knot at the base of his neck to keep it off the body of the instrument. His left fingers pressed the strings down with asymmetrical precision, each knuckle a mountain peak in a jagged landscape. His right hand held the bow with the gentle expertise of a man caressing his lover's body.

Leaning forward, I tried to see his dark eyes. To catch the intensity of an artist simultaneously creating an experience and experiencing his creation. But the closer I got, the more the photo exploded into meaningless specks of ink.

"What are you doing?"

Peter's voice yanked me out of the moment so violently I gasped. He stood three feet away in nothing but a waist-tied towel. His bare feet on thick carpet had made him as silent as an intention.

"I was—"

"What is that?" He pulled the book off my lap.

"It's from college."

"I can see that." He stuck his thumb in the page I'd been looking at while flipping through the rest.

"It's... here." I held out my hands for the book.

He passed it down, standing over me, bare-chested and damp. He showered when he wanted sex, and I hadn't taken the hint and taken care of business in the other bathroom.

"The way he played reminded me of..." I glanced quickly through the italicized names beneath the pictures. "Shelley." I tapped on a violinist with thick tortoiseshell glasses and a French braid. "She played the cello too. Do you remember? From USC? You came to a recital where she played."

"I only remember one woman from that night." He took the book and made a show of inspecting Shelley. Gabriel was one of many inky blobs. He had no reason to turn his attention to Gabriel. None at all. Unless he suspected I was hiding the contents of my heart.

"You met her." I pointed at Shelley's picture. "I was just reminding myself of her last name so I could look her up."

Peter snapped the book shut, losing the page, and handed it back to me. "Is Shelley why you were leaking tonight?"

"Leaking?"

"Sweaty hands. Crying eyes."

"It was the music. You know that's my favorite piece." I wasn't lying. Not entirely.

"Where else were you wet?"

Without trust, sensual questions were no more than filth wrapped around a threat.

I couldn't bear him right after hearing *Ballad of Blades*. That concerto was love, longing, and loss. His hands on me were none of those things. His needs erased beauty and turned it to agony.

"I haven't showered." My excuse would prove inadequate. I was here. This was my life. I'd chosen it and now I had to live it.

"Pull up your dress." He bent over me, a hand on each armrest. His breath was laced with mint toothpaste. "And open your legs."

I did as I was told, pulling the skirt fabric over the tops of my stockings and parting my knees.

"Why were you crying?" he asked in a low, even tone.

"The music was sad."

"You've never cried over a song before."

His hand was cold inside my thigh.

"I have."

"You're supposed to tell me everything."

"I know. I just… I forgot about it until tonight. Shelley played that song—'I Will Always Love You'—at an event. A USC patron fundraiser my father asked me to go to." His icy fingers wove past the crotch of my underwear, and though I tried not to flinch, I failed. "It was so… moving."

When his hand nudged between my legs and found me soaking wet, he smiled. "Did you fuck Shelley? Did you eat her pussy?"

"No, it wasn't—"

He slid two cold fingers inside me. "So, she ate you? Did you sit on a chair with your legs spread and watch her crawl to you? Did she kneel while she sucked your hot, little clit?" He buried his fingers down to the webs. "Did she make you come?"

"I barely knew her."

"Then why are you wet?"

"The tears were for the music. The rest is for you."

"Wrong." He pulled his hand from between my legs and held his wet fingers up like a surgeon after scrubbing. "It's all for me. All of it."

"Yes," I said, skirt hitched, knees apart, wishing away my dread. "It is."

"Get in the shower, my love. When you're clean, I'll give you something beautiful to cry about."

CHAPTER 6

UNIVERSITY OF SOUTHERN CALIFORNIA - 1993

*D*etermined to lose the violinist's number, I spent the hundred-dollar bill in the university bookstore, passing it to the cashier as if it was just another big bill she had to inspect under the light. She didn't say anything about it being defaced before she slid it into the register, and I didn't change my mind and take it back.

Not that I was going to call him. I'd already been accepted to grad school, but I still wanted to graduate with high marks, as if that would prove to my family I had more to offer the world than babies and a happy marriage. I was too busy to go on dates or start a long-distance relationship I couldn't finish. I figured getting rid of the cash was the best way of moving toward my future.

Taking the long way around the escalators, I spent fifteen minutes distracted by a table of art therapy titles, then I went down an aisle of materials for a course it was too late to take until it was so close to class time I had to rush back to the escalators with my heavy plastic bag of books on my wrist.

They swung in an arc as I turned a corner, knocking a bag out of someone's hand.

"Sorry!" I cried.

I looked back.

It was the guy. The money-mutilating violinist. Gabriel. Long and slim with straight shoulders and a disarming smile of surprise. His bag had ripped open, spraying a fan of yellow-stickered sheet music and notebooks all over the industrial carpet.

"Hey," he said. "Hundred-dollar girl."

"Don't call me that."

"Sorry," he said, tossing his ripped bag into a trash can. "I didn't mean to insult you. But you didn't tell me your name."

People were stepping around the spilled books. The mess was my fault. I couldn't leave them there. I got on my knees to pick them up. Out of the corner of my eye, I saw him join me, but I didn't look at him. If I did, my annoyance would drain away, and I wanted to hold on to it as a defense.

Accepting his apology would lead to a conversation that would lead to that warm, buzzy feeling, which would lead to a distraction. Rejecting his apology would be plain rude. So, I said nothing, grabbing his receipt, then piled Philip Glass on top of Bach.

"Hello?" he said.

"Here." I placed the pile I'd gathered on top of what he had, my eyes away from his. "Your bag's ripped. Take mine."

I reached into my bag to empty it, but he put his hand on my arm. "It's fine."

When I twisted away, still looking at the space between his chin and his collar, he pulled back his hand. But avoiding looking at his face meant I focused on his body, from the throat exposed by his open collar to the patch of hair disappearing under his shirt. My mind built a whole from what little I could see.

"I have to go," I said.

"Me too."

I got on the escalator. He was right behind me, books in his arms, hand on the rail near my head. His fingers pushed on the surface in a rhythm, as if they were practicing their movement on violin strings, as if the music was in his muscles, not his mind.

God. What was wrong with me?

I didn't look back, heading for the glass doors. The security guard nodded me through.

The door was half-closed behind me when I heard the guard bark, "Wait."

I turned, thinking he was calling me. But he'd stopped Gabriel.

"Can I see your receipt please, sir?"

Gabriel didn't have a bag, and as the door closed while he shuffled through the books and music, I realized he didn't have his receipt.

He'd have to deal with it. It wasn't my problem.

I was down the steps when I knew I had to at least vouch for him. I'd held his receipt in my hands and put it... where? Looking in my bag, I found two strips of paper. One was for the series of books on autism and Asperger's I'd bought out of sheer fascination. The other was longer. Music. Music. Staff notebook. Music. All discounted.

I ran back to the door. The security guy was on his walkie-talkie, and Gabriel looked as if he wanted to choke him.

"Hey!" I said, holding up the receipt. "I found this in my bag."

"Okay, miss?"

"It's his. We got mixed up."

The guard looked at me suspiciously.

"Look," I said, taking out my receipt. "This one's mine. Books match. This is all music stuff."

He took the first receipt, read it, and went through the confiscated pile.

"Thank you," Gabriel said quietly as the security guard checked each item on the receipt with each item the guy in his custody had tried to take out of the store.

"You're an asshole, not a thief," I murmured.

"An asshole? That's a little harsh."

Maybe. It could be that in trying to avoid getting involved, I'd overcompensated a little.

"Thank you, miss," the guard said when he finished. He handed Gabriel the pile. "Stay out of trouble."

"I didn't do anything."

He hadn't, but the older man had to make a point. "Do we have a problem, kid?"

Men were trouble. All of them.

"Come on," I said, pulling Gabriel's sleeve. Finally, I looked him in the eyes. I couldn't avoid it anymore. A pissing match wasn't getting anyone anywhere. "You're going to be late for class."

He came when I tugged, letting me lead him down the outside steps. But he yanked away at the bottom, giving me a hard stare before turning to walk away.

"Hey!" I shouted.

He stopped. Dropped his shoulders. Looked at the sky. "What?"

I didn't actually have anything to say.

"Nothing. Never mind."

He turned toward me, sun blasting his face into a mask. Students passed between us but didn't break whatever it was that made it so hard to walk away.

"I'm not an asshole."

"Okay."

"And I'm sorry you're not comfortable with your money or your beauty, but that's on you. Not me."

"What? That's…"

Presumptuous.

Disrespectful.

Screw him.

"That's one hundred percent correct." He came closer so passersby couldn't walk in the space between.

"And you!" I shot back. "Hundred-dollar girl? You're not

comfortable with me either. Which means you're not comfortable with yourself."

"Thanks for the therapy session." He said it as a final retort. A goodbye-and-thank-you. But his body didn't obey the tone of his voice.

"You're welcome," I said with the same finality.

"Fine."

"Good."

"Are we done here?" he asked.

Yes. We were done. Very done. "Time's up" done.

"I don't know. Are we?"

"Yes." He twisted his lips to one side as if he was trying to keep words from leaving them, then failed. "For today."

"What's that mean?"

"We're reconvening on the matter tomorrow."

It wasn't a question.

"Really? When?"

"Lunch."

"Well," I said, feeling my control over the situation slip through my fingers, "I'll see you at Heritage Hall at twelve thirty."

"Great. Can you tell me your name?"

"Carrie," I said, intentionally leaving off the last name. Money was money. Drazen money was something else completely.

"See you tomorrow, Carrie."

***

I got to Heritage Hall early and sat on a wooden bench in the shadows. I never thought much about why I always looked for dark corners or why I got uncomfortable sitting in one place for long. People noticed me, and I didn't like it. I hadn't asked why I didn't like it or why it mattered.

The California sun shot dusty beams through the windows, laying bright oblong slabs on the marble floor. Slim pedestals lined the center of the entry hall. Heisman Trophies, busts of famous coaches, jerseys with retired numbers sat on them, brass plaques describing the athletic or strategic feats they'd accomplished.

As usual for lunch, students streamed in. They didn't look like the students in my department. They were taller. Wider. Tighter. They came in knee braces and school jerseys. They didn't carry as many books but hauled duffel bags of gear. I liked watching their power and grace. Special creatures built to be gladiators but consigned to sports in a time of peace.

As he came in, Gabriel was almost mowed down by a refrigerator of a man who, with split-second reflexes, kept him from falling. There was laughter and an apology. Gabriel picked up the instrument case he'd almost dropped and scanned the hall for me as if I were one of the trophy pedestals lit by the angles of the sun.

In Heritage Hall, it was obvious he wasn't a gladiator, but he was power and grace just the same. He owned the space he was in, with broad shoulders and a way of moving that dared defiance and dismissed it at the same time.

I stood in the light and waved. He came toward me with an easy gait and easier smile.

"So," he said.

"So. Second session."

"What are we talking about?"

"Your criminal past," I said with a smile.

"Trying to take my own stuff out of the store without a bag."

"That. And defacing money. That's a federal offense, by the way."

"Benjamin Franklin would approve."

"I hear he was an asshole too."

In the single breath of time that followed, we looked at each other. His expression was empty, receptive yet open, all pretense gone. The room that had, seconds before, been a hollow echo chamber of voices and footsteps went silent. An indistinct haze blanketed the sharp sunlight, putting all of it outside my attention. My body relaxed, and my mind emptied.

I recognized him not from my past, but from my unwritten yet certain future.

He cleared his throat, summoning back the curse of normalcy. "I've never been in here before." He turned his gaze to the trophies and majestic space.

"It's the only decent lunch on campus."

"Really? How did I not know about it?"

"It's kind of a secret. They only serve athletes. But one day I was starving, and I wandered in here. They fed me. If I'm on this side of campus, I stop in. It's not a problem."

"Huh," he said, turning toward the line of gladiators showing ID cards at the entrance to the cafeteria. "Well, I guess we should go in, then."

We went to the back of the line. His violin case took up as much room as a loaded duffel but was the subject of suspicious glances.

"ID, please," the middle-aged woman behind the table said before she looked up. "Oh, hey, Red."

"Hi, Tia."

"Who's this with you?" She bent over to see his case.

"He's—"

"Band," Gabriel interjected.

Tia glanced at me, then Gabriel, then me again. I smiled.

"Tri-tip today," she said. "And the lemonade is fresh-squeezed."

"Thank you!" I went into the cafeteria.

"Thanks!" Gabriel added before following me in. "How did you do that?"

"Do what?"

"That. Get in here by smiling?"

"Where's scowling going to get me?" I handed him a porcelain plate. He bounced it as if checking its weight. "Are you a vegetarian or anything? They always have a veggie option if you ask."

"No. I like meat."

I put a chunk of tri-tip on his plate, then another.

"I can do it," he said, reaching for the tongs of the next chafing dish.

"I know." I got to the tongs first. "Do you like vegetables?"

His hand was still out. He didn't want to be attended like a guest.

"I invited you here," I said. "I serve."

He dropped his hand. "Next time, I'll do the inviting."

"Fair." I loaded his plate with grilled vegetables. Risotto. Rosemary potatoes. I wanted to give him everything.

"I'm good," he said.

"Sorry."

"No, it's fine. Where do we pay? I'm buying."

"No."

"Look, you already invited me and served me. Let me get lunch."

I shook my head. "It's free. Come. This way."

I led him to the outdoor patio and around a corner to a metal table that was always empty. He slid onto the bench across from me and unwrapped his silverware, watching as I plucked mine from the center of the napkin roll.

"Cloth napkins," he said, laying one on his lap. "It's like an alternate universe."

"A lot of money in college sports."

I waited for him to try his first bite. I wanted him to like it. I'd never craved anyone's approval as much as I wanted his.

"Wow, this is delicious."

As soon as I had the approval, my overriding compulsion was to diminish it. "It's good food." I shrugged. "But it all comes out the same."

His laugh was so sudden he almost spit out his tri-tip. "I didn't know you'd be funny."

"I'm not really."

He smirked and chewed at the same time. He had mischief in

him. "I've passed this building a hundred times. Had no idea there was distribution of free food for the physically gifted."

"Wander without a purpose and you'll find new destinations."

"That from a brochure?"

"Sure. You like it?"

"Love it. Keep feeding me like this and I'll travel wherever they want me to go."

"Even if it's across campus?"

"Especially if it's with you."

I was complimented all the time. Sometimes the compliments were sincere. Sometimes they were meant to ask a question or a favor. Often, they revealed a hidden motivation. Gabriel was saying he enjoyed my company and revealed no more than that he wanted it more often.

After I paused too long, he asked, "Was that too forward?"

"Well, I just…" There was no reason not to be completely honest. "I'm going to Duke for my master's."

"Congratulations."

"Thanks. So. I'm really not into anything that's going to get in the way of that. If you want to be friends, I can do that. But right now, I want to graduate and go to North Carolina without attachments."

"No time for charming musicians."

"No."

"Even a charming asshole musician who won't distract you?"

"I haven't met such a person." I popped a forkful of meat between my lips.

"There's a charming asshole musician right in front of you."

"I meant one who wouldn't distract me."

He raised his eyebrows a bit, then put his eyes on his plate to cut a corner off his tri-tip. "Future me is congratulating present me for doing such a good job."

"Of what?"

"Not distracting you in the last months of school and saying a really heartfelt but final goodbye after graduation." He chewed thoughtfully.

I watched him, wondering if I could have a casual relationship with him before a heartfelt and final goodbye.

"He won't tell me how the final concert went," he said.

"Future me loved it," I played along.

"Thanks for coming."

"Thanks for inviting me. You were brilliant."

"I didn't play."

"Really? Why?"

He shook his head quickly. "Scratch that. I remember now. I spotted you from the stage. Did you see me wink?"

"I thought you were winking at the girl behind me."

"That was my sister."

"You have a sister?"

"Nah." His fork scraped against his teeth from smiling and eating at the same time. "My mother's only child is a rogue artist."

"Ah."

"You?"

"Me? Six sisters and a brother."

"Holy... wow. You're never lonely, then."

"It's a big house."

He speared a slice of grilled zucchini and ate it with delightful gusto. Did he do everything with such passion? Or was the food that good?

"I'm at Thornton." He jabbed his fork eastward. "Right that way a bit. You wandered into Heritage Hall one day, so you must be close." He looked at the sky as if trying to recreate the campus map in his head. "Film school's just over there. You seem like the scholarly type so... critical studies?"

"Nope. Psych. Other side of campus. But I walk around a lot. Listen to music. Feel the breeze. Get a little sun. You know."

"I do."

A shadow fell over him. We both looked up at the source—a

tall guy who'd walked right out of douche central casting, complete with side-parted blond hair and a keen sense of who was eligible for the free meal and who was squatting.

"I hear you're in band?" he said to Gabriel.

Band meant marching band. Nutcracker uniforms. Drums on suspenders. Shiny brass horns whipping side to side. Marching band practiced on the game field every day in the off-season. You could hear the conductor berating them through a megaphone all the way to the library.

"Yeah." Gabriel put down his fork and wiped his mouth.

"Haven't seen you on the field."

"We should go," I said into some invisible void where female voices went when men were escalating situations.

"You haven't been paying attention," Gabriel said, standing.

They were about the same height, but Band Guy had more Band Guys behind him. Gabriel had me.

They leaned into each other. We were going to have to run for it. I picked up my bag and the violin case.

Band Guy snarled, "I know every guy on that field."

"Obviously." Gabriel pulled out his wallet and broke eye contact to poke into it. "Obviously you haven't been doing this very long." He took out a card and showed Band Guy, who snapped it away.

"What the fuck is this supposed to be?"

"It's Sammy Daniels's student ID. You know who Sammy Daniels is, right?"

"I do, and it's not you, fucktard." He flicked the card at Gabriel. It hit his chest and landed on the ground.

"We should go," I said, laying my hand on Gabriel's arm. My request was lost in the sea of ambient testosterone.

"No, if I were Sammy, I'd be in baby lit, reading from the seventh-grade canon. He was this close to getting kicked off the march of the wooden soldiers. I tutored him."

"And you stole his ID."

"When I wouldn't write his essay for him, he spilt so fast he left it behind. I've been hanging on to it for him. Now you can pick it up off the ground and deliver it."

"Hey, Chad," a stocky guy said from behind the side-parted blond, "I remember this dude. He tried out for the arrangement assistant."

"Oh, yeah." Chad nodded, turning down the aggression half a notch. "Yeah, the arrangement was pretty all right. Kind of gay but not bad."

Gabriel leaned against the table, arms crossed. "I'll take that as a compliment."

Seeing an opening, I bent down for Sammy's ID and handed it to Chad. "Here. We'll just finish lunch and go, okay?"

Chad averted his gaze to me, and more aggression drained away. I gave him a smile meant to demilitarize a situation. It would work with another little push.

"I know he shouldn't be here. Officially. But he's with me, so we'll just eat." I knew he wouldn't ask me to prove to security that I belonged in the athlete's cafeteria.

Chad took the card.

"Thanks," I said with an appreciative meek smile.

Behind him, his group broke up, finding a table by the door.

"Come on, man," Stocky said.

"Cool, cool." Chad seemed confused by his own compliance.

Gabriel had clearly caught on to Chad's need for a face-saving way out. "Say hi to Sammy for me. Tell him I'm glad he passed. I knew he could."

Chad was pulled away, still confused.

"I'm not hungry," I said.

"Me neither." Gabriel took his violin case from me. "Let's get out while the getting's good."

We put our trays on the bussing station and stepped out onto Watt Way. The sky was clear and blue right down to the horizon, and the air was still and crisp from last night's rain.

"Do you have to get to class right away?" he asked.

"Not until two fifteen."

He leaned into me while we walked, and when the crowd separated us, we maneuvered back together like opposite magnetic poles. We reached a grassy patch where groups of students clustered together.

"There's a shady spot," he said, stopping.

"Let's grab it."

He put his case and bag by the oak tree and shrugged out of his leather jacket. He laid it on the grass for me and held out his hand for my bag.

"Jesus," he said when he took the full weight of the bag. "You minoring in rocks?"

I laughed and sat on his jacket. He set my bag by his violin case against the tree.

"I'm minoring in abnormalities," I said.

"You going to listen to people's problems all day?"

I tucked my legs under me. He put his back to the tree.

"Probably not. I'm just curious about it. People. How they think."

"You'd be great at it."

"How do you know?"

"I saw what you did back there," he said.

"I just made a suggestion."

"You cast a spell over him. You going to do that with your patients?"

I shrugged, plucking at the grass. He was right in one way. In another, he had it all wrong. "It would be a good career, I guess. My friend Lenny's all about social change—one patient at a time. He's a really good person. He and his girlfriend, Andrea, they want to open a practice together to help kids in poor neighborhoods. I'd feel... weird doing something like that."

"Why? You wouldn't feel safe?"

"No, nothing like that." The grass was taking a beating, so I

brushed it straight before I did more damage. "My family has…
we've done well. I'd feel like an impostor or something. Saying I
understood when, really? I can't. Ever."

"So, you really meant to put that Benny in my case?"

"I told you I did."

"I thought you wanted to get rid of me more than admit a
mistake."

"That says more about you than it does about me."

He smiled and nodded a little, looking away. His profile was
just short of perfect, with a strong chin and a slight bump in his
nose that added masculinity to a face almost too pretty to be real.
"Touché, Carrie. Touché. I bet your friends don't get away with
shit around you."

Men had called me beautiful and perfect more times than I
could count, but this compliment—that I saw clearly and judged
well—made me blush.

He rummaged through his bag and came out with two cans of
soda. "Nabbed these from Heritage Hall."

"Slick. I didn't even see you take them."

"Coke or Sprite?"

"Sprite."

He cracked it open and handed it to me.

We tapped our cans like wine glasses and drank. I watched
how he tipped the opening against his lips and poured, closing his
eyes so his long, black lashes brushed against his cheek.

"Where did you learn to play, Slick?"

"Chicago. I'm from Chicago. I'm a card-carrying Midwestern
boy. I had a choice: piano or violin."

"You chose well," I said, remembering the day I first saw him
busking.

"I didn't choose. I love both. All of them. My mother could
only afford one instrument, so I picked violin. Officially. She got
me lessons once a week. Mrs. Forte came to the house. I saved up
and got a thirty-two-note keyboard from Goodwill. Every week,

after Mrs. Forte left, I learned piano from library books, and Mom let me take cello and music theory in school."

"Your mom sounds pretty cool."

"I was supposed to be a lawyer like my father. Or a doctor would have been acceptable. She wasn't paying a cent for music school. I got a scholarship so she doesn't have to."

I had questions. If his father was a lawyer, why could his mother only afford one instrument? Where was he in all this? But objective facts took a backseat to emotional truths. "Is she mad?"

"Yes and no. Mostly yes. That's why I have to be the face of success." His eyes dropped to the ground, then rose up my body, lingering everywhere and nowhere in particular, as if everything he saw was equally pleasing. He landed on my eyes and stayed there, disarming me. "Can I play you something?"

"Sure."

He grabbed his case and snapped it open. "Promise you won't drop a Benjamin?"

"I only have twenties."

He lodged the instrument under his chin. "I wrote this." He ran the bow over the strings and adjusted the knobs. "You'll want to drop all of them."

"I'm withholding judgment," I lied. I wanted to like it as much as I liked him.

His fingers touched the knobs so slightly I couldn't imagine anything had actually changed. But his ear was tuned, and he found his pitch. He made a final adjustment and brought out a long, mournful note.

"Okay, here goes," he said, checking me with a smile before dropping his gaze and giving all his attention to his instrument.

His fingers articulated on the bow with gentle power. He slid it against the strings like a call to attention, turning it into an invitation, gathering the space around him in the rhythm of a gentle mandate. A plea and a demand layered with the promise of splendor. The air vibrated with music, trembling in his hands, under his control. The notes blossomed into grandeur with such precision they sneaked up on me, elevating my heart from tight expectation into the release of a promise kept.

The music drowned out even my attention on the way he moved, veiling my sight with the hum of the tender conclusion, cupping me in his care and dropping me back to earth.

When it was done and he looked up, the circles of students all applauded with me. He got up, held his arms out with bow in one hand and violin in the other, and bowed.

I didn't keep the time, but it couldn't have been more than four minutes. It felt like a lifetime had gone by.

"That was great," I said when he sat back down.

"Glad you think so." He finished his Coke. "Unfortunately, it wasn't good enough."

"What do you mean?"

He shrugged, but obviously the thing he was trying to shrug off stuck to him. "It didn't get picked for a solo."

It seemed impossible that another piece of music could have been better, but I didn't know anything about anything. I only had ears and a heart. "Why not?"

"My piece was too... what did they say? Wait." He snapped his fingers as if trying to remember but made it an act. He'd memorized it. "'Too experimental for the audience.'"

"That's kind of a compliment."

"Well, I'm not doing the recital at all." He put the violin and bow away as if every movement was a punctuation on the end of his decision. "This isn't the required show. My mother can get her ticket refunded."

"I'm sure she wants to see you anyway."

"I haven't told her yet. But I'm not asking her to come all the way here so she can watch me sit with the orchestra and play someone else's piece. The entire Thornton School of Music can kiss my ass." He snapped the case closed, locking his disappointment away for safekeeping.

"You should play," I said.

"Why? They're fine without me. They have enough strings." He pretended he didn't care while daring me to convince him.

"Who got the solos? Anyone you know?"

"We all know each other. My good friend Shelley, and I'm happy for her. I'll go to the concert and clap for them, but especially her."

"She needs you behind her, not in front."

He tapped the case, looking at me, holding my stare. He pressed his lips together so hard that when he relaxed them, they were pink. "You're doing it. That thing."

"What thing?"

"Making me want to do what you say, to make you happy."

"I'd like to see you up there in the orchestra. It would make me very happy."

He considered. I sensed an opening for a changed mind. Without thinking, I put my hand on his. It was warm from playing, heated from the inside, yet frozen still from the surprise of my gesture. After a second, he moved his calloused finger over my palm, leaving a path of shuddering nerves in its wake.

"And I bet your parents would like to see it too," I added.

"My father's gone..." He spaced out for a split second before continuing. "Cancer." He waved his free hand as if he knew unwanted condolences were coming, then placed it over mine. "I have an extra ticket if you want."

"I can get my own ticket."

"It's already sold out."

The Drazen Foundation donated enough to the university to guarantee any of us a spot at any event we wanted, from fifty-yard-line seats at a championship game to John Williams fundraising concerts. I wasn't ready to tell him my family name or explain the dynamics of our money. Once I did, everything would change.

"Trust me, if you play in the orchestra, I'll be there." I gently squeezed the hand under mine. "Will you?"

"Maybe." He leaned closer to me, hands still sandwiching mine. "I'll go anyway. Just to spite you."

"You wouldn't."

"I would." I leaned into him enough to catch his scent of sanded wood.

"Not to spite me," he whispered. "You're manipulative, but you're not malicious."

I should have been insulted, but I wasn't. He spoke truth without judgment.

"You don't know me."

"That doesn't make me wrong." He was so close I could feel his breath on my lips.

"Test me." My words were no more than an exhale of affirmation.

Too soon. It was too soon. We had a few hours between us. Barely a date. And already I was almost kissing him on campus grass, wishing we were alone.

I didn't do this. He was a stranger. His mouth might fit on mine like a puzzle piece, and he might taste the way I imagined sex would, but I didn't know him.

I shifted away from him. "I'm sorry. I have to get to class."

"Sure, sure."

We stood. The weight between my legs moved half a second more slowly, as if subject to different physical laws.

"Can I walk you?" He handed me my bag. "I can carry this tonnage."

"No, I'm fine." I slung it over my shoulders.

He picked up his jacket. "Can I call you?"

"You'll play orchestra?"

"Is that the price of seeing you again?"

"Yes." I dug around my bag and came out with a pen. I clicked the top. "Give me your hand."

48

He held it out, and I wrote my number on the palm.

"I'll try not to sweat." He grabbed his case and stepped back.

"Try." I stepped back.

"Okay, then." Another step back. "This is a heartfelt but not final goodbye."

Why was it so hard to walk away? It was as if there was a string between us and every step pulled it tighter. How far could we go without snapping it?

The only way to know was to turn and walk to class.

I waved, turned, and walked. When I was on the brick path, following traffic to my methods class, I looked over my shoulder. Gabriel was standing there, watching me go.

Professor Gannon passed him, waving to me with his tattoo sleeves exposed to the spring air. "Hey, Carrie." He looked back at Gabriel. "Am I interrupting?"

"No."

"You going to Mudd? I'll walk with you."

"Okay."

With a last wave, Gabriel walked toward Thornton, keeping the string that connected us safe.

CHAPTER 7

LOS ANGELES · 1995

"*M*rs. Thorne." Aiden Klerk slid into his chair. His English accent gave him an air of easy competence, and his gray hair spoke of decades in the business of unearthing secrets and protecting the wealthy. He'd agreed to see me the same afternoon I called. The office was so close to the airport the scream of landing planes was constant background noise. "What brings you?"

"I understand you know how to be discreet."

The insides of my thighs ached where Peter had bruised me the night before. He didn't always hurt me, but when he did, it was to prove a point. I was his. Other men might look at me, but I was his alone. A musician might move me to tears, but he owned my orgasms. The previous night, we'd seen Adam Brate. When Peter sensed a part of my heart belonged to the ghost of another man, he'd claimed me with unusual brutality.

"Depends on the assignment."

"Have you heard of the composer Adam Brate?"

"Not much of a music person myself."

"He's famous for a three-movement concerto called *Ballad of Blades*."

"That rings a bell, but I haven't heard it." He didn't shrug, but his tone was the equivalent.

"In a few years, he's going to be as famous as Yoyo Ma, but he doesn't show his face. No pictures. No interviews. No one knows his real name. He came out of nowhere."

"Sounds like he doesn't want to be found."

"Does that matter?"

"Not to me. But it matters to him. What I don't know is why it matters to you."

The abrasions at my elbows where Peter had tied me down were covered, but I tugged my sleeves anyway. "It does, and that's all you need to know."

"Not if you want me to find him. I don't work in the dark, Mrs. Thorne." His crystal-blue eyes were noncommittal. He didn't need another client. He wasn't desperate or hungry. I needed to appeal to his curiosity to convince him to take the job, but the novelty of knowing a musician's identity wouldn't cut it.

"This conversation is confidential. I need your word."

"You have it."

"Not my husband or family."

"Your maiden name is Drazen? Right?"

"Right."

He put his elbows on the desk and folded his hands in front of him. "Full disclosure, your father has hired me before."

I cleared my throat. Nothing came out.

He waited.

"It's not a problem," I finally said.

"Good."

A deep breath later, I began, "I have reason to believe his name is Gabriel Marlowe, and he's supposed to be dead."

CHAPTER 8

LOS ANGELES - 1993

I found out later that the Thornton School's composition recitals didn't just attract family. Film and TV music supervisors came to see what new talent was doing. They were known to buy original pieces right there, which explained some of Gabriel's disappointment when his piece wasn't chosen.

"I didn't know you were so interested in classical music," Daddy had said when I asked him to get me tickets to the spring concert. I'd called him from the phone in my apartment the same day I'd sat with Gabriel in the grass.

"A friend of mine is playing."

"Who would that be?"

Daddy could hold his tone in check, but there was no hiding the piqued interest or underlying suspicion. If I said Gabriel's name, he'd assume romantic interest, and he'd be right.

Instincts are unconscious calculations of minute data acquired from learned experience. They're your body telling you what your mind hasn't consciously analyzed. So, when my skin tingled and my lungs constricted at the thought of telling him I wanted to see a guy named Gabriel Marlowe, I knew something wasn't quite right.

"Shelley. I don't think I've mentioned her."

"I look forward to meeting her, then."

"You're coming?" The tingle on my skin turned to sweat.

"Of course. Do you want to bring a friend?"

The tickets were so scarce I hadn't anticipated bringing anyone, but a buffer wouldn't hurt. "Andrea. You remember her?"

"I do. I'm bringing someone I want you to meet."

My breath exited my lungs, and I forgot how to replace it. Daddy often brought business associates over for dinner. He sat them next to my older sister, Margie, who spent those meals rolling her eyes and cutting the men apart with a wit so sharp they didn't feel the blade. Daddy used to sit me across from his guests, as I was the next oldest, but when Trevor Stoneman spent the meal ignoring my sister and staring at me, the next dinner had me sitting out of the line of sight of Brandon Wein. Which was just as well since he wound up in prison for mail fraud.

"Who?" I asked.

"I'll see you there."

I hung up wishing I hadn't promised Gabriel I'd go.

***

"Thank you," I said to Andrea in the Bing Theatre lobby before the show. The event was formal. I was in a soft-pink evening dress I'd worn to a LACMA event in January and heels so high I'd instantly regretted them.

"You don't have to thank me. It gave me an excuse to wear this again." Andrea twirled in her corseted Victorian-style red gown that would have looked like a costume except for the black boots and hand-knit rainbow scarf. Her hair was tied in little knots with scraps of gingham fabric. Somehow, it all worked.

"Now remember," I said. "We're here to see Shelley."

"Right." She sipped her whiskey sour from the skinny red

straw. "Second solo. Your friend. Not the hot violinist who returns hundred-dollar bills."

"Yes."

"Why can't you tell your father about him?"

"There's nothing to tell. Half a kiss."

"You can tell him he's your friend."

"No." I poked my club soda. "I can't."

"Why?"

"He'll know. Daddy. He'll know Gabriel isn't just a friend, and he's not appropriate for me."

"What does that mean?"

"It means..." I didn't want to verbalize my instinctual reaction, but Andrea wouldn't accept anything less than my deepest doubts and fears. She was a frustrating friend sometimes. "It means my father is really into how things look. Gabriel isn't one of us. He's not... Money is a thing. A real thing to my family. It's messed up, I know. And he's an artist. Artists don't fly. They're not stable. So, I can tell... I can just tell it's going to set Daddy off. We're going to opposite sides of the country after graduation, so I don't think causing a problem is worth it."

Andrea swirled the ice at the bottom of her glass. "Carrie, that's really fucked up."

"Everyone has a cross to bear, I guess." Not wanting to get sneaked up on while discussing my family burdens, I scanned the room. "He's here."

Dad was already on his way. Six-four, mid-forties, in a custom suit, my father was the epitome of the distinguished older gentleman even without the auburn hair graying at the temples.

"You look like him," Andrea said. "Who's the guy he's with?"

The man laughing with my father as they wove across the lobby was in his early thirties. Another custom suit over broad shoulders. Charcoal with an aubergine tie and gold clip. He had perfect teeth, a dimple in his chin, perfectly parted sandy-brown hair, and when he saw me across the room, his smile faded into something more resolute.

"Carrie," Daddy said, then kissed my cheek. "This is Peter Thorne."

When I shook his hand, Peter met my gaze, and his topaz-brown eyes went as comforting as a predator's as it moved to soothe its prey.

***

The concert was fine. The music was fine. We sat in the third row, four across, with me between Peter and Andrea. I'd never been so uncomfortable in my entire life.

In the lobby before the starting bell, my father had recited Peter's resume as if he was looking for a job. Peter was appropriately modest about his millions, or maybe even billions, in banking. Daddy was appropriately immodest about my acceptance to Duke. And when Daddy made sure we filed into the row in a certain order, I knew that more than the seating was being arranged.

There was nothing wrong with Peter. Not on paper. He was handsome and respectful. As the first solo composition was introduced, he kept his hands in his lap and didn't spread his legs past the boundaries of his seat.

But when Gabriel saw me from the front row of the string section and sent a smirk my way, I resented the banker's presence. He was taking up space in my mind where I wanted to hold the sight of fingers expertly pressing the strings and a jawline stretched to hold a violin in place. Gabriel was in time with the section, doing the job of supporting the solo without adding the flair I knew he was capable of. My smile after Shelley's piece didn't go unnoticed. I caught Peter looking at me with a sense of satisfaction that wiped the smile right off my face.

In twenty-plus years, I'd never told my father no. Not even as a toddler.

First time for everything.

***

There was a reception after the concert, but all I wanted to do was get out of there.

"Let's get dinner," Daddy said as we filed out the center aisle, and suddenly I didn't want to get out so quickly.

Peter was looking at me, gauging my reaction. "I think Carrie wants to hang out with her friends."

"We can go to Tristan's," Daddy argued. "Andrea, can you join us?"

"Sure!" she said from behind me.

"There. She'll be with her friends."

Peter leaned down and whispered to me, "Don't worry. I won't let him drag you out."

His smile was comforting, and his slight nod promised he knew I felt trapped. He understood, and he was going to take care of it.

The press of bodies continued to the lobby. The orchestra members were already out and clustering with family, instruments slung over their shoulders or tucked under their arms. I looked for Gabriel but didn't want to find him.

Instead, we ran right into Shelley, who I recognized from seeing her on stage.

She had two long brown braids and glasses that made her eyes look huge. I walked into her while trying to find a guy I needed to avoid.

"Sorry," was all I had.

She nodded and turned away as if she didn't know me. Which she didn't.

"Hey," Peter said. "Isn't this who you came to see?"

Technically, yes. Actually, no.

"She's busy," I said. "I'll see her later. So how do you know my father?"

"We've done some business together." He shrugged as if it was nothing. "I love orchestral music. I think he's trying to seduce me into a deal. What do you think?"

I cast my eyes around for my father and Andrea. They were chatting by the doorway as people filed out. "I think a concert shouldn't change the terms."

"You're wise beyond your years."

The compliment washed over me like a warm bath on a cold day. My cheeks tingled, and I turned away. Gabriel was two steps away, working against the flow of traffic to get to me.

"We should—" I didn't have a chance to finish.

"Carrie," Gabriel said with a radiant smile and glittering eyes. "You came."

"I did. Hey, Gabriel, this is Peter. He's a friend of my family."

He measured Peter like a young lion deciding if it was time to take on the pride alpha. Peter was handsome, older, wealthier, and in no way a threat for my affections. But you wouldn't have known that from the way Gabriel shook Peter's hand, keeping his gaze on Peter's as if he needed to let him know I was territory he'd defend.

"Gabe," a woman said from behind him. She was short with a straight, black bob. Over an unremarkable navy jacket, she'd wrapped an Hermès scarf so precisely the brand showed at center front. "Who is this?"

"Mom," he said, letting his hand slip away. "This is Carrie. And Peter."

He introduced me as if he'd mentioned me before. I took her hand. It was bird-boned and heavy with silver rings.

"Nice to meet you. My son forgets my name is June."

"Hi, June."

"It was so nice of you to come and see Gabriel play in the orchestra. Could you see him from your seat?"

"I could."

"Did you hear the good news?" she asked.

"Ma, really?"

"What?" I loved good news as much as the next person.

"You didn't tell her," she said to him in mock surprise. "He's so modest. He's a finalist for a Caruso Fellowship."

"Yeah."

I had no idea what a Caruso Fellowship was. "That's great!"

"National prize," she said. "For new artists. He'll study in Italy for the summer and stay on to play in the orchestra at Teatro La Fenice." She put her arm around Gabriel's waist and squeezed him close. "That'll show them who to pick for a solo."

"That's amazing!" I exclaimed, trying to keep the wedge of disappointment out of my words. I'd be in North Carolina, a million miles away, but we'd agreed to part ways after graduation for good reason. I couldn't hold him.

"Congratulations," Peter said with a smirk.

Gabriel's jaw set. "Thank you." He practically growled it.

"Well," I said to break the tension, turning my attention to June, "I bet you'll miss him."

"He'll be back," she said, putting a hand on his shoulder. "Won't you?"

"Yes." He and Peter were still eye-fighting.

"Carrie"—my father's voice came from behind me—"are you coming?"

I had answers. *Yes, we're coming.* Or, *Please meet my friend Gabriel and his family.* Even, *I'm not feeling well, and I have to skip Tristan's.* But I watched June's face change from benignly pleasant to attack-ready. I shot Gabriel a look, but his eyes were on my father's face.

"Dad, this is my friend." My words tripped on the thickness in the air.

"You," June hissed.

"Ma." Gabriel put his hand on her arm.

"You son of a bitch." She let her son hold her body, but her words would not be leashed so easily.

I was confused. What was happening? Without knowing the details, I didn't have the tools to smooth it over.

Daddy was unruffled. Placid, even. "It's been a pleasure. Shall we?"

He turned and went for the door. Andrea took my hand. I tried to will Gabriel to notice me, but he was completely focused on his mother. I didn't know what he thought, and the hole in my knowledge sucked my attention down it.

Andrea pulled me. Peter waited until I was on the way out before he followed, creating a human barrier between me and the woman who looked as if she wanted to scratch out my father's eyes.

"What the hell was that?" Andrea murmured as we walked out.

"I don't know."

The limo driver opened the back door, and we slid in.

"Dad," I said after the door closed. He and Peter sat across from Andrea and me. "Do you know that woman?"

"I know lots of people. Some of them don't like me. Comes with the territory."

"What territory is that exactly?"

"No matter what you do, when you have things other people don't, they're going to resent you. They're going to blame you for their own failures. Get used to it."

"So, you know her?"

"Carrie, if I let everyone's opinion of me ruin my dinners, I'd have starved long ago."

Peter laughed gently. Andrea too.

He was right, in a way. You can't control what people think of you.

But why?

I couldn't let it go without knowing why.

***

After dinner and before dessert, I slipped away to the bathroom and stopped at a pay phone to call Gabriel. Six rings, then his message machine beeped.

"Hey, Gabriel. It's Carrie. I'm just calling to tell you I thought you were great and um… see if everything's okay? That was weird. Okay, bye."

As I hung up, Peter came down the hall.

"Are you all right?" he asked.

"Yeah. Just checking in on a friend."

"I was wondering." He cleared his throat and shuffled his feet as if he were a much younger man. "You. Well, you're very beautiful."

Crap. I'd hoped the silent pissing match between him and Gabriel had been a misinterpretation on my part.

I put on the mask of benign disinterest I'd perfected for when men I didn't want asked me out. "Thank you."

"And smart. I'd like to see you sometime. Get to know you better."

"That would be nice, but I'm leaving for school in August. I'm not dating right now."

His smirk didn't have even a shade of disappointment. It was an expression of cockiness, as if I'd come around eventually, and I was familiar with it. A guy like that didn't take no for an answer.

"I understand," he said. "We can be friends though?"

The answer wasn't an acknowledgement of rejection, and I would have said no to even friendship, but he was an associate of my father's. I had to be nice. "Sure."

"Great."

"I should get back."

"I ordered the black forest cake. It should be there by now."

"I love black forest cake."

"Leave me some." He stepped toward the men's room. "I'll see you back there."

I waved and went back to the table.

CHAPTER 9

LOS ANGELES · 1995

*I*n the mirror, Peter jerked his tie slack as if it were a noose.

"That sanctimonious little bitch is going to pay for that," he growled.

"I thought you handled it well." I took the diamond clip out of my chignon and let my hair fall over my shoulders. The gala to fund arts programs in public schools had gone well, until the chairman of the FDIC joined our conversation and expressed disappointment that the savings and loan crisis was coming to a close with none of the perpetrators facing justice.

"She acts like I'm going to prison tomorrow. I swear, the one place I'm not going? Where my father went. Because he was stupid. Lazy and sloppy and stupid." He could go on like that indefinitely, railing against his father's idiocy and how he'd die rather than get locked up like him.

None of the savings and loan crisis had been litigated. The case had gone to the media, where it had been tried by the jury of popular opinion, and the consensus wasn't that my husband was innocent of bank fraud. Actually, the evidence of fraud was pretty clear. But like most of the culprits, he'd walked with more money than he could burn.

After we were married, my father had bought his bank, closed it, and hired the man who had made it insolvent. Instead of being grateful, Peter acted as if he'd been wrongfully ruined.

Don't get sold, Carrie.

"Don't let one silly comment by a government employee wreck your night." I took off my diamond earrings. "She's not worth it. You're better than her."

I didn't believe that, but in the interest of appeasing him, I needed to say it.

He stopped and looked at me in the mirror. Had I said something wrong? He came up behind me, lifting his hands. The best thing to do was go slack and passive. Fighting only made it worse.

He placed his hands on my shoulders, tenderly running them under my hair, down my back, to the top of my zipper. "You're right." He unzipped my satin dress, amber eyes watching the bodice loosen in the mirror. "You're always right. But it looks bad, and looking bad erodes trust. Business is built on trust."

He unhooked my bra and ran his hands under my dress, pushing both off my shoulders. My arms crossed in front of me, holding up the gown. He laid his palms on my arms until I dropped them. The dress and bra fell, exposing my breasts.

"Look at you," he said. "You're so beautiful it hurts. Can you see how stunning you are? When we go out, I see how men look at you. They want to fuck you, but more than that, they want to worship you. Collect you. And women hate you on sight. But when all of them look at me, I can read their minds. They're thinking, 'What did this asshole do to get a woman like that?'" He cupped my breasts with reverence.

"You're not a gold digger," he continued. "You don't need my money. You have your own. So, they think… maybe Peter Thorne is worth something. Maybe we can trust him. But, Carrie… beautiful Carrie…" He broke our reflected gaze to whisper in my ear.

"Why doesn't anyone look at you and wonder if you're worthy of trust?"

My trustworthiness hadn't come up before. He'd never implied I'd betrayed him, and I'd never given him a reason to. Even when he repulsed me.

"I am worthy of your trust," I said.

"Ron Davitch from LA Opera was there tonight. He said Aiden Klerk's been asking questions about Adam Brate."

I didn't want him to feel me go cold. I pushed his hands off me and picked up my hairbrush.

"The investigator?" I ran the brush through my hair. "That's interesting."

Peter took his hands off my body and leaned on the dresser, facing me with his arms crossed. "Bernie swears by him."

"Is he the one who got those pictures of his wife?"

"Yes."

"And what does this have to do with me?"

"I just find it interesting since we just saw him perform."

"So did a few thousand other people."

"The effect Brate had on you was noticeable. By everyone. You left the hall with your mascara running. People saw. Two days later, Aiden Klerk shows up asking questions about the identity of the man who brought you to tears. If Davitch made the connection, who else did?"

I laid down the brush. He'd gotten close enough to the truth to frighten me, and fear made me bold. "You know why people aren't questioning my trustworthiness, Peter? Because they're normal."

He picked up the brush and turned it to the back, then the front again. "Maybe." He ran his thumbnail over the bristles. "Normal people don't look past the surface."

As I turned away from the mirror to leave, he stepped behind me and held me still in one move.

"Let me go."

"I'm sorry, Carrie, but my instincts are telling me things I don't want to hear." He shoved me down, bending me over the dresser. "My gut is always right."

"I'm not cheating on you."

"Maybe not. Maybe not yet. Maybe never." He tapped the bristle side of the brush against the back of my thighs. "You need to know what I feel when you hurt me."

Holding me down, he hit the space between my bottom and my thigh with the brush. Each bristle was a white-hot needle, opening the tender skin.

"When everyone thinks I'm shit compared to you." He turned the brush around and struck me where I was raw.

"Stop! Please!"

"This is how much it hurts me when people think I married a whore."

He hit me repeatedly, pulling down my panties when he needed to mark my skin.

When I thought it couldn't hurt more, he made sure his pain was seared into my skin.

In a big stone house at the end of a long driveway, standing behind hedges and concrete walls, no one could hear me scream.

CHAPTER 10

*G*abriel didn't answer my calls. He never picked up the phone, and I'd have sworn, the Monday after the concert, I heard a violin playing as his roommate picked up.

"You gave him the last message?" I asked.

"Yeah."

"Tell him I'm not calling again."

"Will do."

"Thanks."

I hung up and went outside into the crisp early-spring afternoon. Andrea was on my patio, studying like I should have been. She straddled a lounge chair, bent over an array of open books. I had a penthouse apartment downtown that was quieter than any library or shared dorm room.

"That was a long bathroom break," she said.

I sat at the text-covered wrought iron table. "Yeah. Have you covered Cognitive yet?"

"You called him again."

"I just want to know. I have to know. If he's over me, that's fine, but I can't think."

The study materials swam in my brain. I read the words, but I couldn't discern the connections between them.

Andrea put down her pen and leaned back. "Let's do a little therapy."

"We don't have time for that."

"Have you ever been rejected before? Romantically?"

"I don't see what that has to do with it."

"You're avoiding."

For a psych major, I distrusted the whole therapeutic method when it was directed at me. "No. I've never been rejected. But he's not rejecting me. He's rejecting my father."

"Maybe. You don't know that. But I know something. What's happening to you? It sucks, but everyone goes through it. You have to embrace the suck."

"Embrace the suck? Is that from Methods 201 or something?"

"It's just normal life."

"I hate being normal."

"That's also normal."

I swung around in my seat, facing my books.

This whole normal thing was for the birds.

***

The Cognitive midterm the Wednesday after the concert went okay. I didn't embrace the suck or accept normal, but I had to admit that I was powerless to do anything but replay every word between us endlessly. The not-knowing was torture, an ever-growing throb in my mind.

Lenny said the only cure was distraction, and he invited me out for jazz and beers. I was moving my stuff between my Prada bag and something less showy when the phone rang.

"Hello?"

"Carrie? Hi. It's Peter."

"Oh, hey."

Outside of my distraction, dinner at Tristan's had been uneventful. Peter had been charming and nice, but he hadn't been overly attentive or obsequious. I chalked that up to his age. It was kind of nice, the way he didn't fall all over himself.

"I was wondering if I could take you out for dinner this weekend."

"Um…"

"I'm sorry," he said. "Is it a bad time?"

"No, no, I'm just thinking."

How long could I wait for Gabriel to call me back before I gave up? He'd gotten my messages. And really, what was the difference anyway? We'd agreed not to start something we couldn't finish. Nothing was keeping me from going to dinner with Peter.

"I could see that about you," he said. "You're a thinker."

Was I? Or had he mistaken my distraction for deep thought? Did it matter? If he valued a thinker over a pretty face, didn't that speak well of him?

"Is Friday good?" I said, zipping my bag. "I can do Friday."

"I'll see you then."

***

The band was a bassist, keyboards, drums, and a fuzzy-haired singer in a shredded lace skirt who crooned like a siren. We sat at a long communal table with pitchers of beer lined up in the center. A miasma of smoke hung under the stage lights.

Emerson was talking close to me so he could be heard over the music. "So, accounting for every molecule may be possible with a powerful enough computational model, but what's the point when we can take a broader approach?"

He was working hard to impress me, and I wanted to respect that, but more beer meant more confidence. More confidence meant more words with less punctuation.

He refilled our glasses from the pitcher. It was difficult to keep count of how much I was drinking if the glass never got empty.

"This wider systemic approach yields consistent predictive results without the contradictions inherent with quantum particles."

Nodding, I sipped my beer. I didn't know anything about quantum physics, but Emerson thought his knowledge was his most attractive trait. He was a pale-skinned guy with intentionally nerdy horn-rimmed glasses and a pleasant face. And he was wrong. His knowledge wasn't the attractive thing. His excitement for the subject was what made him handsome. For someone else.

Andrea caught my attention. She made the "Do you need to be rescued?" sign, and I gave her the "no" sign. I wasn't going to date Emerson, but listening to him was entertaining.

"So," I said, "you're saying you feel like you're wasting your time?"

His eyes widened a little behind his glasses. "You get me."

"It seems obvious."

"No, no. You really connected with what I was trying to say. Have you ever heard of quantum entanglements?"

"Um, no."

The song ended with a long, raspy note, and the band closed their set.

"Particles are coupled across dimensions, and I believe people,when they have a real connection"—he leaned forward deeply, staring into my eyes—"I believe they share entangled particles."

That, along with legit pressure on my bladder, was the signal the conversation needed to end. I put down my beer glass. "Interesting. I have to go to the ladies'."

"Okay, okay. I'll save your seat."

I walked around to Andrea, who was deep in conversation with her boyfriend. "Bathroom."

"One sec."

She'd catch up. I really had to go.

There was a line for the bathroom. I couldn't wait. I knew where the employee-only bathroom was. Through a hall and out a door to a back building. Just a quick pitstop.

Pleasantly buzzed, I pushed my way back through the crowd and out the back door.

I didn't understand quantum entanglements, but the idea that two people could be connected down to their very atoms sparked an idea. When I'd seen Gabriel that first time, I felt something. I couldn't define it, but maybe Emerson had. Maybe Gabriel and I were linked in a way so small yet grand only music could activate it. His playing touched me. His presence shook me. He couldn't stay away. The laws of physics demanded he call me.

The bathroom was clean but messy with mops and brooms. I did my business, tipsy mind buzzing with the idea that fate was physics. I washed my hands and came out determined to demand Emerson clarify the concept so I could cement the connection.

He was right outside the door.

"Hey!" I said, ready to ask about quantum entanglements and how they related to soul mates.

But he had other ideas about connections. I should have seen it. Should have waited for Andrea. Should have used the customer bathroom.

I saw stars when the back of my head smacked against the wall. His beer-soaked tongue was down my throat, and his erection was pushing against me. I shoved him away, but he must have taken refusal as a breachable obstacle, putting his hand on a breast and using it to pin me.

"I know you can feel it," he said as he caught a breath.

"Wait." I pushed him away.

His hand jammed between my legs, folding the thin fabric of my skirt against the crotch of my underpants. "Just admit it."

I must have been more than tipsy. I couldn't mount a focused defense. Couldn't make words. I slapped at him and missed, which made him come at me harder. I was going to be sick. His hands were everywhere, and they were strong, holding me up and probing at the same time.

Then the hands were gone, and I stumbled forward. My arms crumbled under me, and my face hit the pavement.

"Fuck!" Emerson cried from behind me.

The sound of impact. Skin on skin. Someone grunted. I rolled onto my elbows, facing up. The world swam. My stomach twisted and flipped. Bodies wrestled in the haze. Saliva filled my mouth, and I coughed up beer and chips.

"Jesus, Carrie." Gabriel's face came into focus.

"I knew it," I said, trying to get up. The sharp acidic smell of digestion rose from my shirt.

"Let me help you up."

"I knew you'd find me."

He got me standing and put his arm around my waist, holding me up. I rested my head on him. That was the last thing I remembered.

***

Someone had duct-taped a brick to my head. The tape went under my chin, weakening my ability to stifle a gag reflex, holding the hard block painfully tight.

Also, light was made of knives. When I moved, my brain was half a second behind, banging around my skull as if it wasn't properly attached.

"Hey." Andrea's voice cut through the thick soup of ickiness.

"Unh."

A cool hand rested on my cheek. "How are you feeling?"

"Mmph."

"Sometimes I worry you're going to turn into a party girl on me. Then I see how you handle your liquor and I'm pretty sure you can't."

"Are you sure he didn't put something in it?"

"I didn't think of that. He's Lenny's friend. Or *was* Lenny's friend. So, maybe?"

I sat up. Andrea handed me a glass of water and two smooth pills.

"You never know a person." I took the Advil, holding the water down with effort. "I think I'm still drunk."

"I have to get home."

"I'm okay. Thanks for staying. You're a good friend." I looked at the clock. Five in the morning. She was really and truly a better friend than I could express.

She stood. My vision was clearing. "Well, I wasn't leaving you alone with Gabriel until I knew you were all right."

"I'm sorry?"

"He's in the living room."

I remembered him then, in flashes of wrestling blurs and a strong arm under me. I couldn't smell his sanded wood over the stink of vomit still on my shirt. Ugh. I was gross.

"Am I sending him home?" Andrea asked. "I probably should after last night."

"No. No, I'm fine. He's fine. It's okay."

"Are you sure?"

"Just tell him to give me a minute to get the puke off me."

Andrea went for the door and stopped with her hand on the knob. "I was scared shitless for you last night."

"I'm fine." I swung my legs over the side of the bed.

"It was my fault. I should have gone with you. It's a girl rule for a reason."

Wobbly, but in enough control to get to her, I put my hands on her shoulders. "It's life, and life sucks. Embrace the suck."

She kissed my cheek and left. Through the door, I heard her speak to Gabriel. He was right there. I knew he'd come one way or the other.

As I stood under the shower, I remembered Emerson's theory of entangled atomic particles. How he thought he and I were a law of physics. How wrong he'd been. How very wrong and how very convinced he was of a very wrong thing.

And yet, how right he was about Gabriel and me.

CHAPTER 11

LOS ANGELES - 1995

*A*iden Klerk asked me to meet him in an unmarked warehouse next to his office.

"Mrs. Thorne," he said, coming out from the back area in a gray suit and blue tie. "This way."

The hall was glass on one side, overlooking a space as big as an airplane hangar, with three-walled rooms populated with people-shaped plywood cutouts. In one room, the cutouts were bullet-riddled.

"Don't worry," he said with a perfect smile. "We're training security personnel. Assassination attempts are a big business. Right through here."

He showed me into a windowless conference room with a white screen at the far side of the long table and indicated a seat. A week after Peter had used the brush on me, I could finally sit without pain.

"Can I get you something?" he asked.

"I'm fine."

"Let's get to it then." He slid a blue folder marked CONFI-DENTIAL toward me. "We aren't finished, but there's enough here for a status report."

I opened the folder to a picture of three men getting out of a car. I knew Adam Brate by the scarf around the bottom of his face and the eye mask at the top.

"When we're given a case like this," Klerk said, "we have two ways we can work: Forward and backward. Working forward from your theory of his identity or backward from the man in front of us now. We sent someone to Italy to go forward for a death certificate, but Italians get to things when they get to them. So, we went backward, starting with the man you want to identify."

Flipping through the folder, I found more pictures. None were revealing. None gave a definitive answer.

"Adam Brate is quite a mystery. He covers his face, and we're pretty sure he has his suits padded differently every time he plays so we can't get a bead on his stature. His agent doesn't even know who he is. His manager stonewalled. His lawyers are retained by a corporation, not a man. Overseas travel is by charter jet."

"Always?" I asked. "From the beginning of his career?"

"As far as we can tell."

That was expensive. The Gabriel I knew didn't have that kind of money. Even if he'd made millions as a masked cellist, he would have started with nothing.

Doubt crowded out hope. The burst of song was looking more and more like a coincidence. I flipped through the folder, trying to spark the hope again, but all the forms and reports were noncommittal.

"We're not done," Klerk said. "We're still conducting interviews, but as you can imagine, he doesn't surround himself with people willing to reveal anything."

A soft knock came from behind me.

"Come in," Klerk said.

A woman entered. In contrast to everyone else in the office, she dressed like a hip twenty-something with a striped sweater, jeans, and boots. Her diamond nose ring shone against her dark skin, and her hair was perfectly shaped into a halo of tight curls.

"Mrs. Thorne, this is Danika James. She's a scholar of musical styles."

"Nice to meet you," I said as we shook hands.

"We had Ms. James do an analysis of Adam Brate's style and form."

"I have some video cued up for you." She tapped a black box at the center of the table. The lights went down, and a projector I hadn't noticed before lit up. "Technique can change over time, so I went to the earliest known video."

He appeared, straddling his instrument, face covered by a linen veil. Creepy. Mysterious. And once he started playing, completely irrelevant.

Danika froze the video and approached the screen. "So, I'm going to focus here on his bow hold during a legato. Here, you can see his thumb is placed on the frog join. His fingers are open, and his second finger rests on the bow at the second carpal bone. This is a little unusual, but it's a signature of students from the Royal Danish Academy."

"Always?" I asked.

"No," Danika replied.

"We're looking for clues, Mrs. Thorne," Klerk said. "Not certainties."

"Right. Okay. Go on."

Danika leaned over the table and pressed another button and navigated to another video. I recognized Bing Theatre, and without even thinking about it, my eyes sought out the front row of the violin section, where Gabriel sat. It was the concert where I'd met Peter.

Danika said, "This is violin, so it's not fully analogous."

I barely heard her. I swallowed a lump in my throat, but it stuck.

"And here's a legato section..." She froze the video. Gabriel was a blob of pixels, but to me, he was as clear as a living man. "So, the bow hold is more curved and farther down, but the grip, with the fifth finger slightly raised? This is full-on American school."

My entire brain function was taken up with Gabriel, his body, his head as it leaned into the music with pure love. I knew that look. He'd directed it at me. I wanted it again so badly I could barely sit still.

"When you put them next to each other…" Danika flipped to a side-by-side. "What I see is a host of physical cues in their stance. The body positions, the thumb work on quartertones, the way they work the glissandos…" She stopped it again and faced me. "These are two different people with different core training."

The lump in my throat hardened to a stone.

"Thank you, Danika," Klerk said.

She nodded and left. I was left alone with the detective and the image of two different people on the screen.

"Mrs. Thorne?" Klerk said softly. "I need to know if you want us to continue the investigation."

If Adam Brate wasn't Gabriel, it didn't matter who he was. A privacy-obsessed celebrity. A talented stranger who had played a famous Whitney Houston song on a whim. A mystery everyone wanted to know but no one really wanted to solve. A marketing genius. Maybe he was more than one guy, but if one of them wasn't Gabriel, it didn't make a damn bit of difference.

None of it mattered.

Nothing mattered.

What was the point? What did I want out of it besides a second chance to live a life I'd lost?

How could it be anyone else? Why play that song in the middle of a concert unless I was the target?

Maybe the world didn't revolve around me, but my world was all I had. Even if it was a different person, I had to know why he'd played it.

"Yes," I said, standing. "I want you to continue. I want to talk to him."

***

I had nothing to call my own. I hadn't gone to grad school or found anything to give my days meaning. I wasn't good at anything. I was twenty-two, with a lifetime ahead of me and nothing to look forward to.

Margie called when I was feeling most listless. The sour shit-dump of my voice must have been audible all the way to New York.

"Come visit," my sister said. "Drew's playing some dive bar on Ludlow Street. You can slum it for a few days."

"I'm fine."

"Sure. Come anyway. We have wine."

"I'll ask Peter."

"I'll tell him."

"He doesn't trust you. Not after last time."

Last time I'd tried to run away and failed, Margie had covered for me.

***

Janice Joplin sang about the power of having nothing left to lose. Compared to most people, I had plenty to squander, but not caring about it was about the same as not having it in the first place.

Peter had been an absolute prince since opening the skin on my ass with a hairbrush. He didn't apologize but was sweet and tender—treating me like a well-loved doll he'd snapped the head from, calling me his most treasured thing.

I tried to remind myself of the goodness in him when I met him at his office with a hot lunch our cook had prepared. Meat-ball sandwiches. His favorite. I set it up on the little table by the window while he finished his morning's work.

The reminders fell flat. They echoed in the empty shell of my heart and went silent. Sitting at the table, waiting for my husband to join me, I knew for sure what I hadn't dared to suspect.

I was unhappy. I'd always been unhappy. Since the day Gabriel was killed, I'd walked around like a zombie.

What did I have to lose, really?

A life as a dead person?

Peter leaned down and kissed my forehead. "This looks great." He sat across from me. "Thanks for bringing it."

"Sure."

"Have you watched the news today?" He took a big bite.

"No."

"Wentco CEO resigned over junk bonds in the portfolio. Stock dumped thirty-two points."

"That's terrible."

"We shorted it." He waggled his eyebrows and took a slug from his water bottle.

I pushed my sandwich around the paper as if that would help me digest it. "Hm."

"You all right?"

"I talked to Margie. She wants me to come visit."

"In New York?"

"Her boyfriend's playing a show this weekend."

"Ah, sorry. We have the Capstone thing. Next time." He took another bite.

We had to go to that. It was a huge event. We'd gone the past two years, and since Peter was a board member, it was expected.

"You can go without me," I said, looking at food I had no appetite for.

He didn't answer right away. When I looked up, he was staring at me with bold curiosity.

"How would that look?" he finally said.

"It would look like you in a tuxedo having a good time."

"People talk. Why would you miss this to go to see your... not even brother-in-law at what? Another piss-smelling shithole playing music no one wants to hear?"

I wrapped my sandwich up as if I wanted to get revenge on it. "Come on. What's the problem?"

"Peter..."

"Tell me."

Moments like this, when he was in a decency loop, I'd tell him how I felt. I'd open my heart, and he'd make it all better. He'd be great until the next thing came up to make him jealous or suspicious.

"I want to see Margie. In New York."

He raised an eyebrow... and like that, the decency loop was derailed.

I packed my lunch back up. I didn't want this anymore. None of it.

"Carrie," he said without a shade of emotion in his voice. He was completely flat.

I paused with my hand in the bag, hearing that tone as if for the first time, then I took my hand out. "I told her I was going."

He grabbed the phone from his desk and placed it on the table. "Call her and tell her you can't."

Lowering my gaze to the phone, I considered it. Just to make life easier. Why push a rock up a mountain if it was only going to roll back down and crush you?

Peter picked up the receiver and handed it to me, watching every muscle in my face. I didn't want to die on this hill, but I didn't take the receiver. Because if not this hill, which one?

A knock at the door was followed by the sound of it opening.

"Mr. Thorne?" his secretary whispered.

"What?"

"I have Mr. Drazen on line two."

Peter broke his gaze and put down the receiver. "Fine."

"I'll let you work."

"Carrie," he said with a hint of warning, but the interruption had snapped the tension.

"I'm not—" *Running for my life.* "I learned my lesson last time, honey. I swear it. My sister needs me."

He bit the inside of his cheek, considering. I had a few seconds to convince him.

"She…" I took a deep breath as if the next part was hard to explain. "You know her. She'd never tell me something's wrong. Not directly. I'm just worried about her."

The phone beeped again. He didn't reach for it.

"You have my passport," I added. "How far can I go?"

"Mr. Thorne?" His secretary said over the intercom. "Mr. Drazen's on hold."

"Four days," he said. "On day five, I'm coming to get you."

"Thank you." I kissed him on the cheek, grabbed my stuff, and left. My plane would be in the air before Peter got home.

I'd been saved by Daddy.

CHAPTER 12

LOS ANGELES · 1993

*E*merson's attack had left me with a scrape on my chin that washed down to a light brushing of tiny scabs. I wanted to be my most beautiful and intimidating self when I saw Gabriel, but the scrape was a reminder that I could be broken.

I smelled the toast and coffee coming from the kitchen before I saw Gabriel there. I was showered, mostly sober, and as insecure as I'd ever felt.

"Good morning," he said, dividing four pieces of toast between two plates. He didn't look at me when he spoke.

"Good morning." I slid onto a stool on the other side of the island, letting him run my kitchen.

"You look better."

"Smell better too." I peered into the mug in front of me. Already coffee in it. "Thank you for rescuing me last night."

"I would have done it for anyone." He looked at me for the first time. "I stayed because you were calling me."

Was he saying I meant something to him? Or that I was just another victim that, like Andrea, he felt somehow personally responsible for? I didn't want to know the answer. I wanted him to be in my kitchen because he cared, not because he felt obligated.

"You need milk for that?" he asked.

"Nope." I lifted the hot liquid to my lips, letting it burn my tongue and warm my throat.

"Nice place." He swiped crumbs off his fingers before he opened a drawer and closed it.

"Butter knives are over there." I pointed at the drawer with the expensive silverware he'd note but not mention.

In the moments of silence that followed, he scraped butter on the four slices of toast. The crackling sound was hypnotic. Every sound he made was music.

"I never asked you your last name," he said, eyes on the *kkkch-kkkch* of the knife.

"It's Drazen."

"Well, yeah. I found that out at the concert."

Kkkch-kkkch.

"Does it bother you?" I asked. "The money?"

"I'd be an idiot to say it bothered me now." He sprinkled cinnamon pensively. "You dropped a hundred-dollar bill like it was loose change."

"So?"

"So." He put the toast in front of me. "So, put something in your stomach."

I ripped a corner off the toast and ate it. He lifted the entire square to his mouth and bit into it. We ate pensively. I'd been constructing questions and demands for days, but with him right in front of me, I couldn't think of anything to say.

"Your chin looks pretty good," he said, breaking through the stone wall of silence with a gentle tap.

"What happened?" I blurted. "Just tell me. I can take it."

He chewed, unhurried, thoughtful, as if choosing words and throwing them away.

"My father was in corporate litigation." He opened the refrigerator door and scanned the contents. "He started his own firm. Small-to-medium-sized in the grand scheme, I guess." He found the milk and shut the fridge, occupying himself with the spout so he wouldn't have to look at me. "He had a lot of clients, but his biggest one was a building supply company. See-Safe Windows and Doors. It doesn't sound like much, but I'd bet my right arm every window and door in this building is See-Safe. They're huge. Or they were."

He dropped milk into his coffee, clouding it, stirring. "They got sued all the time. This and that. Whatever. Dad never seemed stressed out about any of it. We had a nice life."

He sipped his coffee and put the milk away, letting his hand rest on the refrigerator door for a moment before coming back to the counter. "In Atlanta, this kid, four years old, Brandyn Rolando, fell out a seventh-story window that didn't lock properly."

"Oh." The syllable was an expression of surprise and sorrow. "That's terrible."

"Pretty much. The parents sued See-Safe, and in discovery, they found out that the windows weren't installed to code. So, the building co-op sued the developer, Piper-Sands, for the cost of replacement. See-Safe maintained Ronaldo fell out the window because of the installation. So basically, it was all landing on the developer."

He finally looked at me as if checking on my attention.

"Go on."

"When all records of the build were subpoenaed, Piper-Sands lost their financing and closed their doors."

"Wait."

"What?"

"Because of the subpoena? Or it just worked out that way?"

"Both? I don't know. What I do know, and this is from the papers and my dad's partners, is that project was financed by a shell company out of the Caymans, and when the developer's doors closed, the financier was the next liable entity. The first thing to do was find out who owned the shell. ODRSN. Just nonsense letters. Which my dad should have left alone. He should have just dropped it, but that kid was dead and he wasn't letting Piper-Sands close and walk."

"Okay. This is more involved than I thought it would be."

"Yeah." He smiled and took a sip of coffee. "Isn't everything?"

"No." I drank, watching him over the rim of my cup. He had to know I was talking about us, but I wasn't sure he agreed.

"Right about then, my father's firm started losing clients. He never brought his work home. At least, not in a way that upset anyone. When he was home, he was home, you know? He'd talk about work but not *unload* about work. I was ten. All I wanted was for him to sit in his chair and listen to me play, or throw a Frisbee around, or build snowmen. And he did. He did."

Gabriel cleared his throat. "So, my dad was the last man standing, and he was chasing the money. The attacks... they were subtle at first. Local paper 'exposés' double-dealing on a 1979 settlement. Accusations from old clients. Then the lawsuits started. Like a fucking... My dad, of all people, bribing the entire school board? Nah. They had nothing, but they spent every waking moment attacking him. From nowhere, all at once. Stuff that could be refuted with a phone call. It was dirty. So fucking dirty. He spent a ton of money on a PR firm, but it was too late. They just kept coming for him. They wore him down so hard."

He turned his back to me and dumped his coffee in the sink, gripping edge of the counter. "I lied to you because I didn't want to explain. I didn't want you to think I was... I don't know. Unstable."

"I don't think—"

"He committed suicide."

I didn't know whether to get up and comfort him or give him room. I didn't know if he wanted words or gestures, so I froze, silent and still.

"Hanged himself in his office. And all that time, he was the same with us. Never brought it home. I should have seen he wasn't right."

"Gabriel. No."

"We went broke settling the lawsuits. My mother just wanted it all to go away. Me? I mean, I was mad at myself. I dug all this up later because if I let it go away, I was letting him go away."

"It's not your fault."

I went to him, but when I put my hand on his back, he recoiled. I tucked my offending hand to my chest.

"I was in high school when I found out the shell company was behind the attacks." He put his back to the sink and crossed his arms. He seemed taller, more upright than he ever had. "And who owned that company."

"What did you do?"

"What could I do? We had no money and no proof." He looked right at me. "We couldn't go up against one of the richest families in the country."

Families. Not men. Not companies. But a family hiding behind a shell company to stop a lawyer from following the money to a child's death.

"The Drazens," he said.

My name, sticky and unwelcome, hung in the air like a tune you couldn't get out of your head.

"It's not my fault," I said.

"No." He dropped his arms. "It's not. But that doesn't change anything."

"How do you know? What if you're wrong?"

"I'm not." He slid his jacket off the back of a chair. "I don't know much, but I know your father as good as killed my father."

"You don't!" My desperation raised the volume of my voice. "You don't know anything. You need someone to blame because you blame yourself. But no one's to blame. It's not anyone's fault. Sometimes things just happen."

"Not to you though." With his jacket draped over his arm, he headed for the door.

"What's that supposed to mean?"

"It was all clear the other night." He opened the door but didn't go through. "You get people to do things for you because that's just how your life works. But I'm not going to be a part of it. I'm not going to call that man sir or Mr. Drazen. To be with you, I'd have to submit to him, and I won't. I'm not playing a game I can't win." He went through the door.

"Wait!"

The latch clicked behind him.

CHAPTER 13

NEW YORK - 1995

The club had black walls and mismatched chairs.

Even three glasses of whiskey into the night, Margie spoke in clear certainties. "If Aiden Klerk's team says it's not him, it's not him."

Her boyfriend, Drew, had just finished playing. Their hands were clasped in her lap, but he was turned to a bandmate, talking about the set. Another band was setting up. It was later than I usually stayed out, but I was running on powerful fumes.

"It's him," I said. "I just know it."

"He's dead. You know it. You saw it happen."

I had seen him die. It was violent and ugly, and I'd made it my life's work to not relive it.

"You're right," I said. "I just... It's too much of a coincidence."

Margie leaned across the table. A fall of red hair dropped over her shoulder. "What I want to know is why you care so much."

"Wouldn't you? If you thought someone you loved was dead and then maybe they weren't? It's like being haunted."

Something in her face went blank, as if her attention had done a one-hundred-eighty-degree turn from my problems to her past. Then, as quickly as it came upon her, the inward gaze turned back around. "What's going on with Peter? Does he know you hired Klerk?"

"He suspects."

One of her eyes narrowed with suspicion. Her jaw shifted slightly right, then she stood, taking my hand and pulling me away. She drew me through the dark room, past the crowded bar and the front-door bouncers, to Second Avenue. A group of black-clad smokers huddled in a doorway, and a line formed outside the velvet ropes.

"It's freezing!" I cried.

"Your blood's too thin." She unwrapped the scarf around her neck and handed it to me. It was completely inadequate, but I tied it around my neck. "Talk to me. What's happening with Peter?"

"Nothing." A cloud of steam shot out of my mouth when the heat of my denial hit the cold air.

She looked me up and down. "I'll put us in pledge."

Drazen Pledge was a new thing between the eight of us, but it was somehow already irrefutable. When pledge was called, we had to tell the truth plainly, and nothing said in pledge left the lips of the people present. It could not be refused, making it the perfect way to speak of things we'd never otherwise mention. I'd never been asked a question in pledge, but there was a first time for everything.

I held up my hand. "Open pledge," I said through chattering teeth.

Margie held up hers. "Opened. Talk to me. Peter. What's going on?"

"I don't..." What was going on, really? Faced with the prospect of putting into words what I'd denied was even happening, I was at a loss.

Margie waited, arms crossed, feet shifting on the cold ground.

No. I wasn't at a loss. I was afraid.

"After I got back from Belize, I thought things were going to change." I hesitated, remembering Peter's promises under the blue sky of the southern hemisphere, the beach at his back, eyes red-rimmed and puffy from hunting me down.

"But?"

"He was nice. He said he understood he could be a hard man."

The smoking huddle broke and the group passed too closely for my taste. They were strangers, but I didn't want them to hear.

As if reading my mind, my sister waited.

"Then it started again," I said.

"How?"

"I was reading *The Thorn Birds*, and it was so good. He was talking to me, and I wasn't paying attention. So, the next day, he threw all our books away."

"Are you serious?" Her eyes were wide, neck pushing her face forward.

"Yeah." I shrugged. "It wasn't that big a deal at the time. I thought it was just... It wasn't the same as before. Right? He wasn't hurting me. I still thought running away had worked. That he'd gotten the message."

Her scoff was silent, but the cloud of cold condensation made it unmissable.

"But lately, since we saw Adam Brate? He's been..." I drifted off again.

"Been?"

Down the block, a car alarm wailed.

"Can we close pledge?"

"Hell no. Carrie. Something's going on with you. And you know it stays between us."

"Can you promise not to go crazy?"

"No."

Inside the club, the headline act went on. I hadn't noticed the line outside the velvet ropes disappear, but we were more or less alone, just three bouncers standing out of earshot.

"When we have sex... it's always been... uh... He'll slap my butt, and it's fun, and I kind of liked it. At first."

I gauged her reaction. If she was judging me, she hid it.

"But after a while… and since the concert, he's been…" I cleared my throat. "When I told you he was controlling and I wanted to get away, I didn't tell you the whole truth. He's mean. He…"

Puts things inside me.

Beats me raw in places no one can see.

"He punishes me, and it hurts." The hurting wasn't the point. The hurting was because he knew what I'd refused to say out loud —that I loved a dead man. That love would exist in the world once I told Margie. "I shouldn't have married him. I did it too quick. I was so upset about Gabriel that I rushed just to feel something besides sad all the time. And I think he knows."

There. I'd said it.

Margie looked into the traffic of Second Avenue and said nothing. She said nothing so loudly I wanted to shake her, but I was already shivering so hard I looked like a jackhammer.

"Margie?"

She turned to me, swallowing something so thick I saw the muscles of her throat move. Behind her, a limousine stopped in front of the club, and the driver got out, carrying a long wool coat. He approached the cluster of security guys.

"Pledge means we aren't critical," she said. "And I'm not. Not of you. But you need to get away from him."

"He's my husband."

"Yeah, well. That can be corrected."

I didn't mention Daddy, the fact that Peter worked for him, or the way the Church disallowed divorce. We didn't do that. Margie knew that as well as I did.

Behind her, one of the bouncers walked up to us.

"Ma'am?" he said to me.

"Yes?"

He handed me the black wool coat the limo driver had been holding. "This is for you."

89

"What? From who?"

The bouncer looked over at the street, scanning for the limo, but it was gone. "They were right there. Sorry." He stepped back, shrugging. "Put it on. You look cold."

"Pretty Girl Syndrome," Margie said. "Your cross to bear."

I slid my arms through the satin-lined sleeves and clutched the collar around my neck. "Can we close pledge?"

"Stay here with me," Margie said. "In New York. A week. Get your head together."

"But Peter said four days."

"I need you. I'll tell him so. He's afraid of me."

The shivers were in their death throes, shaking my body a few last times before surrendering to the warmth of the coat.

"I shouldn't," I said, knowing I would. My sister knew too.

"Close pledge," Margie said, holding up her hand.

"Closed." My hand was hidden in the too-long sleeve.

"Come on." She headed back to the club. "It's fucking freezing."

I followed her back in, jamming my hands in the coat pockets. I felt a little wad of paper and took it out.

It was a gum wrapper. Big Red.

Big Red was a popular gum. Millions of people bought it, chewed it, and kept wrappers in their pockets for later. It didn't mean anything.

When we got back into the club and my senses warmed, I smelled cologne on the coat, and past that, a shock of wood, freshly sanded, like the body of a lovingly made string instrument before it was stained.

CHAPTER 14

UNIVERSITY OF SOUTHERN CALIFORNIA - 1993

*O*ur study group huddled in the reading room, books spread over the long oak table, under green lamps.

The USC Doheny Library reading room had set the scene for a hundred movies. Dark wood. A ceiling made for echoes. High, narrow windows. Through the double doors behind the librarians' desk were five stories of stacks inhabited by tightly packed utilitarian metal shelves.

Not that I ever had to go back there. The librarians were always willing to get me what I wanted even when I said I'd go myself.

Our Ethics in Psych class was harder than it seemed. Doing the right thing always took a little more than common sense. We had to know precedents set by the courts, and even then the case studies left plenty of room for interpretation.

"What's wrong?" Lenny asked after marking up an answer I'd made to a previous year's question.

I skimmed his red marks. I hadn't been careful. I was always careful.

"Nothing." I looked behind me.

It had been barely a week since Gabriel stormed out of my

apartment, and I could still feel his presence in my life like a semi-circle of glue stuck from a Band-Aid that had been ripped off. I felt him every time a bit of classical music played in a counselor's office or I saw a group of students carrying their instrument cases around the Thornton School. When I sat in the grass with my friends, I plucked at it and thought of his lips close to mine and the feel of his gentle breaths on my cheek.

And when we sat in Doheny, I felt him for no reason at all. He was that last stubborn bit of glue on my skin, capturing an open wound in a parenthesis I wouldn't rub off.

How could I miss someone I'd only known for a few days? Was it him I longed for? Or was he held to me by the ties of unfinished business?

I looked at Rhonda's paper and clicked my red pen. I was supposed to mark her errors, and finding them would require my full attention. She was close to perfect—always. I went through her long, near-perfect answer so I wouldn't hold up the group.

Passing it back, I stretched my neck with my eyes closed, tilting my head right, then left.

Unfinished business. As if I could give him closure with a denial of a belief he held so tightly. My father killed his father. He had his own glue. Nothing I did would rub it away.

Neck still to one side, I opened my eyes. A man dodged behind a marble pillar and into the stacks. He was tall and broad shouldered with hair to his collar.

"Excuse me," I whispered.

The chair squealed as I rose. My heels clacked on the marble floor. Nodding to the librarian, I ran through the doors to the stacks.

I didn't know where I was going or how to get to him, but Gabriel was there, in the library, sharing four walls with me. I wasn't about to let either the coincidence or the intention pass by.

We had unfinished business.

It took only a few minutes to get completely lost. I wandered through Asiatic history, cultural theory, communication, got on a rickety elevator, and went one floor up to the sciences, where I made a left into practical physics, rushed through quantum mechanics, and somewhere in fractal geometry, I stopped. Spun around. Backtracked and realized in calculus that I was too disoriented to find him or anything.

He'd be gone by now, my chance to explain passed, my opportunity lost.

I put my hand on a row of books full of ideas I'd never understand and squeezed my eyes shut in an attempt to hold back tears. I couldn't go back down to my friends with bloated eyes and snot-stained sleeves. Andrea would demand an explanation, and I couldn't lie to her. She had a silent way of making me tell her everything. I'd have to tell her why Gabriel had walked out, and I wouldn't, couldn't, tell her how wrong he was.

Again, I opened my eyes and saw him. Above the edge of the books, on the other side of the stacks, Gabriel's brown eyes watched me trying to keep it together with a raw fascination. They looked hollowed-out, rimmed in the gray-and-red lines of sleepless nights. Something feral had taken him. Eaten him from the inside out.

We froze there, watching each other, afraid to break the moment.

He took something from his pocket. Only when he offered it to me through the tops of the books did I see what it was. A pack of Big Red. He was trying to get me to come to him, but I wouldn't.

"No, thank you."

He took a slice of gum and put the wrapper and pack in his pocket.

"You're upset," he said finally.

"Of course I'm upset."

"Why?"

"Because I'm lost."

"The elevator's right over there."

He didn't move his body enough to shift his gaze. "Over there" could have been anywhere, as if he knew it didn't matter where I was in relation to the elevator.

"I'm so mad at you," I said. "I can't even think. I can't do my work. All I want to do is yell at you for being such a…" Not a jerk. Not an asshole, moron, dick, psycho, or any name that implied intentional emotional cruelty.

"Such a what?"

What could I say to him when the visible slice of his face looked exhausted and worn?

"Whatever."

"Maybe you're not mad at me, pretty girl."

"What am I mad at then?"

He looked down as if he couldn't see me and say what he wanted to say at the same time. "The truth."

"That my father destroyed your father over some windows? Please, Gabriel. That makes no sense. Why?"

"Some people—they just want to win."

Game player's mentality. Everything was a game to be won or lost. Sure. Daddy always won. He always came out on top. Every argument. Every disagreement. He won. So? That was how our family had gotten rich, and it was how we stayed rich.

"And you're different? Mister wants a solo so bad he almost didn't play in the orchestra. Mister almost got into a fight at Heritage Hall. Mister would rather win this relationship than be in it."

"That's not me."

"No, huh? Why are you here then?"

"I'm allowed to be here."

"Isn't music on the ground floor?"

As if I'd given him directions to the place he'd intended to go the whole time, he walked away, out of my sight—but only for a moment. He reappeared at the end of my row with his hands in his pockets. We stood in silence twenty feet apart.

"You want to know the truth?" He took the gum from his mouth and put it in the wrapper. "The ugliest truth?"

I thought he'd already told me more truth than I could handle. "Yes."

He put the gum in his pocket. "When I found out who you were, I was glad." He ran his finger along the books as if the texture comforted him. "No matter what I did, you'd outshine me. I couldn't help how I felt, but the train was off the tracks. You made me feel things. I couldn't help myself. And I knew you'd drown me out. So, finding out you were a Drazen?" He let his hand drop from the books. "Kind of a relief."

"I don't understand. Drown you out how?"

"My father wanted me to be a musician. I have to do that for him. I have to make him proud. I have to be the soloist, do you understand? For him." He ran his hand through his hair. "No matter how bright I shine, you'll always shine brighter."

His voice tested the truth of his words. As if he couldn't believe he felt that way but had to say it to check.

"You realize how ridiculous that sounds?"

"Does it matter? If that's what it is, then that's what it is."

"I don't know anything about my father's business. I just try to live my life. If it's his fault about your dad, then… I don't know. That's terrible. We should talk about it. But I can't change it. And I'm sorry it happened. Truly sorry." I wanted to step closer to him, but the wall of unfinished business hadn't been broken down, and I realized no matter what we did, it would stand strong.

"My mother would never accept us."

He was challenging me. Could I cope? Did I understand what I was asking for? Suddenly, a secret history and a life without family support seemed like too much. My shoulders dropped under the weight of it.

"And I'm going to North Carolina." It was my turn to run my fingers over the book spines.

"It's a lot. It would be like playing oboe because you love it instead of the instrument you're really good at. It's not fair to you. We shouldn't spend our lives fighting everyone. Right?"

I ran my finger down a canvas spine, feeling the texture of the gold-pressed letters. *Feynman Lectures*. He was working so hard to unwind us. Why fight it?

"You should go," I said, moving to the next book, *Path Integrals*.

"Carrie?" He'd stepped away—out of the row and into the aisle—and I hadn't even seen it. "Do you believe any of what I just said?"

He looked down the aisle, toward what must have been the exit, then back at me.

I rubbed resin and dust off my fingers. "Do you?"

He opened his mouth to answer but closed it as if the word was offensive.

"And," I added, dropping my hand to my side, "do you care?"

"I want to care."

"But you don't."

"No. I don't."

He came to me in a rush, like a tightly wound spring abruptly released. Three big steps, arms out, wrapping me in a tight embrace of renunciations and promises.

Renunciations of the world and its expectations.

Promises of something worth fighting for.

His kiss was all-encompassing. My body. My attention. A trap door opened under the tension of our denials, and they disappeared into a void. From that moment on, I'd associate the cinnamon taste of his mouth with relief and release and the roughness of his fingers on my cheek with the tension between what the heart wants and the body can express.

"I'm sorry," he said between kisses. "This isn't the first time I've watched you. I detour through the other side of the school hoping

I'll see you. It's like I can't keep away. Knowing that you're on this campus somewhere, it burns me up. I made up every reason in the book to stay away."

"I thought you hated me."

"I tried." He kissed my jaw, my neck, awakening nerve endings I didn't know I had. "I tried so hard. I needed to know it wasn't just me. Us, being together… it's stupid. It's wrong. But I can't keep away. I'm obsessed. But I can't take you unless you understand what it means to be mine. I need to know you want it too."

I pressed my hands to his cheeks, my soft, uncalloused palms feeling the brush of his unshaven face.

"I want it," I said flatly so he'd know I meant it. "I don't care what stands in our way."

"I should know better," he said, taking my hands away and clutching them between us. "You stand for everything I should run away from. But you do something to me. You make me want to possess you completely, and I'm sorry, but that's what it is. You're mine. I won't take anything less than that."

His intensity shattered me, blowing my will to bits. The pieces of me got caught in the whirlwind of his passion and were reshaped to a fine point that went in his direction. This was what it meant to be alive. To decide things. To choose by submitting to your heart's desire.

"Say it," he growled in a way he never had before. "Say you're mine alone."

"I am yours, Gabriel." I squeezed his hands. "Yours alone."

He kissed me, but it was different. Without desperation or hunger. He wasn't testing the waters. His hand held the back of my head, and his mouth explored mine as if he was mapping the territory he'd claimed.

My fear disappeared. My family. All the obstacles between us. I became his. And when he gently pulled back, flicking his brown eyes across my face, I felt valued and cherished.

"Let's get out of here," he said. "I'm going to play you like an instrument."

***

I ducked out of study group and drove to my apartment. Gabriel met me in the lobby, standing by a gilded mirror with his bag and his violin case. When the elevator doors closed, he dropped his things, then took my hands and put them over my head, pushing me against the back wall. He didn't kiss me.

He stared into me with heated lust. "Do you scream when you come?"

"I…" Before I could decide what to say, he pushed his hips into me. I gasped at the feel of his erection. My thoughts were a seesaw, rocking on the fulcrum of his gaze between "yes, more," and "no, wait."

"You will. You'll sing like a bird."

The elevator doors opened.

There were only two doors, and we kissed all the way to mine. I fumbled with the keys, and we fell into my apartment. He kicked the door closed behind him, pulling my shirt out of my waistband. When his hand touched my belly, I quivered so hard I had to pull away.

"Wait."

We were panting as if we'd run a mile, standing three feet apart.

"Just wait."

"Okay." He said it more to himself than to me.

"I need to talk."

"Okay." He ran his fingers through his hair as he repeated the same word with a more definitive tone. "Yes. I'm sorry."

"It's fine. Just… I haven't done this before."

His head tilted slightly. "This?"

"This…" I waved in the space between us. "This, um…" Words failed. "Can we sit?"

I pointed at the couch, and he looked at it, then around the rest of the penthouse as if he'd fallen asleep and woken up in a strange place. I sat on the couch and put my hand on the cushion next to me. He sat on the edge of the sofa, twisted toward me. I put my hands in my lap and looked at my knees pressed together.

An eternity went by as I chose words, threw them away, chose different ones, and found I couldn't say them. He put his hand on my back and stroked it. I knew, with that gesture, that I could say what I needed to even if it took a few tries.

"So, I know I'm twenty. But…" I cleared my throat. "I've never. You know…"

I wished he'd interrupt me, but he didn't.

"I've kissed guys before. But I never let it get very far."

"Ah," he said, still stroking my back.

"There was always this thing in the back of my head that they didn't really want me. They just wanted to be seen with me. I know that seems really conceited."

"It's a reflection on them. Not you."

"I don't think it's that way with you."

"You have good instincts."

"I want to." I put a hand on his knee. "But I don't want you to be shocked if I don't know what I'm doing."

He slid off the couch and kneeled in front of me, hands resting on the sides of my thighs, face turned up. "You can't not know, because I do."

"If you say so."

"But we're going to wait," he said, cupping my chin. "You're mine to take care of. Not mine to use."

Wait. The wet throb between my legs cried that maybe I'd gone too far. I wanted to know if I'd scream. I wanted what he'd promised in the elevator.

"I won't feel used."

He smirked. "Are you sure?"

"I am sure. Totally sure."

"But I'm not." He leaned back, hands spread on my thighs. "I want to be your first for every bit of this. Every step. Has anyone ever given you an orgasm before?"

His frankness made me blush.

"No." I stared at my clasped hands. "I've done myself."

He laid his hands on mine and pulled them to each side, then he laid his thumbs in the crease between my thighs. "Can I be your first?"

I looked at him as his hands moved over my jeans, upward toward my center.

"Just let me be in charge," he said. "You can trust me. I'll stop any time you want."

His thumbs pressed the inside seam of my pants, and my lips went slack, parting with the pleasure of it.

"Yes."

He sucked in a breath as if the consent itself was the sexiest thing he could hope for. He leaned into me, waiting a second before letting his lips touch mine, and when I responded, he worked our mouths together, straightening his knees until he was on the couch with me. I ran my hands over his body, tensing my fingers against the hard muscles of his chest and abdomen. He got under my bra and cupped my breast, then he stopped kissing me long enough to look at me.

"Yes," I said.

"I love it when you say that." He tightened two fingers on my nipple and gently twisted it. A cable of sensation went right between my legs, and I jerked with pleasure. "I love that too."

We kissed again, and when he unbuttoned my jeans, he stopped again to make sure it was a yes, and again when he put his hand down past my underwear. I was a chorus of yesses when he got on his knees and pulled off my jeans. On my back, naked from the waist down, as he looked at me as if I were a work of art. He pushed my knees open, stopping for a second when they resisted in a force of habit.

"Yes." I opened for him, but the routine of virginity was so strong I blushed again.

He smiled and stretched himself next to me. "I don't think I'll ever be able to resist you," he said between kisses.

"So don't."

His hand slid between my legs, fingertips brushing the nub I'd discovered when I was twelve. "You're so wet." He moved his hands to my opening, and I nearly went blind when he put a single finger inside me. "You like that?"

"Yes," I squeaked.

"Already singing."

Running his fingers back and forth, he worked my clit, and when I thought I'd burst into a thousand pieces, he went inside me. I could stimulate myself, but having someone else touch me brought the pleasure to new heights. He drew it out, getting me close, then pulling back in the most exquisite torture.

"Look at me," he said.

I opened my eyes.

He read me, playing my body as if the sheet music was in my expression. "Say my name."

"Gabriel."

He flicked my clit, and a new shot of pleasure ran through me. "Again."

"Gabriel."

"You want me to be the first man to make you come?"

"Yes. Please."

He shifted so he could grab my wrists in his free hand and hold them over my head. I was so close to losing control in a way I never had before that the restraint felt safe.

"Give it to me," he whispered. "Come for me."

Fingertips back and forth, he led me to the most powerful, hip-thrusting orgasm I'd ever had. I grunted, and just when I was taking a breath, he took his hand away.

"Sing," he growled with a stinging slap between my legs. I gasped, and he ran his fingers along my nub again.

"Oh, God!"

"Who?"

"Gab—" The next syllable was lost in a long note of pleasure that got louder as my second orgasm ripped through me.

Then, and only then, did he stop and lie down beside me, resting his hand on my belly.

"Wow." He touched his nose to mine.

"I'm the one who should be wowed."

"Nope. I'm wowed. You really are a little bird."

"Only for you."

He tucked a strand of hair behind my ear, letting his fingertips drift over my neck and down my shoulder. "I hope I always make you sing."

CHAPTER 15

NEW YORK - 1995

We left Drew at the club, and Margie took me back to her place. They had an apartment with an extra bedroom on the Upper East Side. There was no talk of me staying at a hotel.

Margie tossed me the phone. "Call him. Tell him you'll be back on Friday."

I pushed the green button, and a dial tone came through the receiver. He'd be unhappy, to say the least. He'd say it was fine, maybe use clipped syllables to mention an event I was missing. There would be menace but not threats, and I'd be saccharine sweet for weeks after to avoid further trouble.

I hit the red button and put the phone on the coffee table. The coat was draped over the couch, and the gum wrapper was in my hand, where I rolled it between my fingers like a rosary.

"He's at a dinner," I said.

Margie poured two glasses of scotch. "Do you want to talk about what you told me?" she asked, handing me a short glass.

"No." I didn't drink scotch around Peter. He thought it was unfeminine, but I loved the gentle burn as it went down my throat.

Margie and I clinked our glasses, and I took a sip, relishing the warmth in my chest growing like a drop of ink in clean water. My sister and I dropped onto the couch. She kicked her shoes off and pushed them under the coffee table.

"I'm glad I came," I said.

"Me too."

"How's the job? The law firm? Do you like it?"

Margie didn't have to work. None of us did. So, she had to like it.

"The firm sucks. But the law? I love the law."

"That sounds nice."

"What are you doing?" she asked. "With your days? What do you do with all that time?"

Andrea had asked me the same question when I'd seen her the year before. She had a raw fascination with my boredom, as if it were a choice she could never understand.

"I have friends, people I know. We meet for lunch. Play tennis."

"Nails and hair once a week."

"I plan events for Peter," I replied defensively.

She swirled the amber liquid in her glass, then polished it off. "What about school?" She put the empty glass on the coffee table. "You said you were going back once you were settled."

"Doesn't seem much point." I finished my drink, and my glass joined hers. "I mean, I'm not going to have a practice or see patients. I was just following a childish infatuation."

"With the human mind."

"It's fine. If I want to know something, I can read about it." Inwardly, I flinched, thinking of the empty shelves where my books used to be. "Do you have any more in that bottle?"

She got up and grabbed the Macallan from the sideboard, then poured two fingers' worth in each glass. "Remember that professor you had? With the wire-rimmed glasses and the tattoos? What was his name?"

"Gannon?"

We clinked and drank.

"He believed in you. I remember you at Deirdre's birthday party, beaming that he'd nominated you for some award."

The burn was never as pleasant the second time, but never before had it turned to ice in my chest. I'd never told her the whole story, and I didn't want to. I wanted her to believe I'd deserved that nomination.

"Andrea deserved it. I was happy for her."

"But you were good." She placed her sock feet on the edge of the table. "You loved studying, and you were good. Probably still are."

"Sure."

"I always thought you quit because of what happened in Venice."

My relaxation turned to a spinning weight on my heart, twisting it into a knot of tight muscle straining to beat. "I never said that."

"You didn't. Because it was Peter, wasn't it?"

"He helped me," I said. "He got me through it. He was there for me. All day and all night. If it wasn't for him…"

I'd be alone.

I'd be broken.

I'd be a different person.

I snapped up the phone and dialed Peter's car phone while Margie leaned back with her feet on the table.

"Hello?" Peter said after he picked up.

"Honey. It's me."

"How's New York?" he asked dryly.

"Fine. Great. How was dinner?"

"Finch asked about you. I said you were sick."

"Okay." I looked at my sister, and she nodded as if she could hear both sides of the conversation and knew I needed encouragement. "Listen. Margie's here."

"Tell her to go fuck herself but say hi instead."

He trusted her as far as he could throw a Chevy, and I couldn't blame him.

"She needs me to stay here another few days."

"For what?" he snapped.

"She's…" I'd never outright lied to him before, but if I was going to, it had to be a whopper. "She's having surgery on… Monday. She's got this thing. This…" Margie turned her hand in a circle, telling me to continue. "Tumor."

"What?"

"Don't tell Daddy! She doesn't want anyone to know. Please. They have to take it out. When they see it, they'll know if it's malignant, and then, well, then it's a problem."

"Where is it?"

"Where is it?" I repeated. Margie pointed at the space between her legs. "Cervix. And pushing into her uterus. She's in a lot of pain."

Margie gave me a thumbs-up.

"Well, if it keeps her from reproducing." He laughed. "I'm in favor of them taking out the whole apparatus."

"Peter."

"Sorry, sorry." He wasn't sorry. "Joking." He wasn't joking either.

"I'll call you tomorrow."

"Wait," he said.

"Yes?"

"There are people in New York who'd love to fuck me over. And with you right there and far away from me, where I can't protect you… you need to be careful."

"Like how?"

"Just don't talk to anyone flashing a badge or ID. You call me right away. Don't go anywhere with them. You got it?"

"Okay."

"I love you, babe."

"Love you too."

We hung up. I tossed the phone on the couch between my sister and me.

"Well done," she said.

"He's going to tell Daddy."

"I'll handle him. What was the last bit about?"

"He thinks the SEC is going to question me if he's not here."

"Paranoia's a drug. Drink up. It's a sin to waste good scotch."

I poured what was left down my throat. The burn was back. Margie refilled us. I was getting lightheaded already. Good. I'd lied to Peter. Gone behind his back to get a detective. Separated myself from him for more time than I'd ever had before.

Something was changing.

I gulped the scotch. If I could obliterate myself, ferment the woman I'd been a month ago, jar her and put her on the shelf, some other woman would emerge. A brave warrior who could make a decision about her life. Who could go forward instead of wandering around the present. Who was smart enough to know when she lacked direction.

I pulled the limo driver's coat over me, draping it like a blanket. "Margie?"

"Carrie."

"I think this is Gabriel's coat."

"You're imagining things."

"Maybe."

"The past isn't your future."

"I get so sad sometimes when I think about it."

She brushed my hair off my face. "I know. I really do."

"I'm afraid to let him go."

She nodded as if she understood all too well what letting go took from a person. Paranoia was a drug, but so was hope.

***

I woke up in the guest bedroom, feeling the upside of good liquor. No hangover.

My bag was by the bathroom door. I showered, digging my

fingertips into my scalp when I washed my hair, and dressed in a comfortable skirt and cable sweater. Sunday morning talking heads jabbered from the TV. At the table, Drew drank a cup of coffee and read the paper. The night before, he'd looked like a tattooed musician. Now he looked like a lawyer, even on his day off.

"Morning," he said. "How you feeling?"

"Pretty good." I poured myself coffee.

"You guys put a dent in that bottle." He flipped the page of the *Times*. "Made me a little jealous."

He wasn't jealous the way Peter would be. Drew wanted to spend time with us. That was what a lover was supposed to be jealous about.

"We can polish it off tonight." I sat next to him and slid the style section out of the paper.

"Deal."

"Where's Margie?"

"She didn't say." He looked at me over the edge of his cup and put it down. "I hear she's having surgery."

"That's my story, and I'm sticking to it."

"Eventually," he said as he pretended to read the business section, "it's going to be easier to leave him. And when you do, we're here for you."

"Thank you."

"Nothing gives me greater pleasure than getting between your father and what he wants."

The front door deadbolt clacked, and Margie came in.

"You're up," she said, unwinding her scarf and shrugging out of her coat.

"Yep." I scanned photos in the style section. Denim and plaid. Jeans and flannel. All the same but different enough.

Margie kissed the top of Drew's head and got herself coffee. "I had the most interesting meeting."

"On a Sunday?" Drew asked.

"Orly Wicz from the New York Philharmonic was at church." She sat across from me. "He was thanking me for the donation and—"

Drew glanced up from his paper. "We donated to the Phil?"

She put her hand on his. "The check's in the mail. Anyway. He was telling me that he's booking Adam Brate."

Him.

More pages of jeans and flannel tripping down Italian runways. Same thing, over and over. I saw them, but I was blinded.

"Apparently," Margie continued casually, "he's in New York at the moment."

The jacket I was looking at broke into blobs of ink.

"He get a good look at him?" Drew asked.

"Nope. No one does. He said he wears this piece of linen over his face." When I looked up, Margie's eyes were locked on mine.

"That dude has a talent for gimmicks." Drew folded up the business section and pulled out another. "Who even cares about a cellist except for the mask?"

"He's a composer," I said, insulted that he'd call it all a gimmick. "*Ballad of Blades* is the most beautiful thing I've ever heard."

Drew shrugged.

"Orly said something about that," Margie agreed. "He's got a meeting with him tomorrow about the lighting specs."

"Huh," I breathed. "At Lincoln Center?"

"Yup. Just before lunch." Margie opened the business section. "The SEC's closing another round of banks. They say it's the last."

"All good things must come to an end," Drew said.

Margie turned the page. "So must the shitty things."

CHAPTER 16

UNIVERSITY OF SOUTHERN CALIFORNIA - 1993

For three months, Gabriel and I were happy. I met his friends, and he met mine. We cuddled in bed and got to know each other's bodies, pretending we didn't have disapproving parents or that we'd be hundreds of miles apart by the end of summer.

But as graduation approached, it was hard to ignore the blank slate of our future or stay blithe about an unbearable separation.

"Hold the bow like this," he whispered in my ear with a voice thick with sex. His chest pressed into my back, and his hands were over mine. His violin was tucked between my chin and collarbone. "And don't push into your neck so hard. You're not trying to impale yourself with it."

I giggled and loosened up. We were alone in his apartment. My books were piled on the coffee table, open to where I'd left off studying to take a lunch break. I didn't know how I'd ever done schoolwork without his music lacing the background of my thoughts.

"Ouch," I said when he pressed the tips of my left-hand fingers against the strings. "Not so hard."

"It stops hurting after the first year. Now, draw the bow…" He moved my right arm so the bow vibrated the strings. They screeched. "Like that."

"That sounds terrible."

"Try again on your own." He let go of my right hand but kept my left fingers pressed down.

"Okay. Here goes."

"Go." He kissed my neck, running his soft lips against my skin as I tortured the violin.

"Ugh," I said. "Why does it sound like that?"

"Why do you taste so good?"

I tried the bow again, but it was worse. Letting the bow drop, I surrendered to the feel of his mouth on my neck, leaning back into him. "I guess I don't have talent."

Bending my head backward, I kissed him, letting my left arm drop so he could wrap himself around me.

"You get good the same way you get to Carnegie Hall."

"That's in New York? So... cab, I guess?"

"You never heard the joke?"

"What joke?"

Turning me around to face him, he looped his arms around my waist. "Guy stops a New Yorker in the street and asks, 'How do you get to Carnegie Hall?' and the New Yorker answers, 'Practice.' You never heard that one? Practice?"

"No. Is it supposed to be funny? Or just the Freudian humor of a universal truth?"

"Kids today."

We kissed through smiles, dropping onto the living room chair with me on top, straddling him as he lifted his hips to grind the length of his erection against me. This could go on for hours. Delicious, wonderful, everything-but-sex hours of touching and tasting.

"Gabriel," I said, pulling back.

"Little bird?"

"I want to talk."

"Okay." He reached under my shirt and unhooked my bra. "Talk."

"My graduation party is next week."

His fingers ran along my hard nipples, teasing them. "Everyone knows that." He pulled my shirt up and kissed each breast in spirals that had their peaks at the centers.

"Stop."

He looked up at me, one eyebrow arched high enough to make me wonder if the punctuation mark was designed to imitate that exact expression.

"You can't come," I said. "I know you want to make a joke about coming, but resist the urge."

"I'm resisting a lot of urges right now."

"If you're there and my parents see us together, they'll know."

"So? I mean, just tell them. What are they going to do? Kill me?"

"I don't want to fight them."

"What's the difference? It's not like we're going to be together after we graduate."

I used to get annoyed when he brought it up, as if he'd dumped grapefruit in a perfectly sweet fruit salad. But he was right this time. We couldn't pretend we weren't going to separate.

"I know." I yanked my shirt down, suddenly feeling exposed. "No. I don't know. I don't know anything about anything anymore."

"How do you feel?"

"Bummed out." I reached behind my back and hooked my bra.

"Carrie, I'm crazy about you. Insane. Every night I fall asleep thinking of ways for us to be together, and here you are, making sure we're not."

"That's not what I'm doing."

"Then what are you doing?"

"Being a grown-up."

He scoffed as if I'd said the stupidest thing in the world. Maybe I had.

I got off him and flopped on the couch, a million miles away. "I take that back. It's not grown-up. I'm not a grown-up yet. I have no control over my life right now, and pretending I do isn't going to help."

"I'm ready to tell my mother who I love, and she can deal with it or not."

"That's not a fair comparison."

He spread his arms, elbows bent, palms up, as if in utter incredulity. "We're the same age."

"It's not about age. Look. You're independent. You've been for a long time. Me? I'm reliant on them for everything, and what that means is… there are tradeoffs. I have to keep a certain face on things. I have to go to a few events a year and stay in certain boundaries and—"

"And go on a date with that guy."

"It wasn't a date."

"Sure." He shot up from the chair and paced. "Right."

Gabriel had been blithe about my dinner with Peter three months before. Obviously, that had been an ovation-worthy performance because he kept bringing it up.

"It's not forever," I said, watching him as if he was a tennis ball and I had seats at center court.

"But we are." He plucked up the bow I'd dropped and stopped and faced me. "Carrie. That is a fact. You can put a bag over your head and pretend you can't see the truth that's right in front of you, but that doesn't change it. We. Are. Forever."

He stood stock-still on the other side of the coffee table, fingering the bow for comfort, eyes a little wide as if he was shocked by his own words.

"Aren't we?" he asked.

"You could have mentioned it to me before you decided."

His Adam's apple jumped even as his face remained impassive. "I didn't mean to do that."

"Right now, I'm dealing with my parents having too much control over me."

"I know."

"And I don't need—"

"I know."

"You trying to dictate stuff to me."

"Carrie, I get it."

"Because here it is. I'm going to just say it right here." I took a deep breath, about to say things to him I hadn't dared to articulate to myself. "I don't think I'm qualified to manage my own life, and what's going to happen is I'm going to go right from their power to yours. And when you say stuff like that, it makes it hard to trust that won't happen. And, you know…" Everything was about to come out, like a dam bursting, and like a child who needed regulation and management, I had no control over it. "Letting you boss me is really super-appealing because I trust you and I love you and I—"

Shit.

I froze.

"You love me?" he said, laying down the bow.

"So?" I crossed my arms. "What do you think? I let every gorgeous musician I meet get his hands in my pants?"

"Wow."

"Shut up." I grabbed the corner of a couch pillow and flung it at him. It spun on a trajectory over his shoulder, but he caught it midair with one hand.

"You."

Me… what? Did he not love me? Was my slip of the tongue cute? Like puppy-dog cute?

Was "we are forever" about control and not about love?

"No, really," I said. "Let's talk about something else."

"I'm going to that party." He paced again but with a smile. "You don't have to invite me. And I'm not going to crash. No, no. I'm going to be there for you somehow."

"Why is this important to you? We're going to Shelley's thing so…" I shrugged as if he could insinuate the rest of the sentence by the position of my shoulders.

"It's important. It's me reminding you that when you separate from your family, I'll be there. When you can make your own decisions, I'll be there." He sat next to me, twisting around to face my profile. "I'll be there, however long it takes. As long as you choose me, I'll be there loving you, Carrie, just loving you."

I put my face in my hands, muffling my voice. "I'm going to cry."

He reached for my shoulders, tipping me into him. "Because I love you?"

"Yes, you big stupid." I pushed him away and sat up with my hair all over my face. "Because you love me."

He laughed, and I smiled. "You're a strange bird."

"I know. Now. I have to study. And you…" I pointed at the bow. "You have to get to Carnegie Hall."

***

Daddy had rented out the entire club grounds for a class graduation party. There was a photographer, a string quartet hired from the music school, a team of people on the grass to keep the kids occupied, and an open bar populated with the parents of the graduates, our professors, and Daddy's business associates.

"Would you look at her?" Lenny said, pointing across the room at Andrea. She was in a vintage lace dress and thick plastic glasses, laughing with a couple of our classmates. "She's gorgeous."

"She is," I said.

"I'm going to propose."

"That's amazing!"

"Shh! Don't tell her. It's a surprise."

"I'm going to burst." I was on my toes, ready to launch.

Lenny put his hand on my shoulder as if he were calming a pogo stick. "Promise, Carrie."

"Okay, okay. Promise."

Andrea moved, and I saw Professor Gannon talking to my father. As far as I knew, they'd never met before, so they should have been shaking hands and exchanging shallow pleasantries. But they weren't. They were serious, hushed, talking like two men with a common interest. I craned my neck to see Daddy put his hand on my teacher's arm.

"I'll wait to let her show you the ring," Lenny said from somewhere as far away as Montana.

Daddy led Gannon through a door that led to a restricted hallway.

"I can't wait," I said, already stepping toward them. "One second."

I headed toward the door the men had disappeared behind. I nodded to people I knew, looking rushed so they wouldn't stop me, and backed into the hallway. Behind an office door, I heard my father's voice.

"Thank you for your help," he said. "It gave me peace of mind knowing you had your eyes on her."

"She's terrific. It's the easiest twenty grand I ever made."

The door had a little window just above eye level. I peeked in long enough to see Professor Gannon take a thick manila envelope.

"There's a bonus in there. For the nomination. The prize... What is it again?"

"The Fischer, and it was my pleasure."

They shook hands, and Daddy put his hand on the doorknob. I ran down the hall, away from the party, and flattened my back against the wall.

"You helped make sure she's known as more than a pretty face," Daddy said as they walked in the opposite direction. "That goes a long way."

The sounds of the party got louder when the door swung open, then were silenced again.

What had I witnessed?

It couldn't be that obvious. Could it?

Everything I'd achieved had been bought and paid for. Not just the nomination, but the respect of the head of the department.

It gave me peace of mind knowing you had your eyes on her.

Was that why Gannon had been across campus, tires screeching as he missed a musician running across the street with a hundred-dollar bill? Was that why he'd made himself my point of contact for any boy problems that came up?

And speaking of boy problems… did my father know about Gabriel?

Was that why he'd shown up at the recital, insisting on dinner with him and Peter?

And Peter.

Don't get sold, Carrie. Margie's words haunted me like a piece of advice I'd thought I was taking.

I don't know how long I stood against that wall, fingernails scratching the wallpaper, staring at the hall table with its pot of rare orchids.

The party got loud as a faraway door opened. Voices. Something about the hors d'oeuvres trays being warm. Some professional agreement was reached, then the music and voices were shut out again.

I had to go. I couldn't stay there in a frozen knot. Taking a deep breath, I stood straight, armed with information I didn't know how to use. A loaded gun with a trigger I felt too worthless to pull.

As soon as I got back out into the party, a silver tray was under my nose.

"Hors d'oeuvre, madam?"

I didn't look at the food, because I'd recognized the voice. "Gabriel!"

"Rumaki," he said with a glint in his dark eyes. His black bowtie was crooked, and his jacket was two sizes too big.

"What are you doing here?"

"Liver and pineapple." He held out a pile of burgundy napkins with the letters USC stamped in gold. "Counterintuitive, but I hear it's delicious."

I took a napkin. "How did you get this gig?"

"Shelley's in the quartet." He smirked, eyes sparkling like the sky on the Fourth of July. "She pulled some strings, so to speak."

"You can't be here." I took another hors d'oeuvre.

"I have news, little bird," he whispered, sending a shiver up my spine.

"Tell me." I put a third rumaki on my napkin, moving slowly. "Then go."

"I got the Caruso Fellowship."

My lungs sucked in air as if I'd been drowning.

Gabriel deserved it, but I had to wonder if Daddy had arranged it to get him away from me. I hated myself for thinking that could even be true—he was so talented—but I'd never trust anything again.

And like that, I knew what to do.

"You're going to Venice?" I confirmed.

His eyes glinted as they took in the length of my body, undressing me for him and him alone. "I'm going to Venice."

"Carrie," a man's voice came from behind me.

I spun to find Gannon next to a curvy woman with curly black hair parted in the middle. The manila envelope stuck out of her bag.

"Professor Gannon," I said.

"It's Kevin now." The familiarity of his first name bred nothing but contempt. "I wanted you to meet Terry."

The woman he was with smiled and held out her hand. I took it, looking back to find Gabriel gone.

"So nice to meet you," Terry said. "Thank you for inviting us."

"It's my pleasure. Profess—Kevin's meant a lot to me this past year."

More than I knew and not just to me.

Uncomfortable with everything unsaid, I couldn't help but scan the room for Gabriel.

"Like the rumaki much?" Gannon asked.

"Oh." I'd forgotten about the handful of meaty chunks I'd piled onto the napkin. "No one wanted them, and I felt bad."

"Compassion for the hors d'oeuvres," Gannon said, putting an affectionate arm around Terry. "Delightfully typical for you."

I smiled warmly. *Stop pretending you like me.*

Through the crowd, I found Gabriel taking his tray toward the kitchen.

"Let me just... um... get rid of these. I'll be right back."

Cutting a path through the room, I pushed through a set of double doors to a water station and dumped the rumaki in the trash. A waiter burst through a second set of swinging doors with a silver tray. Another door cracked open.

"*Psst.*"

I was pulled into the closet by the elbow. In the moment before the door closed, Gabriel's face was in the light, then we were blanketed in darkness. His lips were on mine, his tongue exploring, his body pushing mine against the wall.

"Gabriel," I groaned as he kissed my neck, picking up my skirt. I twisted away. "Stop."

"Are you all right?" His brow knotted in the dim light. "I thought—"

"Stop," I interrupted.

I had to tell him, but if he knew I was a shoddy person whose father had to buy her awards and respect, whose looks were traded for approval and favors, he'd leave me. Or worse, he'd stay. But he'd never trust me. Not with his heart. Doubt would eat away at his confidence.

And even if it didn't eat away at his, it would eat away at mine.

"When are you leaving?" I asked.

"Monday, but I'm coming back in December."

"I'll be gone."

His nose touched mine. "It's what we agreed, isn't it?"

"We agreed we were forever."

"We have two days until forever, then."

We didn't. Not even close. There were too many events. Parties. Ceremonies. We had back-slapping to do and tearful goodbyes to savor.

"I'm scared."

"About what?"

"That we're going to drift apart. For whatever reason. And I'm going to forget what it feels like to be loved by you. To be really loved. I never want to forget it, and I never, ever want to live without it."

He pulled away a few inches to take in my full face. "What makes you think I'll let you forget?"

I pushed him away. "Think, Gabriel. Distance. Time apart. You think you have control over this, but you don't. Neither one of us does. We promised forever, and we can't deliver it."

"Carrie." He was trying to soothe me, and I wouldn't be soothed.

"Don't 'Carrie' me. We have to do something. Like, make a plan. Because…" I gathered the courage to tell the truth and the mindfulness to tell it completely. "Because otherwise the plan's made for me. All I can see is me never deciding to do another thing this good. I'm just so scared all the time now, and I can't do it this way."

His eyes fluttered closed for a moment, and he put his hands up as if he needed to slow me down for a second.

"I can't," I whispered one last time.

"Then you shouldn't." He took my hands. "You shouldn't be scared."

"What are we going to do, then? Tell me."

"What do you want?"

"I want things to be different."

"Then we have to make them different."

I knew that. We had to tell our families we were in love, and our families would have to deal with it. But a deep, silent terror accompanied that option. If Daddy would pay off my professor and ruin Gabriel's father to the point of suicide, how would he react to us loving each other?

As long as I was under their control, the best option wasn't an option at all.

"We can't," I said. "Not yet. I'm not ready."

"When will you be ready?"

A deadline was almost like a plan. The wall behind me was the only thing that kept me from collapsing in relief.

"After summer. We'll both be away. We'll be grown up. We can tell them how it is."

"You and me. Forever."

"It'll be fine. Right?"

"It will be. It already is."

Bad news slid off me as he picked up my legs and wrapped them around his waist, leveraging me against the wall. My skirt hung away, leaving a slip of underwear between the rod of his erection and me. We kissed again, pushing our hips together, circling and grinding.

"God," he said, pulling only his face away so he could hold me tight. "I can't believe you're mine."

"I'm yours. Just don't forget to love me."

He laughed as if I'd cracked a joke, then stopped when he realized I wasn't trying to be funny.

"How could I forget this?" He ran his finger along the neckline of my dress, pushing the fabric aside and exposing my breast before he covered it with his hand, taking the hard nipple between his thumb and finger.

I groaned a coherent thought diluted by pleasure. "Italy's so far away."

"It's only a few months."

Months were nothing in the face of eternity, and a few thousand miles was nothing to a girl with a free summer.

It hit me that I could solve this, and excitement crowded out fear.

"I'm meeting you there," I said before I lost my nerve and ability to speak.

"What?" His hand went still on my breast.

"Shh." I pressed two fingers to his lips. "I'll leave on a different flight and meet you in front of St. Mark's on Tuesday. In the square at high noon. There's a monument. A pillar with a lion on top."

"Just like that?"

"Just. Like. That. I want you to take me, all of me. In Venice, I want you to..."

"What?"

"Fuck me."

He sucked in a breath as if I'd said the most arousing thing in the world. And maybe I had, because my body had its own reaction.

"You're going to love it." Leaning down, he sucked my nipple with a brute ferocity that merged pain and pleasure. "I'm going to make it so good for you."

Easing one of my feet to the floor, he got on his knees and put one leg over his shoulder.

"Someone's going to come," I said, eyes on the door.

"You're right about that." He slid my underwear aside and kissed the swelled nub of nerves. It felt so good he had to hold me up for a second.

My mouth opened in an O as his tongue ran along the head of my clit, pushing gently past the hood, flicking sweetly, filling my body with a pressure so heavy I felt as if the bowl of my hips was a water balloon under a faucet. Expanding as the membrane thinned. The bulbous and warm weight of it.

He put his mouth between my legs, and his free hand spread me apart, entering me again. I couldn't hold it. I feared the explosion. The watery mess. The rubbery shrapnel of my body breaking.

The fear gave way to acceptance, not just of the coming orgasm but of my decision. I was a whole person with forward direction. The balloon broke in a hundred explosions.

I was my own woman, and I had the power to choose him.

CHAPTER 17

NEW YORK - 1995

*M*argie was supposed to be in surgery that Monday, but I was on a street corner nowhere near a hospital with no excuse to be that far west. At all. But once I'd called Aiden Klerk and told him I needed to know about a meeting between Adam Brate and the stage director, there was no going back.

The black coat the limo driver had given me covered me to the tops of my feet. My breath was damp against the heavy scarf I'd wrapped around the bottom of my face, and the wooly cap Margie had loaned me bordered the top half of my vision in shadow. I was almost fully and—once the snow started—quite reasonably masked. He might know me from my eyes, or he might not know me at all.

Aiden Klerk was good at his job. Anyone driving into the staff lot had to register their license plate with security, and of course he knew someone willing to reveal the number associated with Monday's eleven o'clock meeting.

He had me memorize it—*Z1C-136*—and told me the location of Lincoln Center's Amsterdam Avenue staff entrance. The corner where Sixty-Third Street made a T into Amsterdam was the only place I could wait.

I stood at a bus stop with my hands in my pockets, feet stamping as I watched cars turn onto Amsterdam from Sixty-Third. My heart pounded hard enough to keep me warm. The bus came and went.

I was nobody. Neither rich nor beautiful. I was nameless, faceless. No baggage and no privilege. Free to live, to love, to choose a dangerous path. Follow my own heart or break it. Just a cold woman in a New York snowstorm, waiting for a man who didn't want to be seen.

I repeated the license plate number, singing it in my head to the melody of *Ballad of Blades.*

Z1C-136

Z1C-136

Z1C-136

The snow was sticking. Slow-moving vehicles compressed it into a frozen crust. A long car approached in the right lane, close to the curb. It was the right make and model, but white dust hid the license plate. One stroke of my hand would have brushed it away. It came alongside me and idled at the red light, its right blinker flashing. Snow gathered in the corner of the tinted back window. It was inches from me, and even then I couldn't tell if anyone was in there.

He could be right there.

The answer to everything.

The choice between my future and my past on the other side of a piece of glass.

The light was going to change. After that, it would take three seconds for the car to either continue up Amsterdam and make a right onto Sixty-Fifth Street or make an immediate right and disappear into a parking lot.

I bent forward, peering in as if I had a right to know who was in there.

Which I didn't. But being a little rude made going all the way a little cheaper.

I knocked on the window, my mitten making a dull *puh-puh* on the glass. In the shadows, I saw a silhouette. A person who had paid for privacy, and there I was, knocking on the window as if I wanted to ask for spare change.

Maybe it wasn't him.

But it was.

He was that close. I was convinced.

I had nothing but a feeling to go on, but the feeling held me tight. If he could see me...

As I moved the scarf and hood away, I realized the odds that I knew this wealthy person in this limousine. They were extraordinarily good. If it wasn't Gabriel or Adam Brate, there was a good chance they were a friend of my family, or Peter, or a classmate from private school. Showing my face would expose my whereabouts. The news would get to Peter.

He'd figure it out.

And the beat of a hairbrush on my ass would be a mild prelude to what he would do.

I pulled down the hood. My red hair flew in the wind, and snow bit my cheeks as I put my face as close to the window as I could.

See me.

The shadowy figure in the back didn't move. I couldn't tell if they were looking in my direction or studiously ignoring me.

"Gabriel?" I said.

Hear me.

"Gabriel!"

The car moved. I flattened my hands against the window, desperate for an answer.

But none came. The limo turned right into the lot, back license plate cleaner than the front. Blue on white. Readable.

Z1C-136

The limo pulled all the way into the parking lot entrance, disappearing into the warm belly of Lincoln Center.

CHAPTER 18

LOS ANGELES · 1993

*H*aving access to as much money as I wanted granted me just enough freedom to blind me to the fact that I was a captive to it. Legally, I was a grown woman. Realistically, I was a ward of the Drazen family. In particular, my father, who couldn't have planned a more perfect way to delay the onset of mature self-determination.

"Your card won't go through," Lindsay said, pushing up her glasses. She worked in one of my father's offices and had booked first-class plane tickets for me a dozen times. "I'll use the corporate Amex."

"No."

Lindsay tilted her head curiously, her blown-out bangs a ruler-straight line across her forehead. "It's not a problem."

It was a problem. If I put the trip to Venice on my card, I could tell my parents I'd gone to Paris with my friends. Lindsay wouldn't mention the destination in the swell of the organization's business travel. But accounting went through the corporate expenses with a fine-tooth comb. I'd found that out when I was twelve, after Daddy's personal assistant had signed off on my shopping trip to Bendel's. She'd gotten fired for being "sloppy," and I'd gotten my own card. Which no one would check and which wouldn't work. Meanwhile, if he found out I'd gone to Venice and put two and two together… Well, I didn't want him to know about Gabriel. He was separate. Uninfluenced by manila envelopes or business dealings. He was mine, and he was going to stay that way as long as I could manage it.

So, I called the credit card company.

Travel expenses had been restricted by the card owner.

That was my parents.

I found my mother at the tennis club. She was sitting with her friends at a table, having post-match drinks.

"Mom," I said. "Can I talk to you?"

We went to the patio overlooking the pool. The waiter brought her drink out and gave me a menu I put to the side.

"What's wrong, Carrie?"

"I tried to book a trip, and my card got rejected. You said I could go away with my friends after graduation."

"Oh, we were going to tell you this weekend."

"Tell me what?"

"Well." She downed the last of her gin and tonic. "I was going to surprise you with a trip, and I didn't want you booking anything else before I told you." She smiled slyly. "We're going on an African safari! Just you and me."

"When?"

"Next week. June first." She put her hands on mine. "Four weeks. Mindy Callihan did it last year and said it was—"

"Mom! I don't want to go to Africa."

She pulled back as if I'd slapped her.

"I mean… I want to spend time with you, but I made other plans."

"With whom?"

I had a lie ready, but in the face of her desire for four weeks of quality mother-daughter safari time, it was a thin, wan excuse with the firmness of a wet noodle. I'd spent too long propping it up, swapping details, testing them against reality only to find them flimsy and easily contradicted. My silence was already suspect.

Maybe I could kill two birds with one stone.

"Can we change it?" I asked.

"This is the last safari until September. It's too hot after that."

"Can we change the place? It's just... I've been to Rome, but I always wanted to see Venice."

She swirled the ice at the bottom of her glass and got another sip out of it. She didn't say anything until she'd drained it of the last of the liquid. "It's been brought to your father's attention that you have a boyfriend."

I should have known it wouldn't last. "You mean Gabriel Marlowe?"

"Yes." She raised her hand for the waiter. "Can I have another?" She turned to me. "Anything, dear?"

"No." I handed back the menu. When the waiter was gone, I started the first in a series of lies. "I didn't want to introduce him until it was serious."

"Isn't he going to Venice?"

So much for keeping anything from my parents. They had teams of people whose only job was to know things. I was forty shades of red, and I wanted to die rather than get caught in this web of lies. "Yes."

"I'm not taking you across an ocean to see him. That's out of the question."

"He'll be busy. But you can meet him. You'll like him."

"You know your father," she said after a resigned sigh, as if it was all Daddy's fault. "He has seven daughters, and he takes your choices seriously. I mean, in a way, we already lost Margaret, so... you? We're taking extra care with you. We thought some time away would be good."

"I don't understand. Why do I need time away? I'm fine."

"You are fine." The drink came, freshly bubbling with a plump lime at the rim. She squeezed it and dropped the green husk on her napkin, which she pinched to dry her fingers. When she looked at me, it was with a new resolve, as if dressing her drink had given her confidence. "He—this boy? He is not fine."

"Mom. Really?"

"He is inappropriate for you. You know that, or you would have mentioned him."

"How? How is he 'inappropriate' for me?"

"Carrie. You are second oldest. Your sisters and brother look up to you. You need to set an example for the right way. The Drazen way."

"You didn't answer the question. How is he inappropriate?"

She sighed and took a sip of her drink. "For one, artists cannot be trusted."

"That's crap."

"Two, he doesn't have the money to support you."

"He's twenty!"

"And his father committed suicide."

My mouth closed, and my eyes widened. How did she know? Why did she know? And what else did she know?

"Now, it's a tragedy for any family. Look at the Carringtons. Those kids will never get over what their mother did to them. And Louie's a broken man."

"He already remarried."

"The point is, young lady, this kind of disease is genetic. His family is broken. His children will be broken. And if your father and I can help it, he's not going to trap you into that brokenness."

Rage mixed with disappointment and was flash-frozen by shock. In all that, I did a smart thing. Maybe the only smart thing from the range of choices that included dumping that gin and tonic in her lap before storming out.

I took a deep breath and stayed in my seat. Asked myself what she wanted and how I could make her believe she'd gotten it.

"I'm really pissed off," I said calmly.

"I know, and we—your father and I—we knew you would be."

"I'm going home to calm down." I stood.

"I understand. Can you call me later? We can talk?"

"Sure. I'll be mad though."

"You'll see it's for the best. In no time at all, you'll see."

"Bye, Mom."

Walking out with my head down, I gave the valet my ticket and waited for the car. I could go to Gabriel. Explain everything. Promise they wouldn't come between us. We'd meet after the summer.

As the valet closed the door for me and I put my car into drive, I wondered why my mother wasn't worried I'd go see Gabriel right from the tennis club. How did she know I wouldn't pick him up and drive to Mexico?

There was only one answer.

At the solo recital, maybe Dad had heard Gabriel was a finalist for a Caruso Fellowship.

Or maybe Peter had mentioned it.

Maybe Daddy had arranged for Gabriel to win, or maybe he didn't have to.

This was crazy. Insulting. I could tell them a thing or two about what was inappropriate around here.

I wouldn't be treated like a game piece.

I was going where I wanted. I decided what happened with my life. I wouldn't be manipulated or talked into subservience. My parents could try to get me to be their little pawn, but they were going to have to chase me over the ocean to do it.

CHAPTER 19

NEW YORK - 1995

*L*oneliness was a physical thing. Sometimes it hovered nearby, glowering with menace. Sometimes it wrapped around my body and squeezed the breath out of me. Other times, it was small and sharp, pushing against my tender places like a pebble in my shoe.

Standing on a street corner in a snowstorm, rewrapping my sister's scarf, loneliness was a weight shackled to my ankle, slowing me down as I walked south on Amsterdam. The voices in my head needed someplace to go. They told me I was worthless and unlovable. That all the kindness I'd received had been malicious. That I was finally as alone as I deserved to be.

The heavy weight was the wind in my face and the cold ache in my knees. But I pressed on, passing warmly lit coffee shops and department stores, dragging loneliness like a ball on a chain.

My body knew better than my mind, and it led me to Margie's office, where she took me in and gave me a cup of truly bad coffee. It was hot. That was what mattered.

"Okay," she said, closing the door of her tiny office. "What happened?"

She sat across from me, leaning forward with her fingers laced together. She was in a lavender pantsuit and a white blouse, professional and put-together, as if she wasn't just an associate lawyer but a senior partner.

"It was him," I said.

"Which him?"

"Adam Brate. The license plate matched and…" There was so much to say, but I could only feel the shackle loosening. "Thank you."

"For what?"

"Listening. Being here. I'll make it up to you someday."

"When I need you, you'll show up. I know it. Now tell me. Did you talk to him?"

My knuckles ached as they warmed. "I banged on his window like a fool. Uncovered my face. He had to see me, but he drove off. If it was Gabriel, he would have opened the window."

Margie leaned back in her chair. "So. He's dead."

"Yes."

"Nothing's changed."

Gabriel was still dead. I was still alive. Peter was still my husband. Everything was the same as the weeks and months before the concert, when I'd accepted that my life was what it was.

"Nothing's changed," I said.

"Except for you," Margie added. "You've changed."

"No. I'm still me." Even as I said it, I knew it wasn't true. I wasn't me. I didn't even know who that was.

"Do you want to be married to that man?"

"No." The denial was barely a whisper.

"So, that's changed."

"I can't get divorced. I'd be disowned. And Peter works for Daddy."

Margie shook her head and waved at me. "First of all, me 'living in sin' with Drew is a big no-no, but they got used to it. The only thing our parents want is for the family to be together. The end. And let Peter quit. Or not. It doesn't matter."

It all seemed so big. So unwieldy. Wider than my arms could manage. No handhold. Nothing to latch on to and heavier than my own weight.

"He'll find me," I whispered. "I don't know what to do."

"It doesn't matter what you do yet. What matters …" She leaned forward again. "What matters is what you decide. Once you decide, what you do about it is a practical matter."

"Will you help me?"

"Yes."

The shackle popped off my ankle, and my loneliness turned from a dead weight into a balloon. Still present but lighter.

Now all I had to do was make a decision.

CHAPTER 20

LOS ANGELES - 1993

*W*hen I got home from meeting my mother at the tennis club, the light on my answering machine was blinking. I hit the button before I put down my bag.

"Hi, Carrie." Andrea's voice came over the speaker. "I need to talk to you. Lenny's been being weird, and it's kind of freaking me out. Call me, okay?"

In the two seconds between the beep of her message ending and the one that followed, I smiled, then frowned. Was he getting cold feet?

The machine beeped.

"Hey, it's me," Gabriel's voice said. "The fellowship changed the flight date. I'm leaving in a few hours. The plan's the same. Same time. Same place." He paused. "Every time I breathe, every time I blink, I'll be thinking about you. Wear something that looks good in a pile by the bed."

The messages ended.

I had my marching orders.

No credit card? No problem. I opened my wallet. Two hundred and change. I kept an envelope of emergency cash in my night table. Three crisp hundreds. Would that be enough? And once I was there, would I have a dime? There was a good chance that once they realized I was gone, they'd shut the card completely in a fit of pique.

I dug around the bottom of my underwear drawer, past the practical and sweet, where I had an old Prada change purse my mother had given me for my sixteenth birthday. It had had a few hundred dollars in it. Finding it, I discovered with glee that the cash was still there.

Wear something that looks good in a pile by the bed.

I flicked around my drawer. Underpants. Bras. Tights. It was all functional. Piled on the floor at the end of the bed, it would look like laundry.

I called Andrea. "Andrea? Hey, it's—"

"He said he wanted to talk. Did he tell you anything?"

I bit back a denial that would only make her worry more. "Yes, he did."

"What did he say?"

"I can't tell you."

"Carrie, you—"

"Listen, do you love him?"

"Do I love him? Are you kidding? He's my man, and if he breaks up with me, I will die. Do you hear me? Die."

Andrea wasn't the dramatic type, so I believed she considered a life without Lenny a kind of death.

I said, "I'm not going to tell you what he said because I promised not to. But I'm going to say that you have nothing to worry about. Not death or anything."

A slow tempo of deep breaths came over the phone. "I don't like it. I don't like secrets."

"I know. But it's fine. It's not a big deal. When are you talking?"

"Tomorrow night."

"It's fine." I put all my money together. Eight hundred forty-four.

"Is he going to Duke for grad?" Andrea asked. "Because my parents already put in the deposit for Georgetown."

"I can neither confirm nor deny."

"Carrie. Please."

"He's my friend too. And I promised."

"How am I supposed to sit here and not know? I'm going crazy."

"You're supposed to come underwear shopping with me."

"Underwear shopping?"

***

"This is Jean-Paul Gautier." The professional shopper wore a black Chanel skirt suit. Her dark hair was parted in the middle and tightly pulled back into a long ponytail.

The little room had a couch where Andrea and I sat, a coffee table, carpet, soft lighting, and classical music. In front of the mirror, a model—who was exactly my size—showed off the cone bra cups.

"A little postmodern, maybe?" the shopper asked.

"A little," I said.

"I think we have the perfect thing." She turned to the model. "The white Lacroix." The model went back into the dressing room, and the shopper turned back to us. "More tea? We have wonderful English cookies today."

"Thank you," I said, and the shopper smiled and went out the back door.

"I forgot what it was like shopping with you," Andrea said, stirring her tea.

"Did you?"

"Not really." She lifted the cup to her lips.

"Do you want something? I think you'd look great in the red one."

"I don't even know if I'm going to have a boyfriend in two days."

She wasn't. She was going to have a fiancé. But I swallowed the reveal.

"I'm getting it for you." I poured more tea for myself. "They cut off my travel but not my Nordstrom account. And I'm feeling spiteful."

I was actually feeling a deep terror at the unknown consequences of what I was about to do, but spite gave me a reason to give her a gift before I left. She'd listened to my story with the curiosity and patience of someone who wanted to get her mind off her own problems. But it was a long and involved tale. She deserved a medal.

"They want what's best for you," she said.

"I'm a grown woman."

"Using your parents' money to buy lingerie."

I could tell she immediately regretted her words. It didn't matter. She was my best friend. She was allowed to say whatever was on her mind, especially when she was right.

"True," I said before she could backpedal. "But they've been using that money to make sure I stay under their control, so you know what? I don't feel bad."

The model came out in a white lace set. The bra pushed her breasts into soft curves, and garter straps bordered the lace panties. Two little bumps told me there were snaps at the crotch, and like a lightning bolt, I saw myself in that set.

The shopper came back with cookies. "So"—she laid the china plate on the table—"what do you think?"

"It's perfect."

"Excellent. We'll pack up a fresh one." She waved, and the model disappeared behind the door.

"Do you have a size-ten model today?"

"We do."

"I want to see her in the red Donna Karan."

"Done." She left.

"Carrie, really?" Andrea said.

"Really." I put my hand on hers, stopping her objection. "Let me do this. Please. I don't know what's going to change after today. Not with you. You're going to be fine. But with me. And you've been such a good friend to me. A better friend than I deserve. This might be my last chance to show you what you mean to me."

"You don't have to buy me expensive things to prove that."

"But I can. For now, I can."

***

I couldn't sleep. I read until I couldn't keep my eyes open, but as soon as I put my book down, my heart pounded and my mind wove one possible scenario into another, making a web of possibilities ranging from "just fine, nothing to worry about" to "everything's broken."

How mad would they be if I wound up in Venice instead of on safari in Africa? Mom would despair, explaining her failures to the women at the club. If Margie was right, Dad would be furious at the loss of an asset and the harm to the Drazen family brand. I wouldn't feel guilty about their feelings, but what would they *do*?

They could cut off the money, not pay my grad school tuition, leave me high and dry. I'd figure that out. Being broke was such a foreign concept it didn't seem unmanageable.

But what if they cut me off from the family? What if they found Gabriel so inappropriate that I couldn't bring him to Christmas dinner? From Margie and her stupid advice to little Jonathan, who, at eleven, wasn't so little anymore? Theresa with her mannerly poise and Leanne with her crazy hairdos? How could I not be one of them?

What if I really had to choose between them and Gabriel?

What if his mother couldn't bear seeing him with a Drazen? I would blame her less for her disapproval, which was based in grief, than I'd blame my parents, whose condemnation was based on appearances.

And there was Gabriel, with his fingers curled over a bow,

levitating with song. His soft lips. His commanding voice in moments of intimacy. The knowledge in his mouth when it touched my body, the sure stroke of his hands, the rightness of his kiss.

I could lose everything, and yet, by two in the morning, I knew I didn't have a choice.

CHAPTER 21

NEW YORK - 1995

I left Margie's office more settled and, at the same time, more disconcerted. She'd tried to get me a cab, but I wanted to work the decision through my bones. So, wrapped in my scarf and hood, gloved hands shoved deep in a stranger's coat pockets, I walked.

The snow had lightened into fat, vertical clusters that settled onto the wet street until they were stepped on, making a slushy, gray soup. I walked across town, turning randomly, letting my doubts fall and mix with my assurances like the slush on the sidewalk.

When I'd gotten home from Venice, I was a shell of a woman. The Italian hospital had released me when my body was healed, but my mind was at the bottom of a well.

Peter was there. He was always there. When I was in darkness, he pointed upward to show me the bright circle at the top of the pit. He showed me hope. He told me I could climb out. He waited for me, throwing down a rope over and over until I had the strength to grab it.

He told me to take my time, and I did because he was there. He made me laugh, reminding me that bleakness and sorrow were temporary. And when I told him I had loved the man I lost the night we were attacked, he held me without judgment or jealousy.

Peter asked for nothing until I was well enough to accept him into my bed, then he asked for everything.

I gave it to him out of gratitude, and I kept giving him everything out of guilt. I always knew that, but I never accepted it. And when I'd run away in my sloppily planned trip to Belize, I felt more guilt than relief.

The air warmed after noon, and the snow turned to rain, soaking the cold to my bones. The wool coat couldn't protect me from freezing rain. I had to find shelter.

Looking up at a stone lion covered in three inches of melting snow, I felt a sense of relief. I could find refuge in what Peter had taken away.

I carefully climbed the salted steps of the library, where I could feel at home in the presence of things I didn't know.

I hadn't gotten the Fischer Prize. That went to Andrea. I'd used the loss as confirmation that I hadn't deserved the nomination in the first place. That I wasn't that smart, just curious enough to be credibly named. I had curiosity and passion where I should have had brains and ambition.

After roaming the library like a starving woman in a supermarket, I found the psychology section deep in the reference section. The librarian had taken one look at me and let me through to the private stacks.

Pretty Girl Syndrome struck again. My cross to bear was the shame that it was so easy to carry.

Two people sat at the tables, surrounded by piles of books, heads down, working on papers and projects that absorbed them completely. Wishing I could be them and know the things they knew, I unbuttoned the coat and walked down the rows, letting my fingers run over the spines. *A Sociology of Mental Illness, Cognitive Social Psychology, On Aggression*. I could read them. All of them. I could absorb the information and know things. The hows and whys of the mind. The stories we told ourselves, the connections we made, the hundred ways it could all go wrong. I pulled out *The Fantasy Bond, Processes and Disorders,* and *The Social Animal.* Though *The Mind and Memory* made it abundantly clear I'd reached the limit of what my arms could carry, I still wasn't done.

Placing the books on the table and sitting, I opened *The Man Who Mistook His Wife for a Hat* to a random page.

Somewhere in the middle of reading about Anna O., the first woman whose life had been changed with talk therapy, a thought that had been born and raised in my unconscious became a fully formed adult in my conscious mind. It was stubborn, irrefutable, and as accurate as simple arithmetic.

I allowed my mind to say it.

I was leaving Peter.

The how of it wasn't known, but the decision couldn't be changed.

"I am leaving Peter," I whispered to myself, giving the thought a form outside my mind.

There it was.

My hand shook as I turned the page. The words swam before my eyes. I was caught in a whirl of terror over the consequences of a truth that led to action.

I closed the book and headed for the comfort of the quiet rows of books. *The Divided Self, Group Dynamics,* and *Color Cognition* lined up like soldiers waiting to be deployed.

When I reached for *Ghost in the Machine,* I heard a book fall behind me. Turning, I saw a man on the other side of the stacks, rushing away. I picked up the book.

Freud and the Psychology of Music.

A piece of paper stuck out from the title page. I slid it out.

Practice. 8 a.m. 56th St.

The point was the man, not the book.

"Gabriel!" I shouted in the quiet room.

I ran after the man. Camel coat. Hat. Trouser cuffs stained with snow. I was stopped short by the guard.

"Those don't circulate, ma'am."

Confused for a moment, I realized I still had books in my arms. I gave them to him and ran outside. The snow had stopped, and the man in the camel coat was gone.

CHAPTER 22

VENICE, ITALY - 1993

*S*t. Mark's Basilica was packed with tourists, but I saw
him right away, reading a book as he leaned against a
fence surrounding the column of the winged lion.

"*Ciao*," I said.

"*Ciao*," he replied with a smile, folding the book closed. It was
written in Italian.

"Good book?"

"*Si*. I'm brushing up."

So far from the disapproval of our families and the familiarity
of school, we looked at each other as if seeing the other for the
first time. He was the same but different. Older. Or maybe more
complete. Existing outside my memories, without mental land-
marks, bathed in Mediterranean sunlight, he was more real and
yet more pleasingly mysterious.

He tried to hold back a smile as he looked at me.

Was it the same for him?

I turned away, suddenly self-conscious.

"The light here suits you," he said.

"I need a shower. I just got off the plane. There were
two stops."

"You must be tired."

"I was, but now I'm kind of awake."

He looked at the ground by my feet, but it was all pigeons and stone.

"Is this your only bag?" He took my carry-on.

"I don't need much."

Just him and a slinky bit of white lingerie. I must have blushed thinking about it, because he bit his lip and looked at me as if he wanted to eat me alive.

"I hope you didn't get a hotel," he said, putting his arm around me.

"I didn't."

I would have needed a credit card to book a hotel, and my cash was limited.

"Good." He guided me to an archway that led outside the plaza. "Because I have a twin bed and a bathroom down the hall."

"Perfect."

"I'm going to feed you," he said, then leaned down to whisper in my ear. "Then I'm going to fuck you."

***

He fed me little square pizza slices at an empty café. We drank espresso from tiny cups we'd rubbed with lemon rind. He told me about his program mentor, who would only speak to him in Italian. Gabriel imitated his teacher's frustration with how he held his bow until I buckled with laughter. I told him about the African safari I'd never go on and made a joke of my parents' disapproval.

We pretended that this was who we were. Two people in love, with our choice of innumerate futures.

I'd thought I'd experienced happiness in my life. But every birthday and Christmas in my childhood had been a dress rehearsal for those hours in a Venetian café.

***

Squeaky clean from the shower, I padded down the *pensione* hall in a silk robe and slippers, my hair up in a towel. He was waiting for me outside his room, leaning on the doorjamb with his arms crossed, watching to make sure I made it twenty feet unmolested.

"Feel better?" he asked.

"Tons."

I went into the room, and he followed, closing the door. He hadn't been lying about the twin bed. It was made with white sheets, a blue blanket, and a single pillow. He had a sink with two faucets, a mirror, and a little space for his razor and soap. A table and two chairs, dresser with his violin case on top. Narrow French doors led to a balcony overlooking a winding street.

And him. In jeans and a navy T-shirt, the most beautiful thing in the room, watching me as I put my toiletry bag on the table.

"Stop," I said.

"Stop what?"

"Looking at me like that."

I let my hair loose from the towel, and he sucked in a breath as it fell over my shoulders. He brushed my hair away from my neck, letting his fingertips linger.

"How should I look at you?" He kissed my cheek with cautious tenderness. "I can only see the most beautiful woman in the world." Moving his lips down my jaw, he brought my skin to life. "Or is it that I can't believe you want me?"

He moved the robe away from my shoulder so he could kiss my collarbone. If he expected an answer, he wasn't getting one. Words had left me. I was made of breath and need.

He leaned away, taking me in from toes to lips.

Timid, ashamed of both my desire and my inexperience, I couldn't move. He reached for the belt of my robe and, with one finger, released it. It opened, sending a chill past the fabric and revealing a white lace garter set.

"What are you wearing?" he asked.

"I thought you'd like it."

He slid his fingers under the robe, along my shoulders,

pushing it off me. I was suddenly ashamed at my preparation.

"Oh my God." He took half a step back, eyes eating me alive.

I swallowed. I needed him to tell me what to do, but he just stood there with his jeans bulging.

"You like it?"

"Is this how you wanted me to look at you?"

It wasn't. Not a minute ago. I'd imagined something more neutral, but his hunger was exactly what I needed. Muscles flexing involuntarily, eyes drinking me in until my skin was textured with goose bumps and my clit was rubbing against the damp crotch of the panties, his gaze was a physical thing.

"I don't know what to do now," I said.

"Whatever I tell you." He smirked. "I like to be in charge."

"I'd like that."

"I'm going to make this good for you." He bit his lower lip. "You're going to come so hard when I suck your clit that your pussy's going to be jealous."

I laughed, releasing a bit of the tension but none of the desire.

When I reached for his jeans, he took my hands away and opened his fly himself, taking out his erection with relief, as if releasing an animal from a cage.

He was huge. Thick and longer than his fist could hold. My lungs released a breath so fast I squeaked.

His smirk got wider. "I'll go slow and easy. It's going to be worth it."

"Okay."

With his free hand, he shifted my bra strap off my shoulder. Then the other. Languidly, he undid the front bra hook, and I spilled out. He ran the back of his hand over my body, pushing the bra to the floor, bumping my hard nipples along the backs of his fingers.

"I'm going to suck these," he said. "Tell me to stop if it hurts."

He bent down, taking his hand off his dick to play with one nipple as he sucked the other. It tickled at first, but then the pleasure came as if a thick electric cable connected my breasts to the skin between my legs. He sucked harder, pinching the other side, twisting and pulling. I put my hand behind his head to draw him closer.

"You like it," he said as he switched sides.

"I like it."

"You're fucking magic." He stood, leaving my wet nipple to tighten in the cool air. "You ready to come?"

"Yes."

"Sit." He led me to the edge of the bed and sat me down, running his hands over and between my thighs, pushing them apart. Out of habit, I resisted, and he looked down at me. "You want to stop?"

"No."

"Then open your legs, little bird."

The command sent a shudder up my spine, and my legs opened for him. He pulled my knees up, and I fell backward, leaning on my locked arms. He unsnapped the panties. I was exposed, vulnerable, throbbing under the pressure of his gaze.

He stood straight, letting his pants drop to the floor. His dick had a drop of wetness at the tip. If he wanted me to, I'd taste salt in the dense liquid and feel the thin, hot skin on my tongue.

But he didn't want me to. Not yet. He peeled off his shirt, revealing taut muscles and glowing olive skin. He put his hands between my knees and pushed them apart as far as my body allowed and kissed the inside of my thigh, the outside of my vulva, the dark, damp places where my bones joined.

"Please, Gabriel, please."

"Please what?"

"Lick it. Do what you said."

He spread my lips apart. "As beauty commands."

Ever so gently, he ran his tongue up from my opening, lightly over my clit, and back.

"Oh."

"Oh, you ain't seen nothing yet."

He did it again, flicking my nub, then sucking. My arms couldn't hold me up. I dropped to the bed and wove my fingers in his hair. Over the horizon of my breasts and belly, he looked at me with an expression of confidence in the delights he was about to deliver.

Flattening his tongue against me, he watched my face. Sucked. Flicked. Sucked harder. He spread me open, watching me. "You want to come?"

"Please."

"I want to hear you."

I nodded but didn't have a moment to say a word of agreement before his tongue committed fully to its task. I came into his mouth, arching and twisting with my eyes closed, crying out so loudly all of Venice must have heard.

When it was too much, I pushed him away, laughing and panting. I opened my eyes to find him kneeling between my legs and sliding on a condom.

He seemed even bigger than before.

"Don't worry," he said, bending over me with one elbow on the bed. "Easy does it."

"Okay."

"Open wide."

I didn't realize I was clamping my legs shut around him. I opened for him, and he guided himself into me, breaking barriers slowly, gently pushing forward until I thought I was stretched to the limit.

Eyes tightly closed, jaw clenched, he stopped for a moment. "You're okay?"

"Yes. Please."

He groaned and buried himself inside me, opening his eyes when he was down to the root. "Thank God for the condom," he said with a grin. "I'd be done already."

I cupped his jaw, smiling with him as he moved slowly, deliberately.

Through the wall, loud pop music played, making me realize how thin the walls were.

"I think I was too loud," I whispered.

"I always want to hear you."

He pushed deep, pressing himself against my clit and moving to stimulate it, over and over until I felt the swell of pleasure rise again. Shifting his hips, he increased the pressure, moving with the music as if he couldn't help it.

"Carrie," he groaned as he bent his head. "Fuck." He picked up his head. "I want you to come again. Here." He put his thumb to my lips. "Make it wet."

I opened my mouth and took his thumb, not knowing what he was planning but trusting him with my body.

"You're so sexy." He pushed his thumb in deeper, then drew it out. "Wetter."

I gave him everything I had until he was satisfied, then he reached between us, where our bodies were joined, and ran his wet thumb over my clit. I grabbed the muscles of his back, digging my nails into him as if I needed purchase against the shock waves of pleasure.

"Gab—oh."

"Look at me."

I tried to keep my eyes locked on his, detailing the thickness of his lashes and the shape of his parted lips, but as the orgasm swirled and coalesced, my eyes craved darkness and closed. I bucked and twisted with the motion of his thumb, biting back a scream.

His thumb moved away, but his body was still connected to mine, thrusting against me, still slow but less methodical, jerking out, then slamming into me. He moaned in a note I'd never heard before. A groan of vulnerability. Exposure.

A full surrender to the moment. To me.

His orgasm unmasked him and attached him to me forever.

CHAPTER 23

NEW YORK - 1995

*I*t got dark pretty early in New York, which made me feel perfectly fine about dipping into the six-pack of Sam Adams Drew kept in the fridge. It was cold and bubbly, only semi-pissy, and a dead weight in my stomach. Three in, one after the other, and I was high as a kite, swimming in depressive nostalgia and waiting for my sister or her man to come home.

Adam Brate had seen me in the limo window and done nothing. He wasn't Gabriel.

The man in the library wasn't him. I was hysterical. Imagining things.

Gabriel was dead. Completely and utterly dead.

And I was leaving Peter anyway.

"Daddy won't approve," I said to the talking head on the muted television. "Oh, boo-hoo-hoo for you, Declan Drazen."

I picked up the phone for the hundredth time and put it back in the cradle for the hundredth.

One more beer.

I popped open the fourth bottle and dialed the phone.

"Hello?"

"Andrea?"

"Carrie? Is that you?" Her voice carried over the miles between New York and Boston on electric waves of excitement and love. "Len!" she called. "It's Carrie!"

"Hey, Carrie." I could barely hear him, but he was there, and I remembered why I'd dialed her number instead of Peter's. What they had was what I wanted. It was what I deserved.

"How's the baby?" I asked.

"Kicking like crazy. How have you been?"

We'd spoken on the phone but hadn't seen each other since my wedding, a little over a year before. She and Lenny had eloped. Peter and I had had an event that was reported in the society pages.

"Fabuloso." I threw myself on the couch.

"Are you drunk?"

"Hell yes!" I tipped the bottle to my lips and drank.

"Are you okay?"

"Hey. You remember that guy? Gabriel?"

"Duh?" She knew about what had happened in Venice. She'd spent a weekend that July wiping my tears and going out with Peter and me.

"He's dead."

"I know."

"And Peter, my husband, he's an asshole anyway."

"What happened?"

"He likes to…" I got up. The room swam, so I stopped in the middle of it. "I'm leaving him."

"Oh my God."

"Yup. Fucking right. Oh. My. God."

We paused. I set my feet apart so I wouldn't fall over.

"He likes to what?" Andrea asked.

My mouth tasted like a burned match. I took another swig of beer to get rid of it.

"He likes to hurt me." I rushed to finish before she had a thing to say. "And I wanted to tell you… to say it first so it's out there.

Whenever a man looks at me, he punishes me. And I let him. I let him."

"Oh, Carrie."

"It's fine."

"It's not fine."

"When it was nice, I liked it, but now it's not nice, and what I'm telling you..." A bubble of beer came up, making me stop for a second. "What I'm telling you is I don't think it's nice anymore, but he's not stopping, and also? He's a criminal. I thought it was just moving too much money around so whatever, but he had blood on his cuff this one time."

"Jesus."

"Praise Jesus!"

"Where are you?"

"Big Apple with my big sister," I slurred. "Looking for Gabriel, but he's dead. Like I told you. But I'm calling Peter and telling him it's over so I don't have to look at his face or be close enough to..." I gulped. "He can't hurt me if I'm here. Right? It's okay to do it over the phone?"

"Yes, Carrie. It's okay to be safe."

"Are you happy, Andrea? With Lenny? And the baby coming? Is it good?"

"It's fine."

She sounded as if she was sparing my feelings. I didn't want them spared. I wanted them teased out from the corners I'd stuffed them into.

"No. Tell me. I want to know if there's hope or if it's just all shit. Say it's great or it's terrible—or tell me it's somewhere in the middle, but I want the honest answer."

She sighed before taking a long breath as if she needed the time to couch her reply. "Lenny's everything to me. I'm everything to him. It's everything."

"You're happy?"

"Work sucks."

"With him, you dork."

"I'm very happy."

The front door deadbolt clicked open.

"Good," I said. "That's what I needed to hear."

Margie came in and closed the door. "Hey," she said, taking off her coat.

"I have to go," I said into the phone. "My sister's here."

"Can you call me after you talk to him?"

"Yep."

"Please be safe."

"I will."

"I love you, Carrie. You're the sister I never had."

"I love you too, Andrea. You're the sister I never knew I needed."

After hitting the button to hang up, I tossed the phone to Margie, who snatched it out of the air.

"You smell like a brewery," she said, coming close. "Sam Adams."

"Winner, winner, chicken dinner," I said, touching the tip of my nose. "You know why?"

"I couldn't hazard a guess," she replied dryly.

"I made a decision." I took the phone from her.

"Let's hear it."

"I'm not chasing a dead man anymore." I pressed the green button. It beeped and gave a dial tone.

Margie picked up my bottle. It was nearly empty. "I'll get you another."

She went to the kitchen. I took a deep breath, and with an alarmingly sudden flash of sobriety, I called Peter's office.

He wouldn't like hearing this at work. He'd be angry and punish me. He'd make it harder for me to travel without him.

But it was now or the next time I had the nerve. When the line was picked up, my body stopped functioning for a split second.

"Peter Thorne's office," his receptionist chanted.

"Hi, Greta, it's Carrie. Is he in?"

"Left about an hour ago. I can connect you to the car."

"No," I said. "Thanks. I got it."

After I hung up, Margie came back with two open beers and handed me one. "I'm sorry. I didn't know it was bad with him."

Holding up my beer, I said, "Here's to me not hiding anything from you."

"Hear, hear."

We clicked our bottles, and I drank my nerves away before sitting to dial the car. Margie sat next to me.

Having dialed the office first, the car was less nerve-racking. But there was no answer.

"Okay," I said, hanging up. "He's probably already home."

I tried there and got the machine.

"Does he have a pager?" Margie asked.

"Yeah. But I've left enough messages. I don't want him to panic. He's probably in a meeting."

Or meeting a white Honda by the train tracks.

"I'll sit up with you and wait."

I put the phone on the coffee table, next to my beer. The room was swoony and soft, edgeless and curved. My mouth was thick and dry, and my limbs flopped bonelessly. "Where's Drew?"

"Work, then rehearsal."

My body leaned, then dropped in her direction with my head in her lap. "Does he make you happy?"

She put her bottle on the side table and brushed my hair away from my face. "No."

"No?"

"No. Happy is situational. He's my companion of choice."

"I don't get it," I mumbled.

"It's not about happiness." She stroked my hair pensively. "Not for us. We have history together. Lots of ugly shit we don't have to explain. That makes us indispensable to one another."

Even in my drunken haze, I knew she wouldn't tell me her ugly shit. Not that night. Maybe never.

"So," I said. "You love him or no?"

"More than I can ever say."

Her fingers soothed the last of my uneasiness, drawing out drowsy, unfiltered thoughts.

"I thought love was about happiness. It made everything perfect. Blue skies and birds singing. It was music and light. That was Gabriel. He made everything all right, and we would have been so happy. So happy if we could just have had a chance. And then it happened." I swallowed hard, remembering the feel of the cobblestones against my head and the blood... all the blood. For months, I saw it whenever I closed my eyes.

"And I loved Peter," I said. "I know I did. But it didn't make me happy. He saw that. He knew. It made him crazy because he couldn't give me what Gabriel could have. And now... no one can give it to me."

"No one ever could, Carrie."

"Whenever I hear a violin, I miss him. So, I used to hear them in everything, then I just gave up and listened to classical music all the time. It's like I can't let it go. Then that piece came out. *Ballad of Blades*. It made me crazy. It was so... *him*." I sat up and pushed my hair out of my face. It was seven forty-five. Too early to go to sleep. "I keep thinking if I hadn't gone to Venice, he wouldn't have died. I'd have so much music in my life."

"You can still have music." Margie picked up the bottles and stood. "Just not with him."

While she was in the kitchen, my gaze landed on her stereo. I got up and flipped through her CDs. Rock. Rock. Rock. Margie's life. I found a Debussy next to Dinosaur Jr. and pulled it out, slapping the case against the heel of my hand. The desire to play classical music so I could think of him was like the hunger for a drug.

Transported to a thoughtless past where possibilities opened like a flower. Where we could have been anything with enough wisdom and work. His work. My life was always going to be artless and gray without the sound of him. No amount of practice would have made me a musician, and hours of listening didn't fill my life with music.

But that life of troubles and joys had been so close. I'd chosen it, and it had been taken with the fierceness of a knife in the dark. The days and nights of reading while he played the same thing over and over until he got it right.

The stereo lights blinked to life when I turned it on. I flipped open the CD case.

"What are you playing?" Margie asked as she flopped back on the couch.

"Debussy."

"Rock out," she said. "But keep it down. The neighbors have a kid they put down early."

I wanted to do what I always did. Bring Gabriel back to earth, pretend he was in the next room, practicing as if his life depended on it. Over and over. Better and better. Fortifying his muscle memory until you could hear his proficiency with every stroke and he practically levitated while I read about the workings of the human mind.

Jung on the synchronicity of meaningless events.

Maybe even Freud on the psychology of music.

Blissfully reading while he practiced and practiced.

I laid the CD in place and let the player pull it in like a tongue.

"Margie," I said, pressing Play, "how do you get to Carnegie Hall?"

CHAPTER 24

VENICE, ITALY - 1993

*G*abriel wet a washcloth with warm water from the room's sink and cleaned my body with such sweet tenderness I fell asleep.

It was night when I woke with a blanket over me. The French doors were open to the sounds of the street, and Gabriel was playing a melody I'd never heard before.

"What is that?" I asked, still sticky with sleep.

"That's you." He put down his bow.

"Play it again."

He placed the violin in the case. "It's not ready yet."

I stretched as he snapped the case closed and sat on the edge of the bed.

"I'm hungry," I said.

"Me too." He slipped the blanket off me, revealing my naked, satisfied body. "Let's go eat, then we'll have another round."

***

After eating, we took a walk. The streets of Venice were so narrow and the canals so still in the moonlight... they folded us into safety. We didn't have parents, families, or expectations. We met where our laughter mingled in the space between us, the places where our skin touched, the rhythm of our footsteps. We found our way around corners and through cobblestone alleys, wandering arm in arm into the untrammeled part of the city.

Seemingly enchanted by something going on in his head, he stopped at a little store that was no more than a hole in the wall. The store was half the size of my shoe closet in Malibu, shelves of beauty supplies and makeup stacked behind a window.

"Are you all right?" I asked.

"Mm-hm." He took a few crumpled lire from his pocket and spoke in Italian to the woman behind the window.

The woman took a little jar from a rack.

"What are you getting?"

He smirked. One eyebrow twitched with mischief. "Tomorrow night, you'll find out."

He handed the woman the money. She gave him the little jar and offered a brush, which he declined.

"Let me see." I reached for the jar, but he hid it inside his jacket.

"No peeking."

I pouted. "I hate not knowing."

"Now you know how I feel," Gabriel said. "I'm two days into the music program here, and I've learned more than I learned in four years at USC."

"You're changing the subject."

"I'm pointing out that we learn when the knowledge is given. Not sooner."

"You mean you didn't know everything?"

"Not about music," he said. "Playing your body though…"

"You might not know everything about that."

"We'll see."

The alley ended in water. Without deciding, we sat on the edge of the short dock, feet dangling, the voices of residents drifting down from windows above.

"What do you want to do?" I asked. "About us?"

He tilted into me, hand braced on the wooden surface behind me. "We didn't invent this. Romeo and Juliet did."

"That didn't work out well."

"We'll be patient. You go to school. I'll finish up here and meet you there."

"What's a classical violinist going to do in North Carolina?"

"There are musicians everywhere. We'll just be who we are. Your parents will see how appropriate I am."

I had to twist to see his face, blue in the moonlight, darker than dark in the shadows. "Your mother though. If she blames my father for what happened to your father? It's hard to get over that."

"You trying to talk me out of loving you?"

"Could I, if I wanted to?"

"No. Never." He sat up. Down the canal, a lone gondola made its way toward us, the gondolier singing a song that softly bounced off the walls of the narrow street. "There are notes that go together. Play them alone and they're fine, but play them together and it makes music. No matter the instrument or what part of the world you're in, they're linked by a chord. That's us. We were waiting for the moment the world put us together. I can't unhear us now."

We kissed as if we were making that music, notes weaving together in a pattern predicted by science and art. Yet we were doomed by history.

"*Buona sera, piccioncini,*" the lanky gondolier cried as he approached.

We jumped up as he leveraged his oar so the boat came within a foot of the dock. Gabriel spoke in a broken conversational Italian. The gondolier answered, and Gabriel turned to me.

"He has time for one more tonight."

"It's late."

But he'd already jumped onto the boat and was holding his hand out to me. I stepped on, and he helped me sit on one of the padded benches. We were off in the swish of rippling water. Gabriel chatted with the gondolier, and he agreed to something.

"*Grazie*," Gabriel said, reaching for a case at the gondolier's feet. He unzipped it and took out an accordion.

"What are you doing?" I asked.

"He's agreed to let me do the serenading as long as I knew how to play it."

"Do you?"

"Not really." He pulled out the accordion, making it whine. "You're not going to leave me if I can't figure this out, are you?"

"I'll give you a minute," I joked as he fingered the buttons. "But our gondolier might not."

"I think I have it."

The boat turned deeper into the city, away from the crowds, where it was quiet and dark. Gabriel got used to squeezing the bellows and found the right way to press the buttons. Even a goofy grandpa instrument was sexy in his hands.

"What are you going to play?"

"Ah," he said with a series of confident notes. "I think this." He hummed to get the note right, then half spoke, half sang the first line. "*If I should stay…*"

"'I Will Always Love You'!" I clapped. "I love this one!"

The gondolier laughed.

At the next line, Gabriel's voice went from timid to assured, as if the words carried a truth that elevated his voice. He would always love me. He got more confident as the song went on and the canals got tighter.

At the last note, a voice came from a window above. "*Basta!*"

The gondolier called upward, "*Scusa!*" then turned back to us and put his finger on his lips.

We kissed through laughter like teenagers caught behind the gym. Gabriel put the accordion back, thanked our gondolier, and held me close all the way back to the dock. The *swish-swish* of the boat in the still water was the breath between us, and I felt right, calm, and with him at my side, powerful enough to overcome anything.

The boat pulled up to the dock where we'd started. Gabriel paid the gondolier, helped me off the boat, and we walked hand in hand down the shadowed alley.

"Do you know where we are?" I asked. "I feel lost."

"I'm not. Come."

Trusting him, I let him lead me into the darkness of the old city.

CHAPTER 25

NEW YORK - 1995

The next morning, I made my way to Carnegie Hall's Fifty-Sixth Street entrance.

Because practice was at eight o'clock.

Possibility one: I was seeing meaning where none existed. That was the most likely scenario. Jung's synchronicity only worked when no other cause for the connection could be found. But there was a connection, and it was my desire to see one. A random note in a library book that looked more like a reminder to some unknown person didn't bring the dead back to life. "Practice" did not equal "Carnegie Hall" any more than "the road" equaled "chicken crossing."

Possibility two: The man in the library had left the book not for me, but for himself. It was his note, and he had practice at eight on Fifty-Sixth Street. Maybe at Carnegie Hall. Maybe not. The idea that the library man, whose face had been hidden, was Adam Brate occurred to me, but I dismissed it even as I hoped it was true. Adam had seen me through the limo window. Maybe he wanted to see me again and was only telling me where he'd be. I enjoyed playing out that idea on the cab ride but let it go as I got out into the freezing rain.

Possibility three: The ghost of my first love was sending me messages through a living person. I didn't even have time for that, but in the context of the mind's push toward hope, I understood it.

Carnegie Hall was closed for the morning. The Fifty-Sixth Street entrance was a small, deeply set brown door. Just inside it, a man in a black parka sat behind a desk, doing a crossword. His mahogany cheeks were pocked with old acne scars, and his fingers were thick around the pen.

"Hi," I said.

"Good morning, miss." He laid down the newspaper and picked up a clipboard. "Name, please."

"Carrie Thorne."

He glanced at me. "You sure about that?"

My heart sank. I'd let the cab go. Now I would have to hail another one in the freezing rain and go back to Margie's after a wild goose chase. "Drazen? Carrie Drazen?"

"You got ID?"

Bending my face toward my bag so he wouldn't see me smile, I took out my wallet. "It all has my married name, which is Thorne."

"Mm-hm."

I showed him my driver's license.

"Looks like you." He folded the list over the top of the clipboard and handed me the sign-in sheet. "Sign here."

My hand shook as I signed. What was I walking into? The next hours would be an unexpected Christmas present found behind the tree. At worst, they'd be pleasant. At best... I couldn't even guess the best case. I'd witness practicing musicians who didn't know me from Eve, enjoy as much as I found comfortable, and slip out.

The guard gave me directions. Left. Right. Right. Down the stairs and left. I nodded, knowing I'd forget it all and get where I was going anyway.

I was right.

Once I was in the public-facing space, all I had to do was follow the music.

A cello tuning. Playing a few atonal measures. Stopping and playing again to get it right.

The theater was empty, broken into sections of minimal house lights. The stage was arced with chairs and music stands, flatly lit, with a white folding screen stretching across the left half, casting the man behind it into a silhouette. He was playing that cello, and the sound was unmistakable.

Adam Brate. Had to be. Was the note in the book intentional? Should I sit and listen like an eavesdropper?

I walked down the center aisle as quietly as I could.

When I got to the front of the stage, he stopped.

"Hello?" I said. "I found a note. I'm not sure it was for me."

The shadowy arm extended to a metal folding chair on my side of the screen. I climbed up to the stage, heels clopping on the floor like dogs barking in an otherwise quiet yard.

He said nothing as I sat. The chair was so close to the screen I could touch it.

"Are you…" I stopped myself. Saying the name seemed sacrilegious. Louder than the intrusive, cloppy heels. "Are you who I think you are?"

The answer should have been, "Who do you think I am?" which would have softened the sound of the famous name. But he didn't answer. He drew his bow across the strings.

On the first note, I knew what it was.

He was playing *Ballad of Blades* just for me. I sat back, ready to receive his gift for whatever reason he'd decided to give it. I knew the piece. After playing it a hundred times, I'd memorized it, making it the soundtrack of my best memories.

But the movie wouldn't play in my head because this was different. He played it with a sharpness I'd never heard. Maybe the CD recording or the speaker's amplification had dulled the experience. Maybe it was me.

No, it wasn't me.

The notes had an inner life. They were greater than memory, larger than longing. The cello called to me with a voice that spoke a wordless language filled with sadness and grace. My mind emptied. I lost any preconceived notion of what the piece was and let myself hear the humility and ache in the melody. It pierced me. Opened me. Filled me with a melancholy that grew inside my chest until I thought I'd be lifted from my seat.

It was the most beautiful thing I'd ever heard.

When it was over, my cheeks were wet with tears and I could hear him gasping for breath.

I leaned toward the paper screen. "Thank you."

He didn't move. I put my hand on the screen, and high on the truth of the music, I opened my mouth and spoke the truth.

"Gabriel."

My hand flat on the paper, I waited for him to acknowledge what I knew to be true. The shadow shifted, and he laid his hand on his side of the screen, palm pushing against mine until I felt the pressure of it.

"Little bird," he croaked. "I miss you."

"Why?" I asked before swallowing tears. "Why?"

He paused before he spoke. "Because I loved you."

My hand got warm against his. The man on the other side was real and alive.

Gabriel was dead. Gabriel didn't have warm hands. Without the music to tell me the truth, doubts crept in.

"Take the screen away," I said.

"I can't."

"Please. I want to see you."

"No."

Reacting to the cut of his answer, I took my hand away and regretted it. "Why did you call me here, then?"

He plucked a few pensive notes from the neck of his cello as if he needed music to think. "Because I have everything I ever wanted and I'm empty. I saw you at Dorothy Chandler and realized I didn't want you. I want lots of things, but not you. No. I need you. Without you, I have the world. The whole empty, meaningless world I'd give up for one more night with you."

"Take it. Take tonight. Move this screen and tell me what happened in Venice."

"I can't." He laid his cello down like a fact.

"I thought you were dead." The last word came out so loud it echoed in the hall.

"What? No. I didn't know that."

He was surprised that I'd thought that. God. Had I been tricked? Mistaken?

"I did," I said. "But you're not. You're... I can't believe it."

"I am dead without you."

"What happened? Gabriel. What could it be? Why can't I even see you?"

He took a deep sigh, and his silhouette bent at the waist, elbows to knees, one hand in his hair. "Can you just trust me? This one thing. For now. I didn't think you'd come. I didn't think you'd remember me or a stupid joke. But," he said with a resigned laugh, "you were always smarter than anyone gave you credit for. Especially yourself."

"It's not that I'm smart. It's that you always knew me."

"No." He put his hand to the screen again, and mine shot up to meet it. "Things are at work here. Things I can't control. Promises I made."

I shrank inside. Who was to say he wasn't married? And who was to say she wasn't powerful enough to control who saw his face? I'd spent so much energy thinking of my own husband that I hadn't given a thought to who he'd given himself to. "Promises to who?"

"I can't say. Not yet."

"Can you tell me what happened after Venice?"

"No."

"But you lived."

"Apparently. And you?"

"I died." My hand slid away. "Peter Thorne took me on a whirl-wind tour of Europe, and I figured…" I stopped to manage the shame of what I was about to say, but I resolved to say it anyway. "I figured, why not? I had to get married anyway. Might as well get it over with."

"Did you go to Duke?"

Did the woman he was promised to have a life? A career? A degree she'd finished because she was smart and capable and had enough grit to make it past anything life threw at her?

"No," I grumbled.

"Why not?"

"I'm just a pretty rich girl, and that's all I'll ever be. I mean, think about it. Who wouldn't want what I have? What's the point of trying for more?"

"Fulfillment?"

"That wasn't an option after Venice. I know I'm a disappoint-ment. I gave up. That's all there is. I gave up. Married Peter. Being his wife is my job. End."

He rubbed his hands together. I heard the callouses scrape. "Do you love him? Is he good to you?"

"No. He's shit. He treats me like…" I trailed off. He hadn't earned the details. "I'm leaving him."

The scraping stopped. "Are you?"

"Yes."

"Because I'm here?"

The truth was that the decision to leave Peter had been in the oven since I'd heard Gabriel play "I Will Always Love You" and had only been pulled out the night before I'd stepped into Carnegie Hall. It was still warm, but it was finished. I had no intention of undoing it whether Gabriel belonged to someone else or not.

"No," I said. "It's been a long time coming. I just have to figure out how to do it. And I will. Even if I never see you again. Even if you're happily married to someone you love."

My voice cracked so hard on "married" that I barely got to "love." As much as it hurt to say, I had to give him a chance to confirm it.

"I didn't know you thought I was dead," he said.

"But you stayed away? Why?"

"I'll tell you."

He sat up straight with his hands on his knees. I waited. And waited.

"Gabriel."

"I can't. Not now. Not yet."

"If you're with someone—"

"I'm not ready," he cut in. "I just want you to know... to believe that I never forgot you. You're in my mind every day. You take up space in my heart. I tried closing it up so I never had to miss you again, but this piece? *Ballad of Blades?* It's for you. It sounds like you. Every time I play it, you're speaking to me. So, I stopped playing it for a while, and it only got worse. It called to me. I couldn't shut it out. You were there with that voice of yours. I thought I was playing your song, but it was playing me."

Why? Then why did you stay away? The questions came to my lips but couldn't leave them.

"Do you want to see me?" he asked.

"Yes. And not through a screen."

"Okay." His shadow placed the cello between his legs and picked up the bow. "I need to do some things, and you need to think about it."

"No, I don't."

"You do." He drew the bow across the strings. "I'm at the Waldorf. Room 2220. Call me there tonight if you want to see me. No." He stopped himself as if changing his mind midstream. "We'll meet at the library lions at three, and you'll have one more chance to walk away."

171

He played the first few measures of "I Will Always Love You."

"I won't."

"Then you'll be mine again." He abruptly stopped playing. "But you'll walk when you see me. Anyone would."

He played the song, and I knew that no matter what I said, he wouldn't be interrupted.

I stood, and with one look at the screen and the outline of the man behind it, I turned and—

"Wait!" The silhouette of the man stood. Head down, hands fidgeting at his sides, he continued, "You have to know."

"Know what?"

He came from behind the screen and stood with his back to me, hands balled into fists at his sides, and I gasped.

CHAPTER 26

VENICE, ITALY - 1993

I hadn't realized how many turns we'd made through the city, but every time Gabriel guided me around a corner, we passed something I recognized. A particular box of flowers. A configuration of the stones. A little storefront that had been open when we passed the first time but was now shut for the night. I fell into a relaxed state of submission to his sense of direction.

"Hey," a man called from a doorway twenty feet in front of us. He stepped into the center of the street, silhouetted against a bare bulb behind him. *"Turisti! Vi sieti persi?"*

I couldn't understand what he said, but there was no language barrier for his tone of menace.

"No." Gabriel stopped short, pushing me behind him.

"Questa è la mia strada," the man called, speaking slowly enough for me to understand that it was his street. The man stepped forward into a shaft of moonlight. He was in his late teens, maybe early twenties. Young enough to do a stupid thing.

"Bene, prego," Gabriel said, then turned, his body close, facing mine as he looked over my head. *"Ce ne andiamo."*

I followed his gaze. Two men had appeared on the other side of the alley.

"What's happening?" I asked.

"Stay close, little bird."

Even as the men came toward us, I assumed we'd walk away. Our wallets might be lighter, but we'd be together the next day and the days after. Some things were inviolate. We'd established our future as one of them.

"*Dove stai andando?*" a fourth man asked from the shadows of a doorway just a few feet away.

I jumped.

Gabriel pulled me away from him, but he was running out of ways to protect me.

I threw my purse on the ground between us and the two approaching figures.

"Take it!" I said, not knowing if they spoke English.

It didn't matter. The men didn't even look at it. The first man was a few feet away now.

"*Grazie,*" he said, "*Ma avrò il tuo sangue come pagamento.*"

The moon glinted on the blade.

It happened so fast my perception sped up, making the attack play in slow motion as my muscles froze into helplessness, as if they'd submitted to spectator status. All I could do was cling to Gabriel as they pulled him away and despair when he let me go to save me.

Four of them. Two of us. One on me, pulling me away by the arms, the hair, my legs pulled from under me as I flailed. I thought I was screaming, but I couldn't hear myself. Couldn't see anything for a moment. Then in the next moment, I saw Gabriel with utter clarity—on his back, straddled by one of the men, and the blade coming down on his face.

Finding strength I didn't know I had, I broke free and lurched for him.

The blade came down again on his throat.

Blood everywhere. His face covered with it like a mask. The thick, viscous jet from an artery.

Stars crackled in the frame of my vision. I tilted sideways until the stone street met my cheek.

Gabriel and I were face-to-face, locked in a split-second eternal stare. My head hit the ground again, and the street and sky swung around me, our eyes the hub of a spinning wheel that turned into blackness.

CHAPTER 27

NEW YORK - 1995

My gasp echoed in the acoustics of Carnegie Hall as I recognized the man I'd heard behind the screen.

It was Gabriel even from the back. The shape of his body under his shirt. The way his jeans sat on his waist.

It was him. Risen from the dead.

"I'm going to turn around," he said.

When I didn't answer, he rotated slowly with his neck bent downward, his hair dropping over his face. I approached and pulled up his chin so I could see him.

I swallowed a sharp inhale so hard my body jolted. "Gabriel?"

The left side of his face was divided by multiple scars a short beard did little to hide. One closed the side of his mouth in a quarter inch of web. Another ended in a boneless divot in his cheek. His left eye was covered with a light-brown patch made of cloth.

But the right eye was framed with black lashes, and it was brown and warm. He didn't see how I was made but who I was. He didn't look at my face. He looked at *me*.

"You're still beautiful," he said.

I ran my fingertips over the scar on his cheek, and he shook with discomfort, but he didn't stop me as I found the lump of a scar on his throat.

"Is this why you gave up violin?" I asked.

"Yes." He pulled back and stilled my hand. "It's... a sensitive spot. It almost killed me."

When I pressed my hand to his cheek again, he grimaced, as if keeping still for the touch took reserves of willpower.

"Your eye," I said.

"Gone."

"I'm sorry."

"Don't be."

"Show me."

His smile was nervous and cut short on one side, but it was his. "I should have known you'd be curious."

I touched the patch. He went taut, holding his breath, swallowing hard. I could practically hear his heart pounding.

"It's okay," I said.

His mouth tightened shut as, with a shaking hand, he moved the patch aside.

The eyelid was sewn shut and sunken into a misshapen socket.

"I know..." His voice shook. "I know I'm horrible."

"What happened to you was going to leave a mark. I just..." I shifted the patch back down, more for his comfort than my own. "You're alive. Gabriel. I've never seen anything as beautiful as you being alive."

I raised my other hand to the undamaged side of his face, still in a state of disbelief. He was here. Damaged but here, and all the feelings I'd stuffed away blew the lid off the box.

The last two years folded into moments as if he'd never left. As if I hadn't married Peter in desperation and endured his abuse as a way of punishing myself for surviving. As if Gabriel and I were kids in college with nothing to do but fall in love.

"You needed to see me before you decided," he said.

"I feel like you were never gone."

"But I was."

"What happened? Why didn't you come back to me?"

"I didn't think... I mean, look at me."

My hands slid off his face. "You could have let me choose."

"Please be mad," he said. "Please be so angry you hate me. Tell me it's my face or what I did when I didn't come back. Don't give me a reason if you don't want. Just tell me you never want to see me again."

He thought it was going to be that easy, did he?

He wasn't playing the pathos card with me. I wasn't as impressed with the state of his face as he was.

"I have some things to take care of first." I backed away. "Don't go anywhere, Gabriel Marlowe. Adam Brate. Whatever you want me to call you. I know where you are now, and I know why. You can't hide. I will find you, and I will love you the same as the last day I saw you. Do you understand?"

"You scare the fuck out of me," he said through a smile that, even cut short on the left, could melt the ice caps.

"Good. Then I'll see you at the lions. Don't be late." I turned on my heel and left.

***

Margie handed me the hot tea I didn't ask for. The warmth of the mug was welcome against fingers running with Los Angeles-thin blood.

"And you're one hundred percent sure it was him?" she asked, pouring boiling water in her own cup.

"One hundred percent."

She leaned against the counter, tapping her ring against the porcelain. "Who told you he was dead?"

"Daddy."

"Just him?"

"He had some lawyers, and a doctor was there, I think."

She sighed. "Yeah."

"Yeah?"

"You got sold, Carrie."

Our conversation in the bathroom came back to me. I'd refused to believe it was possible for my family to change the course of my life without my approval.

Yet, there I was.

"Even if you're right," I started.

"I'm right."

"Even if you're right, what am I supposed to do now?"

"What do you want? If you could do anything, what would it be?"

"Am I supposed to believe my own parents lied to me? To make sure I married Peter? That's crazy. I can't even deal with the fact that Gabriel's alive now, and when I looked at him—"

"With the scars. Were they that bad?"

"Terrible. And I love him. Same as the day he die—was attacked. All the love was just waiting. I was waiting, and I didn't even know it. I'm going to be with him, Margie. I'm not going to let Peter be a consolation prize or put up with his crap out of guilt anymore. This is it."

"It's not that easy."

"You said it was just a practical matter."

"How does that equate to easy?" She put down her tea and rubbed her hands together. "Want to know a secret?"

"No. I can't stand it. Please."

"Remember when I went to study abroad? In Ireland?"

"Barely."

"Kind of sudden, wasn't it?"

"Maybe? I was twelve, and there were a lot of us running around."

"I was pregnant."

"Margie! What?"

My older sister didn't have children. She'd never have children. And even though she lived with a man she was obviously sleeping with, to me, she was as sexless as a Barbie doll.

"I know you think I have it easy. But I didn't. Ireland wasn't a semester abroad. They shipped me off to a convent in a country where abortion was illegal."

"Did you have it?"

"The baby? Yes."

"What happened to her? Him. It. Whatever."

"He was born, and he was taken away." She came close to me and held up her finger to stop more questions. "That's all you need to know. My point is this. Listen closely. What I'm about to tell you is true." She lowered her hand and leveled her eyes to mine. "Our father will do whatever he has to do to make this family into his image of perfection, and our mother will allow it. Sometimes that protects us. Sometimes… it breaks us. But it's never, ever with our consent. So, I'm asking you. What is your image of your life? What do you want? You can't fight him by flailing blindly. You need a plan, and you need to execute it around him. And you need to know this. If your vision isn't his, he will do everything he can to get in the way."

I felt like a pinball springing between bumpers.

Finding Gabriel. Leaving Peter. I had no control. I was subject to the physics of my decisions. Now this? A life-altering lie perpetrated by my own family?

"So," she continued. "Before I'm late for work. What do you want?"

"Gabriel. I don't care how."

"And Peter Thorne. Are you done with him?"

"Yes."

"Okay. Take that. Hold it. That's your direction. Daddy's going to do everything to prevent you from leaving and not just because Catholics don't accept divorce. Your marriage is something he made, and he's going to defend it."

***

My sister and Drew were at work, and I sat on the edge of Margie's couch with my decisions made, coffee cold on the table in front of me, waiting for Los Angeles to wake up. At noon, I picked up the phone. I didn't need Aiden Klerk anymore. I'd take care of that first.

"Hi, this is Carrie Thorne. Is Mr. Klerk in?"

"Hold please."

As if a past hope called to me, the hold music was *Ballad of Blades*. I was about ready to throw the phone when Klerk picked up.

"Mrs. Thorne."

"Mr. Klerk. I wanted to thank you for helping me. But I don't need your services anymore."

"That's fine. We've had a bit of a bump in the road I need to mention before we cancel your retainer."

"A bump in the road?"

"Did you tell your husband you retained me?"

Could a person freeze and melt at the same time?

"No."

"He approached me last night at a client dinner. I'm quite sure his presence there was not a coincidence."

Small again, living with the fear of consequences I couldn't predict, I pressed my knees together and put my elbows on them as if I wanted to curl into a ball. "What did he say?"

"He said he knew you hired me, and he wanted to know what for."

"Oh, God." I was going to be sick.

"When I told him it would be unethical to reveal my client list, he said it was his money paying me and thus his right to know."

I couldn't make a sound.

"Mrs. Thorne?"

"I'm here."

"I don't, as a rule, talk about clients. No matter where their money is coming from. He was escorted out. Now, I'm not a betting man, but if I was, I'd put a few dollars on him making it a point to talk to you personally very soon. He was not happy."

"Okay." My agreement was tinged with fear. I wasn't ready to deal with Peter.

"We have a team in New York," he said. "Do you need security?"

"I don't know."

I'd denied hiring Klerk, but I obviously hadn't been that convincing.

"Can I give you a word of advice?" Klerk asked.

"Please."

"The truth is a weapon. It neutralizes whatever's being held against you. Some people… a certain kind of person… they get vicious when disarmed. There's no harm in protecting yourself."

"Let me think about it." Having his offer in my pocket gave me the strength to stand up. I wasn't alone. I didn't have to take it all on myself.

"Don't take too long," he said.

"Do you know how he found out I hired you?" I took my cup to the kitchen and poured more coffee.

"No. But we found something. We followed the money into Adam Brate's past. To the beginning of his career. When he— quote, unquote—'came out of nowhere.' We found his first booking agent out of London and interviewed him. He said Adam Brate already had enough money to launch, and he, the booking agent, said before Adam Brate got his own fees, he was paid… sounds like for six months, through a shell company." He paused as if he needed to read it to get it right. "ODRSN."

The coffee was cold and bitter. I nearly choked on it.

"Does that ring a bell?" Klerk asked.

I hadn't known until that moment if Gabriel's research into his father's death and the money behind it was correct. My body bent so I could sit, but there was no chair in the kitchen, so I slid down until I hit the floor, back to the cabinet, knees pressed to my chest.

"It's my father's," I croaked.

"Are you sure?"

"Yes."

"Would your father have any reason, two years ago, to give an unknown cellist payments?"

That night. In Venice.

I never had any proof he was dead.

Had Gabriel faked death for the money?

It was one thing to chase the fantasy that Gabriel had lived through that attack. And another to think… No. That hadn't been faked. No one could fake that much blood.

The screams were real.

Or had they been mine?

"Mrs. Thorne?"

"I have to go."

I wasn't going anywhere. I was never going anywhere. I was trapped.

I wanted to do what Gabriel had done. Disappear into the world with a fake name. Break the life I was given and create a new one from the pieces.

But that was a childish fantasy. What I needed was reality, so I called my sister.

"Klerk said Adam Brate got his start with Daddy's money," I told her before saying hello.

"How do you know?"

"It's a long story."

"I'm off the clock."

I sighed and sat on the edge of the bed. She needed as much information as she needed and no more. "Gabriel's father was in a lawsuit over some buildings in Atlanta. The money was funneled through ODRSN. It's a—"

"I know what it is. Are you sure?"

"One hundred percent. Our father's involved. I don't know how. And the other thing—Peter knows I hired Klerk."

"Jesus."

"I know. And he still hasn't called back. He could be anywhere."

"I shouldn't have to say this," Margie said, "but I will. I didn't tell Peter or our father anything."

"I know it wasn't you. He was already suspicious."

"So, where is he?"

"I don't know."

"Great," she muttered. "Think like an abuser, Carrie. Where's Peter?"

My chest seized before the answer crossed my lips. "On his way."

"Is it alarmist to suggest you leave my apartment?"

"No, I…" I stopped. I wanted to wait for him. Get it over with. Say what needed saying and be done with it. Running away would just prolong the agony. But it was more than possible that I was drunk on the confidence of a decision.

"Carrie," Margie said when my pause went too long, "get a hotel. I have cash in the top drawer of my dresser. Don't use a card."

Even after everything, I didn't believe Peter would hurt me any worse than he ever had.

No. He'd hurt me. But he wouldn't harm me. He wouldn't do anything he couldn't get away with. He had too much to lose.

"I'm fine," I said. "It's cold out."

"I'm sending Drew home," Margie said.

"Don't waste his time. I'm going to call Peter again in an hour, and he's going to pick up. Trust me."

"If he doesn't pick up in an hour, then?"

"Then you send Drew, or I get a room at the Plaza."

"Cash," she said. "Pay cash. And lock the door."

"Fine."

"Carrie," she said before I could hang up. "If you could do anything, what would it be?"

I laughed at the impossibility of my fantasy, then spoke it out loud.

***

Peter didn't pick up at one or even two in the afternoon. Each time his secretary said he was out, I was relieved because I knew I'd call him again and eventually I'd leave him.

I was less sure about Gabriel.

A shower would warm me up and get the scent of rage and shame off my skin.

The hope I'd held since getting to New York seeped from my heart to my skin, washing off like sweet-smelling filth. Nothing replaced it. It had expanded inside me like a balloon and left hollowness where it had been. My lungs compressed, choking out a breath wet with snot. Tears exploded, mixing with the hot water. All my energy went into my sorrow, draining my legs of strength until I was crouching on the floor of the tub with my face between my knees. I wept at Gabriel's rejection. The loss of hope. The way I'd been used by people who loved me.

My fingers were wrinkled and my eyes were painfully swollen when I turned off the water. I knew what I had to do. My path was laid out before me, but I'd walk it with a broken heart.

I went out to get a late lunch, passed a pizza place, sandwiches, bagels, sushi, barely registering my options as I paced past. The idea of food eclipsed my appetite for it. My mind was on a hamster wheel of what I had decided, what I didn't know, and what hurt me the most.

I was leaving Peter and starting fresh. School. A career. My own life. My own decisions. It would be hard at first. My husband had control of every dime in my trust. I didn't have a salary to sock away or a credit card in my name.

And my father. My family.

I didn't want them to finance a new start.

But Adam Brate had gotten his start with Drazen money.

Gabriel was Adam Brate.

If Gabriel had survived and been bought off, he could kiss my ass too. He could take the solo career he'd always wanted and shove it right where the sun didn't shine. Whatever he had been paid to fund his ambitions, I was worth more.

Nothing had changed, right?

Gabriel was as dead to me as he'd ever been.

He'd been in the world the entire time, and everything he'd said he felt for me?

He'd sold it.

He was alive, and he'd sold what we had together.

I stopped at a pay phone and put a cold quarter in the slot for the Waldorf Astoria, room 2220.

***

The lions at the entrance of the New York Public Library were named Patience and Fortitude. The stone steps were wet, and the pedestal under the lion to my left—wasn't sure which virtue he was named for—was covered in a crackling of ice. The sidewalks were packed with people who had their heads bent over coffee cups or up toward a gray sky cut by angles.

A limo pulled up on Fifth Avenue and was barely at a complete stop when the back door opened and a man got out in a hat and sunglasses. His scarf was pulled over his face.

I was so angry at him I couldn't bear giving him the courtesy of a "how do you do."

"Take that off."

"What happened?" he asked, condensed breath huffing through the fabric of his scarf.

How dare he hide? How dare he cover himself after turning his back on me?

When I reached for him, he didn't pull back. Even when I dragged the scarf off his face and jerked the sunglasses away, leaving him bare except for his hat and eye patch.

"How much?" I growled.

"How much?" He looked truly baffled.

"How much did my father give you to…" To what? Break up with me? It had been so much worse, and the difference between a breakup and the loss of hope gathered into a breath-hitching sob. "To leave me there by myself and just fuck off."

He said my name like a prelude to an explanation, but he could shove his excuses right up his ass.

"How much were we worth to you? How much to break me? How much did that get you? You left me. You turned your back and cashed your check. You had your money, and you were done. That was it the entire time, wasn't it? Money."

Until I saw the way he glanced at the people who stopped and stared, I hadn't realized I was screaming. Nor did I care.

"Did it make you happy?" I yelled. "The money? How much was it?"

"What's the difference?" he shouted back. "Look at me, Carrie. Look at me. You weren't going to love me. You were never going to be able to stomach this face."

"You didn't trust me enough to even try. You asshole…" I pushed his chest with everything I had. And not just him. I pushed my father. My mother. Peter. All the fury came through a shove that moved him back half a step but made him look as if I'd smashed his heart under my heel.

"I'm sorry," he said. "You're—"

"Is this guy bothering you?" A white woman in a red pompom hat and navy down jacket got between us, looking me in the eye.

Over her shoulder, I saw a guy in a matching red pompom hat in front of Gabriel.

"No! I'm bothering him," I said.

"Are you sure?"

"Lady, I know you mean well."

"Because he looks homeless." She wrinkled her nose when she nodded, as if she didn't like having to tell me that sort of thing, but if I was too ignorant to notice, then she'd reluctantly break the bad news.

Gabriel was wearing a Burberry coat and had just gotten out of a limo, but it was his face. No matter what he did, he'd always have that face. For this lady, that made him homeless. For someone else, it would be stupid, or simple, or angry, or crazy. People would always see that first and put him into a category that made them comfortable.

"He's brilliant," I said, poking her chest. Maybe it was time Red Pompom Lady stopped trusting beautiful women on sight. "And he can buy and sell dopes like you by the dozen. So back up. I'm pissed off enough at him to take it out on you."

Her eyes widened, and she turned to her partner, who was blocking Gabriel with his significant bulk.

"Honey," the lady called.

I pushed her out of the way and got between Pompom Guy and Gabriel.

"Back up," I said. "He's mine."

He put up his mittens, not convinced yet. "Just trying to—"

"Get out of here before I take your eye out too."

They backed away slowly. A crowd had gathered. I could see the heroes among them. They wanted to save me from the scarred man I was yelling at even though I was the aggressor.

I spun around to face him. "And you—"

"Should probably go," he said.

We were so close I could feel him against me. His warmth. His humor. His music. It all emanated from him, pushing against me like a vibrating field.

Yes, I was turned on because he was Gabriel and I was Carrie… and this was meant to be.

"No, you stay right here and take my forgiveness like a man."

"You forgive me? I can't forgive me."

"Ma'am?" another voice from behind me. Beauty's savior on a fine white steed.

"Is this going to happen all the time? With these people?"

"That's why I hide my face," he whispered.

"Ma'am, we called the police, so…"

I laid my hands on Gabriel's cheeks and kissed him hard—to make a show of it. The scar tissue on one side was stiff and rigid, but I didn't let go. I kissed him until his hands slid around my waist. The sweet softness of his lips turned to urgency and the show for the Samaritans became a real thing between us. Slowly, he accepted control. I surrendered my mouth to his, and he claimed it with his tongue and the rattle of a groan in his throat, holding me up when my legs went to jelly.

I'd forgotten what it was like to be kissed like that, and I never wanted to forget it again.

When we came up for cold, foggy breaths, he leaned his forehead against mine. "God, Carrie. Little bird. I'm so sorry."

"Actually"—I leveled my gaze on his—"I kind of understand. But," I dropped my voice to a whisper, "I'm still pissed."

"I kind of understand." He pulled me close. "But I don't want to let you go."

"You have to. I have things to take care of."

"Things." He said it as if he knew I was talking about Peter. "Are you safe?" He pressed his lips to my cheek. "Is he going to lose his shit?"

"It'll be a phone call."

"When?"

"As soon as he picks up."

"And then?"

"I'll tell him it's over."

"And then?" His kisses were warm on my neck.

"Then I'll call you."

On Fifth, a police car pulled up behind his limo.

"I'll wait, Carrie." He loosened his arms. "I'll wait as long as I have to."

"You should go," I said, pointing at his car.

"You okay to get back?"

189

"Yes, please go before I threaten to gouge out someone else's eye."

He smiled, turned, and jogged down the steps. His driver opened the door, and with one last wave and a smile that turned a cold day into spring break, Gabriel disappeared behind tinted glass.

***

When I got back to Margie's, I took another shower to warm up, smiling as I remembered Gabriel's kiss. I could be kissed like that for the rest of my life and never get bored. Never be afraid. All I had to do was call Peter until he picked up.

Which turned out to be unnecessary.

When I padded out of the shower in my robe, he was there.

Peter.

Sitting on a chair in a three-piece suit, an ankle over a knee, resting his arms on the chair with his Rolex glinting in the morning light.

I sucked in a breath as if I'd been drowning.

"Sorry," he said without a drop of regret. "There's a key that says 'Margie' in the junk drawer, so I figured I'd give it a shot."

Telling him to get the hell out would only make him mad. I had things to say, and he needed to be calm to hear them, so I modeled what I wanted from him. "It's okay."

He stood and buttoned his jacket. "No, Carrie. It's not okay."

I stepped back, knocking into a side table so hard a vase fell over.

"How did Margie's surgery go?" Peter asked. "Don't answer. There was no surgery."

"Back up," I said, holding out my hand.

"Carrie"—he stopped his advance without stepping back—"we need to talk, don't you think?"

"We do." I tightened the knot on my robe. It was the only thing between him and my naked, defenseless body.

"So. Talk." He put up his palm as if yielding the floor to me, but he was a few feet too close. I slid sideways to get away. He turned to follow my direction but didn't come closer.

"I don't think we're working," I said. "Us. As a marriage."

"Because one of us is lying."

He was trying to trap me into a conversation about my lies because they were fresh, but his were baked deep, rotting our lives from the inside.

"You knew, didn't you?" I said. "When I woke up in that hospital, you were already there."

"Your father told me you were in trouble. I was there for you. I'll always be there for you."

"He told me Gabriel had died. He didn't die. And you knew." Holding back another round of tears, I pointed an accusing finger. "You knew the entire time."

"He couldn't take care of you."

"I don't need anyone to take care of me."

"You did." He came closer, his voice softening with the memory of those months when he took care of me. "You did and you do. You're a beautiful woman, but what does that add up to in this world? Just a sad, beautiful girl with a sad, broken heart. And he wasn't worth it. Do you want to know how much it cost to get him to walk away from you? To turn his back on your forever? It was a pittance, really. There's more in our couch cushions."

"That was my decision to make."

He smirked and stepped away, shrugging off his jacket. "He didn't love you." He threw his jacket on the couch. "He wanted your money."

"You don't know anything."

"Maybe a little revenge for his father." He unbuttoned his cuffs.

"He loved me. You turned me into a trophy."

"I'm the only one who loves you." He rolled up his cuffs to the elbow. "Who else would spend three months taking you all over Europe to get you over a dead man? Who else could support you when you gave up grad school? When you decided—yes, you

191

decided—to be nothing but a trophy. I gave you that. I gave you what you wanted in life." He yanked on his belt to release the notch, then pulled it through the loops. "He took the money, baby. No one's going to buy me off." Snapping the belt free, he wound it in one hand. "I own you, and you're not for sale."

"No, Peter," I said, my palm facing the belt. "No."

The muscles around his eyes twitched—not in anger, but as a way of receiving my denial and reconsidering his strategy. The buckle clinked when he tossed it away.

"What, then?" He stepped close to me. "What?"

"I want a divorce."

He should have been hurt, but he wasn't. He was suspicious. Curious. Estimating my intent.

"I don't love you," I said, knowing it didn't matter to him one way or another. He wasn't there to be loved. He existed to be admired and feared.

"Carrie."

I backed up when he came to me, but the wall kept me from getting away.

He reached for the belt of my robe and, with one finger, released it. It opened, allowing a chill past the fabric.

The motion and result were so close to what Gabriel had done in Venice, and his intent was so different that a deep sense of wrongness cut through me.

Peter was stealing my memory and twisting it into something ugly. That night in the Venice *pensione* was mine. It wasn't his to corrupt, and fuck him for trying.

My hands shot out, pushing his chest. "Don't you—"

He didn't let me finish. He was faster and stronger, grabbing my jaw with one hand and squeezing so hard my bones cried out in pain. "You know what your problem is, *wife?*"

I tried to wrestle away, but he only gripped harder.

"Your problem," he growled in my face, "is you're too beautiful for your own good."

With his free hand, he yanked the robe over my shoulder. I fought him, bending away, but I wasn't a fighter, or I would have known he'd use my imbalance to get my feet from under me. It only took a moment for him to gain complete control of my body, restrict my arms in the sleeves of the robe, and leave the rest of me naked and bent over the back of the couch.

"Stop!" I cried.

"I'll stop." He pushed his hips against my bare bottom, his cock hard through his trousers. "When you get it through your head that you don't lie to me."

With one hand, he twisted the robe so the sleeves held my arms tightly behind me. With the other, he jammed the flat edge of his hand between my ass cheeks.

"Please," I whimpered.

He curved his body against mine and spoke in my ear. "Another man might think you're beautiful when you're all dolled up. They have an undeveloped aesthetic. Not me." He removed his hand to release his dick from his trousers. "When your mascara's running down your face and your mouth is full of spit. When you're crying in pain. That's when you look like an angel."

The warm skin of his dick pressed against me, pushing me hard against the edge of the couch.

"I won't stay with you," I said. "No matter what you do. It's over."

"Wrong." Without preamble or preparation, he put his thumb in my ass.

I bit back a scream. "I won't cry for your pleasure. Never again."

Pinning me with his hips, he pulled my head back by the hair, twisting my neck so he could see my face. "Let's see about that."

He maneuvered his cock to my ass and had to bend close to keep me still. His cheek was so close to me I could smell his cologne and, under that, the stink of his humanity. He was just a man with soft parts and vulnerabilities.

Maybe he'd kill me, but he was just a man.

When he shifted to push against my anus, I found the room to bring my face closer to his.

Just a moment. No more. Decide. Now or never.

I brought my open mouth toward him in a puckering, sucking, open-mouthed kiss to the cheek. In the split second I had once I could taste his sweat and feel the unshaven points of hair on my tongue, I clamped my jaw tight.

He yanked away with a roar, but I held on, bolting upright with him, throat vibrating with a warrior cry of my own. He pulled my hair to get me away, but that only tore the skin in my teeth. His hands locked on my face, pushing me back with slippery palms.

I tasted the thick metal of my husband's blood as skin and tendon crunched between my teeth. He punched me in the stomach, and I opened my mouth to suck air, thrown back against the wall with the force of it.

He was bent at the waist, hand over one side of his face, flaccid dick hanging out of his pants, blood soaking his white collar.

Getting my legs under me, I wrestled my arms out of the robe.

Slowly, still bowed, he looked at me with a terrifying calm.

There wasn't a single hard or sharp object in reach. He was between me and the exit, and a sidestep would put him between me and the bathroom door, which I'd have to close and lock. Knives all the way in the kitchen.

Peter stood straight, letting his hand fall away from his wound. It flowed thick red.

He wasn't going to kill me.

He was going to break me.

Well, that was it for me. I'd spent every penny of my good fortune, shaken the dust out of the change purse, and counted all the money in the cushions.

He came for me so quickly I perceived it in slow motion.

Putting my arms up did nothing. He wrestled me to the floor and put his hands around my throat.

Tightening. Cutting off my air. Bruising me where people could see.

That was when I knew it was all over.

PART II
GABRIEL

CHAPTER 28

NOWHERE

My first girlfriend was Creole. She had moved to Chicago from New Orleans. Babette. We met in our music elective. I was in ninth grade, and she was a senior. She was a brilliant guitarist, and her take-zero-shit attitude was a turn-on. Nothing was going to be easy with her. I liked the challenge as much as I liked her accent and the way her fingers flew across the strings. Getting her into bed was easier than I'd thought it would be, but after a few turns, I realized I was the one who had been easy. She knew what she wanted and demanded it, putting me in control. That role was easy, and I fell into it whenever we met in her empty house.

The rest wasn't. I'd been too immature to separate her submission in the bedroom from the take-zero-shit girl I fell for in class, and she wasn't having any of it. Not for a minute. That ended in tears. Mine.

But before she kicked me to the curb for trying to boss her around in the cafeteria, I met her family at a Mardi Gras party. They had a tradition. Everyone had a slice of king cake. A little plastic baby had been baked inside it, and whoever got the slice with the baby had to prepare the next year's feast or suffer a year of bad luck.

Of course, I got the baby, and though Babette and I didn't last long afterward—certainly not long enough for me to make the next Mardi Gras meal—I never forgot that inch-long plastic infant, facedown, pushing out from the edge of the slice like a figure half-carved in marble. How it was encased so tightly in soft dough, coddled as if in a womb yet suffocating in the unmoving mass.

I'd plucked it out as if rescuing it to do CPR, leaving a grave-shaped hole in the cake.

Maybe the consequence of not hosting the next party wasn't a year of bad luck. Maybe I was doomed to travel far away and become that plastic baby. Half-stuck facedown in a blackness specially shaped for me but aware that ahead of me was light and freedom and movement. Behind me was a dark alley with men, and dull blades, and the smell of copper, and my life draining onto the stones. Behind me was a failure to protect what I loved.

When I came out of the blackness, would I leave a trough? When the unconsciousness stopped pressing against my face, would it still exist inside me? Would I leave it in Venice? Or would it be broken into pieces and digested into nothing? I couldn't imagine it hadn't always existed, unformed, unbaked, rising to meet me when a knife flashed and came down. Suffocating me, trapping me inside it with only my stifled questions to keep me company.

Where is my little bird?
Is she all right?
Did they hurt her?
And if they did, will I live to kill them?

CHAPTER 29

LOS ANGELES - 1993

A full scholarship to USC took care of tuition, but food and shelter was another thing entirely. The assistant jobs had been given to other students, and the schedule at the Thornton School didn't leave much room for even a part-time job off campus. My mother gave me an allowance, but as usual, the money had run out. Again. Much of my father's life insurance had been eaten up by legal fees against his firm, and my mother lived on minimum-wage jobs and Prozac.

She was bitter, and I couldn't blame her. So, even though I knew she'd send what she could, I didn't ask for more money. After four years at USC, I knew how to survive. I went to the University Village mall, where Earl the security guard liked to hear me play.

I needed to practice anyway.

"Play that Stravinsky thing, would you?" I'd educated Earl in the ways of classical composers, and he turned out to have a great ear. He always had a request.

"You got it."

"Gonna miss your playing after you graduate," he said as I set up my case.

"I'll miss the acoustics in here."

"Where you going?" he asked.

"New York." I drew the bow across the strings and made an adjustment.

"Big Apple. You got a job there?"

"Not yet. But that's where the opportunities are."

He shook his head not as a negation, but with a rueful look back at youth.

When I started playing the piece Earl liked, I wasn't looking to fall in love. I wasn't looking to get tied down.

If I wanted sex, I could get it. There were enough women in my life who were as disinterested in emotional attachments as I was. They'd take their clothes off when I commanded it and writhe with pleasure when I allowed it. We wouldn't ask for anything of each other outside the bedroom.

If nothing else, I'd grown up enough to separate who I was sexually from who I was on the other side of the door. I hadn't fallen in love since Babette, and that was fine. Making a name for myself as a musician would take up all my time.

The acoustics in the front hall of University Village were outstanding. My eyes were closed as I played, listening for off tones and missed notes. I was in perfect flow. My fingers acted before my mind could correct, so my ears made adjustments. The conversations, the clattering food trays, the dim Muzak in the speakers were miles away.

There was no reason for me to open my eyes, but I did, and that changed everything.

She changed everything.

Standing with her friend, red hair covering her face as she rooted around her bag, she looked up just as I saw her, as if my gaze had called out.

USC is full of the children of actors, models, and athletes. My friend Danny said you couldn't swing a dead cat without hitting something fuckable.

But she wasn't fuckable.

Not exactly.

She was more.

Calling her beautiful illustrated the inadequacy of language. She was a melody. A perfect symphony. The final crescendo in a masterpiece written by a genius. Taking my eyes off her would be impossible. All the air in the room bent in her direction and emanated from her as if she owned it.

And still, my fingers did their job, filling the room with music that had been written for her before she was born.

She was impossible. Eternal. Divine.

Nothing like her should have existed anywhere but Olympus.

With a little smile, she dropped a bill in my case and walked out with her friend, getting momentarily lost in the afternoon sun.

I stopped playing to watch her go.

"You got a day's worth out of her," Earl said from behind his podium.

"Yeah," I said, assuming he was talking about her looks.

"You gonna get greedy and keep playing?"

"Huh?"

He pointed at my case with its dotting of loose change and a single rolled-up bill. I picked up the cash. Benjamin Franklin stared at me with a sly smile.

That couldn't be right. Even if it was, I couldn't take it. Not from another student. Not from anyone who wasn't Bill Gates.

Looking out the glass doors, I saw her and her friend make their way to the crosswalk and wait for the light.

"You okay?" Earl asked with a knowing smile. "Or did that pretty thing shake you?"

"I'm shaken," I said, grabbing the pen off his clipboard. I scrawled my number on the bill and handed back the pen. "Save my spot."

"Will do."

I dropped my violin in the case and snapped it shut, losing a spray of pennies and dimes, grabbed my bag and case, and ran after her.

Behind me, Earl shouted, "Good luck!" right before the doors closed.

I managed to not get run down crossing Jefferson, but I was going to lose her.

"Hey!" I called, but she didn't hear me, and we were in a world of *heys* and *yos*. I needed to be more specific. "Hey! Miss! Red Hair! Beautiful!"

Her friend, who had the quirky pixie-girl thing down to an exact science, turned around. "Hello again, Mr. Stravinsky!"

I stepped it up and got to them, out of breath.

"Are you all right?" Hundred-Dollar Girl asked. A glossy blue headband held her long, candy-red hair behind her ears, but the breeze blew it across her face anyway, sticking a single strand to her pale lip gloss.

To be that thread of hair clinging to those lips.

"You… you left this… in the…" I held out the money. "The wrong bill."

I was making the worst first impression ever. Out of breath. Barely making a complete sentence. I stood straight, trying to get my shit together.

"No," she said. "It's the right one."

The insanity of her action played against the sound of her voice. She was gorgeous. I'd established that. But her voice? It was in direct contrast. It was rough and rattled. In five words, she'd ranged an octave and a quarter in the strangest places, phrasing like Björk with the vocal fry of Axl Rose.

She'd gone from magnetically pretty to irresistibly interesting.

"It's too much," I said.

Her eyes were a blue I'd never seen before. Bright but with a hint of gray. For everything I thought I saw, closer inspection revealed another layer.

"I've never heard anyone play like that," she said with a shrug.

"Like what?"

Was it possible she found me interesting too?

"Like they were about to levitate."

I laughed because she'd said something so unexpected… and because I was a goner. Total fucking goner.

"Really," I said, holding out the bill again. At this point, it was more about giving her my number than returning the money. "It's my pleasure. A dollar would have been enough."

"Keep it. I have to get to class."

She was turning away. I was going to lose her. I didn't know her name, and USC was huge. She could be any of forty-four thousand students.

"I'm going to throw it away if you don't take it."

If I sounded desperate, I was. I gave her friend a desperate look, which, in retrospect, could have backfired.

"Like hell," Miss Quirky said, taking it. "I'll stick it in her bag when she's not looking."

"Thank you," I said.

"If you busk again, I'm putting in another hundred, and I'm going to run away so fast you won't catch me."

Two solid octaves in flats and sharps with fry in the most counterintuitive places. Her looks were one thing, but I could listen to her all day.

"I'll catch you," I said. "Don't you worry about that."

"What if I don't want to be chased?"

I started to promise her she couldn't run fast enough, but that was the kind of thing Babette had gotten fed up with, so I shut the fuck up.

"Great," Quirky said, pulling her elbow. "Thanks. Come on."

"Bye," the beautiful girl said.

What if she didn't see the number?

"What's your name?" I called.

"Bye," she said back.

She didn't want me to find her. I could accept that. But I could leave the door unlocked if she changed her mind.

"I'm Gabriel!"

The only Gabriel at Thornton. She could figure it out.

"Bye, Gabriel!"

I could walk her to class. Spend a moment. Listen to the warble and wave of her voice.

But I left her alone, and that made all the difference.

***

"Okay, wait." Danny was stretched the length of the couch, game controller in both hands. He didn't stop playing for a single second. "A hundred? US dollars?"

"Yeah."

"And you gave it back?"

"Dude. She's a student."

"And that's where you wrote your number. Fuck!" He threw his arms up in mourning for a dead video game character. "You get a name?"

"No."

"Who *are* you?"

Danny swung his legs off the couch, standing to his full six foot six. His straight hair was cut evenly all around, landing at his jaw. When he tucked it behind his ear, the gesture was almost feminine. "I'm making a sandwich. You want one?"

It would be peanut butter and jelly. House favorite.

"Nah."

He walked to the attached kitchen in three steps, the distance made shorter by the size of the apartment and the length of his legs.

"You still need your night?" he asked, getting the bread from the top of the fridge.

We kept a schedule of nights for when we had plans with women and needed the other to make himself scarce. I was set that night to be with Nancy, a women's studies major who, every time I told her to spread her legs, made it a point to tell me it could be the last time I could tell her what to do.

That worked for both of us.

But now?

"Take it," I said. "I'm going to cancel."

"Cool." Danny's hair flopped over his face as he made his sandwich.

"Let me know if she calls tonight."

"Who?"

She'd never told me her name. As if waking from a fog of love-struck stupidity, I remembered our last words. She hadn't just said, "Bye, Gabriel." She'd waved a big, red flag with the words "I'm not calling you" written on it.

"Jefferson. The girl from Jefferson. Whatever she says. You'll know."

He tucked his hair behind his ear as he looked at me. "What's with you?"

"With me what?"

He cocked his head before wrapping up the bread. "You look like a guy who never got laid before."

"Shut up."

"Whatever. Gerry and I are gonna start looking at apartments in Silver Lake. Last chance to room with us as free men."

Danny was eager to start a life as a starving Los Angeles musician, but my career was elsewhere.

"Pass."

"Your loss."

"I'll crash when I'm in town."

He came back to the couch, lunch in hand, and picked up the controller. He started the game again and played with the sandwich wedged in his mouth.

CHAPTER 30

CHICAGO - 1995

I had six rules.

One: My face was my own. If I never showed it in public, I wouldn't have to explain it. That meant scarves, sunglasses, hats. It meant being outside only when necessary and usually at night. It meant I was a pain in the ass to work with.

Two: The name Gabriel Marlowe was forbidden. Anyone who worked for me worked for the Adumbrate Corporation of the Cayman Islands, and anyone who spoke to me called me Adam.

Three: Separation of roles. My manager didn't know my agent. My assistant lived in Chicago but worked from home. She didn't ask questions, but when she was in trouble, I helped her with her tuition. She never met my driver, Herv, who agreed to never look at my face, even when I was right in front of him.

Four: My mind was a pressure-sealed container with a single valve. I was never, ever to think of Carrie Drazen unless I was playing *Ballad of Blades*, when thinking of her was unavoidable. It was composed with the rise and fall of her voice to tell our story. Once the bow left the strings, the valve was shut again.

Five: Control the mental narrative. Even in my mind, my

dreams, the subconscious river of my thoughts, I was not allowed to complain about losing her.

Six: Los Angeles belonged to the Drazens. Stay away.

It all started when I broke rule six and played Dorothy Chandler Pavilion right smack in the center of the Drazens' LA.

She was there.

Right there.

Third row center, casting her own light. Finally summoned by the concerto I'd written for her.

I'd thought I'd never see her again, but when I did, she was like a magnet. She drew me, but more than that, she changed the shape of everything inside me.

Grief became hope.

Despair became courage.

Without thinking, I played something for her, only her.

How else would it all go to shit?

Playing that song was foolish. Reckless. Unavoidable. I should have made a rule against it, but how could I have known she'd slip through my defenses?

"I got the Lincoln Center contracts," my manager, Lori, said from the other side of the phone. She was a forty-two-year-old shark who wore misleadingly feminine pastel suits and didn't care if I called her in the middle of the night about an unruly cameraman in Latvia. "They added a rider. You're liable for licensing and legal fees as a result of you going off-script with random pop songs."

"It wasn't random."

"Sure," she said. "I guess it could be worse. Everyone's talking."

A year ago, I would have been happy with that. Last week, even. But now? I had the sense that my entire life after Venice was going to fall between the night I'd spotted her in the third row and everything after.

"I'll sign off on the Lincoln Center rider."

"Good. Lighting and sound design are on the twenty-third."

Impatient, I got to the one thing I wanted to ask. "Did you get anything on what I asked about?"

"Carrie Drazen?"

Hearing her name spoken aloud vibrated inside me. "Yes."

"Married to Peter Thorne."

"That guy," I grumbled.

"He works for her father, but before that, he ran Anchor Savings and Loan right into the ground. He's being investigated by the SEC. It doesn't look good for him."

My fist clenched and unclenched as if looking for a bow to hold. The scar on my neck ached the way it always did when I was irritated.

"Who is she?" Lori asked. "To you, I mean."

I'd made promises, and I kept my promises. Always.

But now?

This one would be hard to keep.

"No one," I said. "It's nothing."

"Fine," she said without suspicion or concern. My secrets were mine, and she knew it. "Let me get you a copy of the Lincoln Center rider before you go."

New York. Far away from her.

Exactly what I needed.

CHAPTER 31

VENICE, ITALY - 1993

he blackness took a shape I understood not as a sticky, heavy mass around me, but a deep, dreamless sleep I sometimes woke from. I heard voices far away, then closer. But even fully conscious, my eyes wouldn't open and my mouth wouldn't move.

In those wakeful hours, I made music. From the way her hair twisted in the breeze, I wove melodies. From her voice in the throes of ecstasy, I chose the scale. From her heartbeat against my ear, the throbbing percussion. From the stages of our time together, starting at the moment we met to these hours of separation, I constructed movements. When I fell into unconsciousness, I woke to darkness, remembering everything, and what I forgot, I rebuilt, adding more until I came to the music I couldn't avoid. The accordion on the gondola. The dark street. The cobblestones hard on my back, and the flash of a knife in the moonlight.

My ambition to get well came from my desire to play the *Ballad of Blades* for her.

My Italian was rudimentary, but I could catch the doctors and nurses saying *scarring* and *blood loss*. When the English language reached my ears, my brain fired and the haze was shot through with sunlight.

"Don't be alarmed at the bandages. He's stable."

"Is he in pain?" My mother's voice quickened my heart, and a stinging erupted behind sightless eyes.

"No, *signora*."

"Gabriel, my angel," she said. "I'm here now. It's going to be okay."

My voice box rumbled her name with the hum of a mental orchestra behind me.

Carrie, Carrie, Carrie.

But my lips were sealed, and my jaw was immobilized.

My voice and the music were silent.

***

They prepared me for what I'd see when the bandages came off. The sharpest points of pain were the sites of the worst damage.

My eye.

My cheek.

My jaw.

My throat.

They all felt as if the knife was still in them, and as the doctors spoke, my mind searched for Carrie's voice, but it never came.

CHAPTER 32

CHICAGO · 1995

*H*ow easy is it to lie to your mother?

If you tell her you're giving music lessons to kids in your home, why wouldn't she believe you? Especially if your face is so shameful you can't leave the house without covering it? Especially if she's as ashamed as you are?

Lying was easy enough.

I could, but that didn't answer the question of why I didn't tell her I was Adam Brate.

Adam was everything she dreamed I'd be but without my father's name.

His success was in spite of the Drazens, but it was also caused by them.

The anonymity was necessary, and it would hurt her the most.

I couldn't bear telling her what her dreams for me had cost us both. I kept promising myself I'd tell her, but she wouldn't react the way I needed her to. She wouldn't jump for joy and tell me how proud she was. There would be questions with answers she didn't like.

So, payment for my cowardice, I gave her money and bought her things but not enough to tip my hand.

"I had the most interesting conversation with a man in the coffee shop," she said, sitting across from me. *The* coffee shop was the one she managed in Wicker Park. As a lonely extrovert, she found comfort in being the chatterbox at work.

"Really?" I cut into the steak, finding it pink and perfect inside.

"He said he went to Thornton when you were there. Turns out he knew you!"

Looking at my plate, I chewed, trying to hide my expression. I didn't like old contacts. They tended to ask questions I didn't have lies for. "What was his name?"

"Danny."

My old roommate.

"Tall guy?" I asked.

"He was sitting, so I don't know. But he asked what you were doing. How you were."

You couldn't miss Danny's height whether he was sitting, lying down, or curled up in a fetal position. He wore it like a skin. That was my first clue something was wrong.

Still, I asked, "How's he doing?"

"He was in town on business. I told him you were teaching, and he said he's working for some record company and travels a lot. I gave him your number. I hope that's all right?"

"Mom."

"What? He's with a record company—"

"I haven't seen him since USC." I pointed at my face as if it was the subtext she wasn't getting.

"I didn't tell him about the accident."

The "accident" was a mugging in a Venetian alley. Mom had flipped it to a strange misfortune the same way she called Dad's suicide a "death." I never corrected her. She needed her illusions as much as I needed my lies.

"What did you tell him?"

"We talked about how talented you were."

"Before I was a grotesque freak?"

She put down her fork. "I didn't mean it that way."

"You're the one who didn't tell him."

"So? Neither did you." She balled up her napkin and put it next to her plate. "I'm sorry if I wanted to talk about your talent. I'm sorry if fate dropped a record executive in my lap and I tried to use it to your advantage."

I felt like a defensive teenager again, trying to find fault with my elders without dealing with my own shortcomings. And like a teenager, I was helpless to get myself out of it.

"That part of me is gone."

"No," she said. "It's not. You'll always be a musician. I didn't get used to the idea so you could turn around and deny it."

I could deny having the ambition to pursue music further, but Adam Brate's ambition made it a double-stacked lie. I was tired of lying. I was going to tell her the truth. Soon. Maybe today.

"That Drazen girl." Mom put her napkin back in her lap. "She messed with your head."

Today was not the day for truth. She was really running for the third rail. Why now? Was it this visit from Danny? This miraculously not-noticeably-tall Danny who was probably on an unmasking assignment for a sleazy paper?

"Do you need help getting the Christmas lights down?" I asked.

"Sometimes I think it's her you're upset over. The way she ditched you when you needed her. She was shallow. All she cared about was beauty she could see. Like that whole family. They'd kill to keep up appearances."

"Mom. Stop." What I couldn't say was that she was just as concerned about appearances but not powerful enough to destroy lives over them. Nothing about that would help.

"I know this therapist." She stabbed a piece of meat. "She comes into the shop on Tuesdays."

"I don't need therapy. And before you even start, I don't need a dating service or a matchmaker or anything."

She left her fork on the plate with the meat still on it, staring at the napkin in her lap.

"What, Ma?"

"Nothing."

"Just say it." It was wrong of me to demand honesty from her when I had so little truth to offer her. But the facts wouldn't help her feel any better.

"All I want is for you to be happy."

"I am happy."

"You should have a family. A wife who loves you."

I sighed. There would be no wife. No children. Not without Carrie, who existed behind a wall of vows, contracts, and money. My mother needed to accept my solitude the way I had. Isolation was the defining characteristic of my life, and it hadn't killed me yet.

"I have you," I said.

"You do. Always."

"I have friends," I lied. "I have my students."

"You can play again. Get out there. Do some composition?"

I had to give her something to hold on to. She'd never been ambitious for herself, but for her children, she strove for great heights.

"I've been thinking of it," I said cheerfully.

We continued on a lighter note, and I fed her hope.

But inside, my mind turned over the possibility that Danny wasn't really Danny at all.

***

I had a message when I got home. Female. Identified herself as Danny Mankewicz's office and left a New York number with a request to call back. Click. Beep.

I listened again. She didn't say the company. And—of course —"Danny" didn't call himself, because whoever it was knew I'd know my friend's voice. I could just call back and ask. If they were reporters, they'd have to identify themselves. Except a guy had already lied to my mother.

I called my assistant, Cherie. I'd found her through the Bienen School job board, and we only worked over the phone. At least she wouldn't break my balls over a song.

"Mr. Brate," she chirped. "Hi. Your flight to New York is set."

"Thanks. Any calls?"

Calls to the business number went to Cherie, and she listed the usual suspects. I gave her the number that had been left on my machine.

"His name's Danny Mankewicz," I said. "I knew him in college. Give him an hour. Let him pick the time and place."

"Okay. I got it." She cleared her throat. "One more thing. I have my audition for the Phil on the seventeenth."

"What are you playing?"

"Dvořák. Got any tips?"

"Slow practice. And the…" I stopped myself. I couldn't actually show her the difficult thumb positions. When we'd started working together, she asked me for lessons as payment, and I'd snapped at her like an impatient parent. I didn't want to do that again. She was a great assistant who understood my work and my needs. "Dvořák's about endurance. Working out isn't a bad idea."

"Slow practice. Endurance. Got it."

"Good luck."

"I'll call Danny now and get right back to you."

Something important came to me as I was about to release her. "Cherie, to him, my name is Gabriel Marlowe."

That was the first time since Venice that I'd told anyone my name, and the syllables terrified me.

CHAPTER 33

VENICE, ITALY - 1993

*W*ithout sight, I relied on my mother's visits and the warmth of the sun on my body to determine the time of day. She read the *International Herald Tribune* to me. Told me the Caruso Fellowship board had approved me for attendance the following year. Chatted about the weather and sometimes wept.

"Today is the day," she sang one morning. "Bandages off. Tap your finger if you can hear me."

One for yes.

I heard the doctors shuffle in. I'd learned to identify each of them. The best English came from a woman doctor's voice. Dr. Perla DeMineo went by her first name. I later learned she had round features and deep brown eyes that she lined with a bright blue that matched the velvet headband keeping the tight curls off her face. But in the darkness of those first days, she was the doctor who stuck her tongue on the roof of her mouth when she was thinking and released it with a *tk* before she spoke.

"How are you feeling today, Mr. Marlowe?" Perla asked as they shifted me to a sitting position.

One for yes.

"Are you ready?"

Two for no.

She made a little laugh.

"He's ready," my mother said.

One for yes.

"*Bene*, I'm going review this again. All right?"

Outside the bandages, in the real world, a cart was wheeled in and instruments clicked.

One for yes. Tapping twice was pointless. She was going to do it anyway.

"You experienced wounds to the left side of your face."

I experienced. Passive voice. As if the *polizia* hadn't come around asking me a hundred yes or no questions until I thought my finger would fall off.

"Your left zygomatic arch was smashed and partially reconstructed. The blade pierced it and entered your orbital cavity. The eye has been lost."

She paused, waiting for my reaction. I didn't have one. *Yes* or *no* couldn't tell the story of my fear. I was in love with a woman so beautiful she could have any man she wanted.

When those bandages came off, I would be ugly, scarred, damaged.

Carrie. Curious Carrie. A tender, compassionate soul who would pity me. How could I be her equal in life and her master in love? A one-eyed freak who could only ever see half her beauty would never be worthy of her.

If—by some miracle—she was alive, I had to leave her. Let her find a man she could be seen with. Someone she wouldn't have to explain to her friends. That was the noble thing to do.

I didn't know if I could ever be so honorable, but for her sake, I would try.

The doctor had explained the destruction half a dozen times, and the shock had worn down to a smooth, hard anxiety, but she went through it again as if she knew she was wearing down a stone.

She'd saved the eyelid so I could have a glass eye, and even though she kept her voice flat and businesslike, I heard her pride in the rescue.

"The left side of your jawbone was cracked," she continued. "It's still wired shut, so you won't be able to open your mouth even after the bandages are off. Trying to speak may stress the hardware, so you'll have a pencil and paper to communicate. The most concerning injury was to the left carotid artery. The scarring there is significant, and healing has been slow. So, what you'll be seeing, if you want to see today, is all that damage to the left side of your face. But I want you to know that with surgery and care, you can have a normal face. Don't look at yourself today as if this is the final product. All right?"

One for yes.

"*Bene.*"

In Italian, she requested scissors. The bandages shifted right before the familiar snipping *shh-click*. Layers were unwrapped, and light filtered through.

"Your brain is an amazing thing," she said. "It will become accustomed to seeing from a single eye. It will make adjustments to your field of vision."

"Last layer," my mother said, holding my wrist so she wouldn't keep my tapping finger down. Her voice was thick, and I knew she was crying.

My skin felt the prick of dry air, and a shade of dim orange light came through my right eyelid.

Mom was trying to keep it together, but her gasp was a sound I'd never forget. I listened for her as the staff removed gauze from my neck, muttering in Italian medical terms I couldn't understand outside "yes" and "good."

"Keep your eye closed for a moment," Perla said before she told the nurse to shut the room lights and close the blinds. Then she took the last bit of wrapping from my eye. "Okay. Open."

Their masked faces hovered in the dimness. I held up my hand and pantomimed writing. A nurse placed a pencil in my hand and a pad in my lap.

I wrote one word.

CARRIE

Perla glanced at my mother. Pain shot through my neck when I tried to see her reaction.

I wrote again.

CARRIE

I scratched a line under it.

"Gabriel," Mom said, coming around to face me.

I feared the worst. She'd been murdered. She'd spent her last moments a few feet from me, and I couldn't help her. She was gone. Dead. Snuffed from the world.

"She went home," my mother said, poorly hiding a hot rage. "She left you here."

Hope is the key signature the song of despair is built around. Without it, everything falls apart.

I'd hoped that when I showed her my ugly face, she'd say it didn't matter.

I'd hoped to keep the girl and get credit for my noble offer to leave.

She'd spared me the trouble of hope, and at that moment, I hated myself for it.

CHAPTER 34

NEW YORK - 1995

*C*herie had gotten me a chartered flight to Teterboro so I could meet with the technical crew at Lincoln Center. I was allowed to drive without depth perception, but I told myself it still wasn't safe. The fact was… I didn't want to retake my driver's license photo.

So Herv went to New York ahead of me to get a car. Too much of my money was spent maintaining my anonymity, but it was my most precious possession. And now that I'd seen her and played for her, the woman I loved in the third row, I had to protect it more jealously than ever. Not from any identifiable outside threat, but from my own temptation to unmask myself so I could see her.

"Transport's on its way, sir," the pilot's voice came over the loudspeaker.

I looked out the window, shoving a stick of gum in my mouth. To the west, piles of sand and rock were lined up as a border for the construction of a new runway. Big machines dug and scraped while a water truck was filled from a reservoir.

A long, black car coasted along the tarmac. I assumed it was mine until it stopped by a Lear with its stairs dropped. I almost turned away, but something kept my eyes on it. Even when a second car came behind—most certainly Herv—I watched the first one as if my curiosity had ever been anything but a punishment.

She appeared at the top of the airstairs, holding the railing with a kid-gloved hand. Bare legs under her skirt. Sunglasses. Knee-length pink coat. Scarf around her neck. Red hair flying in the winter wind. She was dressed as if she didn't know how cold winter really was.

And she didn't.

She'd never know how cold it could get.

She smiled with a mouth I'd kissed a hundred times. I'd kissed them a thousand times in my dreams, a million in my despair.

Twice in as many weeks, she'd appeared.

She got in the back of the limo.

Twice in as many weeks, she was gone.

And for the first time since I'd signed on the dotted line, I knew I wouldn't allow it again.

***

Drazen was an unusual enough name that my assistant could find one. Margaret. Her sister. She had an unlisted number, not that I'd call it. She also had a desk at a law firm.

I wouldn't call there. That would be insane.

But I'd wait outside.

"Do you want to get out?" Herv said over the intercom between the back and front of the car, his voice gruff from decades of cigar smoking. He was an egg-shaped man in his sixties with a full head of hair and black-rimmed glasses. He had a family he adored so much he'd tried to quit working for me when his wife got breast cancer so he could take care of their daughter. I wouldn't let him. I paid for his wife's care and canceled all my appointments for a month while he stayed home with her.

I did all that for my own good, but also to beat back my envy.

"Wait here for a minute."

What did I want from her? She'd moved on. She didn't want to see my face. Didn't want to know about the surgeries I'd refused so that I could punish myself for losing her. I had nothing to offer her but awkwardness. Nothing to offer myself but regret.

Bile bubbled up in my throat. More gum to mask the taste of loss. I stuck the wrapper in my coat, watching the glass door of the building for signs of life.

The doorman hailed a cab, and the redheaded sisters came out, chatting apparently happily.

It was getting late. I needed rest.

I knocked on the glass between Herv and me. "Go where that cab's going."

"Yes, sir."

We followed. There was little chance we'd be noticed in the Manhattan traffic, circling the block around the nightclub where they'd gotten out. Every time the club was out of sight, I wondered if she'd left, but like a man possessed, I kept sending the car around the block. Even as I told myself this was wrong— disrespectful to her, unhealthy for me—I did it anyway.

Just another glimpse. One more and I'd know if she'd been disgusted by me.

Maybe her husband would show up. Maybe I'd get a sense of them. Maybe I'd get high on the rage of seeing them together. Drink my impotence like a thick, green liqueur.

"Stop," I said.

She stood on the sidewalk, arms crossed, shivering like a tuning fork as she talked to her sister. No man came. No husband to put his coat over her shoulder.

If I'd asked myself what I was thinking when I took off my coat in the back of the limo, I would have told myself I was thinking of her comfort. Of making her world right for a moment.

That was what I was thinking.

It wasn't what I was doing.

I pressed the button to roll down the glass between my driver and me, sitting behind him so he couldn't see me.

What I was doing was acting on a decision I hadn't admitted to when I saw her at Teterboro Airport. A decision that was taking shape even as I denied I'd made it.

"The woman with the pink jacket gets this," I said, pushing the coat to the front. "Give it to the bouncer to pass to her and come back."

I closed the window before he could turn around to see me.

I watched as he got out, gave the coat to the club's security, and dashed back.

"Go," I said as the bouncer approached Carrie with my coat.

Herv drove off as she received the gift… and before she could try to thank the stranger behind the tinted window.

CHAPTER 35

VENICE, ITALY - 1993

The men came to the hospital before my mother came for the day, soon after the wire was removed from my jaw. Two lawyers. I knew their profession from my father's firm. The way they swaggered as if they'd already won a war I didn't know was being waged.

"Mr. Marlowe?" one of the lawyers said once the door closed. He didn't have a trace of an Italian accent. American. He'd flown across an ocean to stand in my hospital room.

"Who's asking?" I said, trying not to move my jaw too much. Talking still hurt.

"We represent someone who would like to help you."

"With what?"

He smirked as if anyone with eyes could see what needed help around here. "You're going to need surgery. Quite a bit. Strictly aesthetic procedures aren't usually covered by insurance."

"So?"

The second man stood by the door with his hands folded, and I started to doubt he was a lawyer at all.

The first man said, "My client is prepared to offer you a choice. Both options are very generous."

"Who's your client?"

"He's offering all the reparative work you need at no cost to you. Alternately, you can take a lump sum and use it to start a new life. Jump-start a career. Just about anything."

Just about. The vague restriction wasn't lost on me.

I looked him up and down. I didn't need both eyes to see the creases in his jacket where it would have been folded in a garment bag. He'd come straight off a plane. This offer—whatever it was— was important to his client.

"In exchange for what?"

"Simply," he said as if he was about to propose a new brand of toothpaste or a promise to swear off eating hot dog turds left on the sidewalk, "you agree to avoid all contact with Carrie Drazen."

Nothing was as gut-twisting as the white-hot rage that filled me when I heard the lawyer's proposition.

She'd never love me like this, and I had to leave her. It was the noble thing.

But on my terms. Not her father's. Not the lawyer's.

My terms.

"Tell your client to shove his offer up his ass."

***

Nighttime was the most frustrating. Hospitals were a terrible place to rest. Nurses felt no compunction in waking me to check vitals and ask questions. The lady I shared the room with groaned in the middle of the night from the other side of a curtain.

The beeping of the instruments fell out of time, making it hard to listen to the music in my head. The last movement of the *Ballad of Blades* was a deep pit of minor chords and spiraling gloom.

He came in the dark hours of the morning, after a shift change.

I knew who he was right away.

Carrie had her father's eyes.

I'd always remembered Declan Drazen in a snappy suit and imagined that his trousers were cut to make room for a tail. As a kid, I'd wondered how he'd style hair to hide his horns. But the second time we met, he wore a polo shirt under a sports jacket. He had an unremarkable manila envelope tucked under one arm and looked too exhausted to be the devil.

"Gabriel." He smiled with a disarmingly warm sincerity. "I believe we've met."

"Yeah."

"May I sit?"

"Suit yourself."

He suited himself by sitting on the edge of the chair with the envelope dangling between his legs—looking right at my face. No pity, which I was grateful for. But no compassion either.

"I'm the client," he said.

"No shit." I tried to look away, but his stare pulled me back. "How is she?"

"She's fine."

"Did they hurt her?"

"Bump on the head." He touched a place above his ear as if it was important to know her face wasn't injured. "Carrie. My daughter. She's sensitive but strong."

His tone and word choice were clear. These were facts. Like the square footage of his house or the number of dollars in his bank account. She was his property.

"You didn't come out of it as well," he said.

"I just wanted to know if she was okay."

"She is."

The honorable thing to do would have been to send a message back with him. Say goodbye. Tell her it was over. Eat shit for the sake of her life. So what if it made Declan Drazen happy? Or if it satisfied his sense that his way was the only way? Or that Carrie was his property? What right did a monster have to pride?

"Tell her I was asking about her."

"No."

The refusal was so flat it was like a slap in the face.

"I'm not going leave her for money."

He scoffed with a tight laugh he couldn't suppress. "You seem like a smart boy, so I'm not going to insult your intelligence. I'm going to do you the favor of being honest with you."

"Don't do me any favors."

"Your father was Keith Marlowe?"

"Yes," I growled, angering the wound in my throat.

"A decent lawyer. I knew him."

"You killed him."

He looked down as if he didn't want me to see him smile but did it a second too late, as if he wanted to make sure I did. "You know," he said before looking up, "the Catholic Church isn't full of creationists. We can follow the Canon, be devout members, and still believe in evolution. Which is good. Sensible. Because I see evolution at work every day. The strong survive. The weak fall in line. But when the weak overestimate their strength? When they fight with lions? That's when they find out they're as weak as lambs."

The damaged artery in my neck beat so hard I thought my sutures would break.

My father hadn't been weak, but nothing I could do would prove otherwise. He was dead, and Declan Drazen was alive, looking at me from the winner's perch.

"Get out."

"Don't take it personally," he said. "It is what it is. No insult was intended."

"Get out." My voice dropped an octave but squeaked at the end as if it couldn't sustain a show of strength.

"I haven't told you what I came to tell you."

"Say it and leave."

He nodded, satisfied with the terms. "My daughter wanted to make sure you were all right. Once she knew you were alive and well, I told her what you…" He waved toward my face. "I described your injuries. At first, she was strong about it. She made a compelling case to see you, but then… let's just say she's no lion. She's a lamb."

I wasn't going to fall apart in front of him, but setting my jaw hurt like fuck.

The woman on the other side of the curtain moaned loudly, shocking me out of self-pity.

"I can see it in what's left of your face," Declan continued. "You think you can power through me and get to her. But she's my lamb to protect. Don't make me defend her."

"I can fix my face. There's no cure for you."

"You can fix your face? With what money? And after how many years? By the time you look like a man again, she'll be married with children. But…" He stood, holding the envelope in both hands as if it was now the most important thing in the room. "Once the best plastic surgeons in the world are finished with you, you can find someone else. A nice, pretty lamb. Maybe even a lion who won't leave you when you need her."

He dropped the envelope on the tray next to my bed. It was fat with heartbreak and loneliness. I'd been rejected like a warped bow. Unusable. Substandard. A mistake to be forgotten.

"Let me know," he said before turning to leave.

"Wait," I said as I picked up the envelope.

"Yes?" He turned back to me and took a single step in my direction.

I untwisted the string fastening and pulled out a contract.

"I still hate you," I said, scanning it. There was a place to check my option. A normal face or a career. Neither with the woman I loved.

"Understandable." He handed me a pen.

I took it and checked my choice.

If she didn't want me, what could I do? Chase her down? Force her to want a grotesque mask of a man?

"And I'm going to fucking bleed you." I found the amount offered to start my career and added a zero to the end.

"Oh, really?" Declan said, sounding bemused.

"No," I said before changing the first digit to a nine. "Want to patronize me again?"

"I don't think I can afford it."

"Initial it." I gave him the pen, and he initialed the change.

I'd checked the box to choose my music instead of my face, leaving myself unlovable for another woman, then I signed her away, restricting her to my past as she'd banished me from her future.

He signed in his space and folded the contract back into the envelope. "I wish you well. Truly."

I turned to the window, where the black night and the light in the room met, reflecting my face on the glass. "Turn the light out when you leave."

In the reflection, he flipped the light switch down before he closed the door behind him. My face dissolved, and the gray sky appeared in the window.

My roommate moaned.

The machines beeped.

I was alone.

CHAPTER 36

NEW YORK - 1995

*M*usic works because the tones fall into patterns we're hardwired to find pleasing. Then culture steps in, refining the expectations until we become consumers with expectations of what music is, how it should sound, what marks need to be hit, and what conventions should be present. That's why when people hear a musical genre they aren't familiar with, they're apt to say, "It doesn't sound like music to me."

Music tells us what we already believe.

A con man does the same thing when what you already believe is false. He learns who you are by observing you and, with a sharp sense of human nature, feeds you your own lies, giving you a way out of the trap of faulty assumptions.

It didn't occur to me that Declan was lying, because he'd told me what I knew was true.

Carrie couldn't love an ugly man. She'd never settle for someone damaged.

Wholeness cannot love brokenness.

Beauty can only love beauty.

A weak lamb loves weakly.

That was my truth until she appeared in the car window, unwinding her scarf to expose objective perfection.

And it was her. Bounded by the dark frame of the car door, it was her. Even with cold pink at the tip of her nose and flecks of snow on her red lashes, it was the same Carrie I'd only known in California sun, her breath now condensing into winter smoke and her ginger mane circling her head like a fire.

The first time she opened her mouth, I was too stunned to accept her face and my name together. Then she shouted it again with such fierce intention that the sound pierced the glass, driving into my heart, silencing a reply with the bang and crack of my shattering reality.

How had I not seen it?

She was a lioness.

***

I told Herv to turn the car around and out of the lot. The snow slowed us enough to make following her to the library discreet. When she went in, I stopped myself. My face was a wild card. She might recoil.

No. She would freak out. Who wouldn't? The patch over my left eye couldn't hide the destruction of my cheek or the scar that closed the corner of my mouth.

Like a regal, unpredictable animal, she could not be approached from the front.

The guard was distracted enough to let me slip into the research section, and I spotted her right away, red hair flowing over my coat as her fingers brushed the book spines the way they'd brushed the bones of my back on our quiet nights together. I ducked away when she turned.

What was I going to do about this?

Nothing?

Not an option. She was mine. She'd always be mine. Even if she didn't know it. I played her song every night, and every time I did, I molded the air into the shape of her.

Pinching a piece of scrap paper from the librarians' desk, I scrawled a note she'd only understand if she remembered me, and I stuck it inside a book on music.

I sensed her on the other side of the shelves. Through the space in the stacks, I saw her chin tilting down to read as she caressed pages like a devotee. That piece of her, so close, was all I needed.

I pushed the volume through the space above the books before I slipped away.

A hundred things had to go right. She'd have to pick up the book. Read the note. Understand it.

None of it worked unless I was on her mind. The old me. The normal boy with brown eyes and a future with her. The one who hadn't sold his love.

***

I didn't like looking at my reflection, but I'd cut myself shaving too many times trying to avoid it.

In the hotel, leaning into the bathroom mirror, I said all the usual horrible things to myself because they were true. There was objective beauty, which meant there was objective ugliness, and I was looking at one of the two. And to some extent, it had been a choice.

No reconstructive surgery. No glass eye. No skin grafts. Nothing. This was me. This was my face. Not one dime of Declan Drazen's money went into people seeing me. Every penny left after I paid for living expenses and whatever I could get away with giving my mother went into making sure I was heard. I'd built a persona, an apparatus to hide it behind, and a career.

After a while, the idea of plastic surgery had seemed like an insult to what I'd built and a dishonor to what I'd lost.

I realized I'd decided to break my contract the moment I played "I Will Always Love You" in LA. My resolution had grown from an irritating grain of sand to a pearl that got so big I cracked open. I had no room for the ring on her finger or the promises I'd made. I only had to consider how I would do it, and fully exposed —in public—wouldn't work.

I took off the patch. Would I be okay with her seeing the deep recess where my eye had been? The sewn-shut eyelid with the lashes preserved so that one day a glass replacement could be inserted? I touched it. Would she want to? Would she run her fingers along my face and stop where no hair grew? The wound on my neck had damaged the nerves so badly even I couldn't touch it without a buzzing pain. Would she feel cheated?

Would she ever leave a handsome husband for this minefield of knotted tissue?

"Can you walk away?" I asked my half-normal reflection.

I had to embrace the possibility that nothing would change, but I had to know.

Maybe it wasn't a reporter looking for me, but an investigator.

That rich girl had wound up on a New York street corner, peeking into the tinted window of my limo. And maybe an investigator had shown up looking for me.

It hadn't been an accident or coincidence.

It was all so clear I could barely pay attention to the conversation.

She didn't just happen to be on that corner in a blizzard, knocking on my window and saying my name. She'd found me.

She was always inquisitive.

Maybe playing that song for her had ignited no more than curiosity about her old college love. Maybe she wanted to catch up over coffee. What then?

If she'd banged on the car window in a snowstorm so she could make small talk, I'd eat my cello.

"I'll walk away," my reflection said back. "I'll respect her, and I'll leave her alone."

It would leave me solo forever, but I wouldn't try to capture a lioness who didn't want to be caged.

But if she didn't open the book and meet me at Carnegie Hall? What then? Had I been too cryptic?

When I left the bathroom, Cherie called. "I spoke to Danny Mankewicz."

"Him? Or his assistant?"

"Him."

"Did he admit he was a reporter?"

"No. He said he was a record exec."

His story was consistent. Maybe it was him? I'd cut off everyone but my mother after Venice, but with the possibility that my friend was real and not the result of diligent, if sneaky, reporting, I smiled at the thought of a cup of coffee.

"When are we meeting?"

"I said you were really tightly booked with students. He said fine. He's home in New York anyway, but he'll be in Chicago March fourth."

"I'm in Seattle that week."

"Right. I didn't say you'd be gone, but I asked for a backup date. He suggested the following week. Saturday the twelfth."

"San Francisco."

Weird that he'd only suggest days Adam Brate was scheduled to play. I wanted to see him, but the real him. I'd almost been tricked into a meeting before.

A reporter would know Adam Brate's schedule. If Gabriel Marlowe agreed to meet him when Adam was supposed to be across the country, Danny would show up. A reporter would reschedule.

"Call him back," I said. "Tell him the fourth is okay."

"You'll be in—"

"I know. Just tell him that. Tell him I look forward to hearing all about how he leveled up in Chrono Trigger."

She said "Chrono Trigger" as she wrote it down as if she'd never heard it before.

"Tell him if he can't make it, he should call me in my hotel room here—2220."

"Got it."

"I'm going to make it up to you for helping me."

"Okay?"

"When I get back, I'll work with you on Dvořák. In person. I'll tell you everything I know."

"Really?" she squeaked. "In person?"

"Yes, but Cherie?"

"Yes?"

"I'm a hard teacher."

"Oh my God, please be the worst, hardest ever! Thank you, thank you!"

I hung up, smiling even though I'd broken two of my rules. She knew my name, and she was about to see my face. But I didn't feel as if I had a choice. To an extent, exposing myself was unavoidable. All I had to do was keep it to a minimum. If she was going above and beyond the call of duty, I could too. Cherie couldn't have made those calls without knowing my name, and those calls were the first notes in what sounded like a much larger piece.

First though, I needed to know if I could expect a call with a bullshit Danny.

Thank God he wasn't named Smith.

New York 411 had no Danny or Daniel Mankewicz listed. He could easily have an unlisted number, but that was out of my control.

Los Angeles 411 had two listings for Danny Manckewicz and one for Daniel Manckewicz.

On the second try, a voice I recognized came through.

"Hello?"

"Hello, is this Danny?"

"Sure is."

"This is Gabriel—"

"Hey! You dumb fuck, where have you been?"

"Around. I heard you were a big-shot record executive."

"Me? Hell, no. If you meet one, give him my number."

It wasn't him hunting my mother down in a coffee shop.

"Man," Danny said. "I was worried about you when I didn't hear from you. You still with that rich girl?"

"No," I said, stopping before I gave an explanation I'd want to change later.

"Whatever." He blew her off like a summer fling that wouldn't tolerate shorter days. "You in LA? If you're still here, we have to get together."

Rule Six was already shot. My problems had gone from wide, high-stakes methods of hiding my identity to the mundane avoidance of a day with an old friend. I didn't have time for it. Not the small talk or the explanations about my face. "There's a lot going on..."

"No excuses. I have a place in Silver Lake. Big yard. Two Great Danes you can saddle up and ride."

I could either give him a definite no or bite the bullet and see him. Go to his place in Silver Lake. Take a dog for a spin around the block. Act like a normal guy for an afternoon.

"Things happened since USC," I said. "I look different."

"I wasn't into you for your looks."

We laughed because of course, why would it matter? Besides the sad story that came with my scars, my face was irrelevant. A friend is a friend, and I'd been friendless too long.

"Then let's meet." I said.

"I need a date. Don't do that LA thing where you make promises you aren't going to keep."

"The twenty-ninth. Brunch?"

"You're on. Whoa, whoa," he said at the sound of dog nails scratching on the floor. "Down, Killer. Bring your violin. I want to hear what you've been working on. We can do a classical jam."

"I don't—" I stopped.

There was no explaining why I'd moved to cello without

telling him about the alley in Venice. And that would have to wait until the dogs were calm and I had a beer in me. But I would tell him. Besides the people who didn't need to be told because they had been there in the aftermath, like my mother, I hadn't told anyone from my life before, and I knew Danny would be the first.

"I'll bring my instrument."

***

After hanging up with Danny, I had Cherie cancel my flight home. I told my manager I was staying in New York until she heard otherwise. I gave Herv a cash bonus to watch Margie's apartment building. If Carrie left with suitcases, I wanted to know, and if she hadn't hired Fake Danny to find me, I needed to know who had.

She wanted to see me. She'd hunted me down. Whether it was out of curiosity or love didn't even matter. Whether she'd changed her mind about being with an ugly man or not was beside the point. I wanted to see her one last time. I wanted to hear her tell me she loved her husband with tones that clicked together in truth.

I needed to hear it from her lips.

Standing at the high windows, looking over the gray-sludge-frosted Manhattan rooftops, I imagined breaking my contract. Doing what I'd dedicated myself to avoiding. Gauging her reaction. Hearing no more than relief that her curiosity had been satisfied. Making small talk about future plans that didn't include each other.

Then what?

Maybe Declan Drazen would sue me. We'd settle. Maybe he'd destroy me out of spite. But I'd have no more reason to be a nameless cellist. Only shame would keep my face hidden.

Shame was as exhausting as anonymity, and I was tired. Very tired. The burden was as heavy as the wet snow on the rooftops… and as temporary. Everything changed. Seasons plodded forth, one after the other, whether I was ready or not.

Walls crumbled, and secrets were revealed. Truth had a way of following a man, hiding under the thick pads of snow until spring. Carrie was the warm sun, and I'd extended winter as long as I could.

I had to find a way to walk away from that night in Venice. Acknowledge it and move on like she had. Let the snow melt and reveal the ground I walked on.

I spent the rest of the afternoon making a deal to get me into Carnegie Hall the next morning.

***

How do you get to Carnegie Hall?

In the fugue between coma and consciousness, darkness and half sight, you compose a violin sonata that turns into a concerto. Every note is a hymn to a moment with a woman you love.

You try to play it, only to find you can't hold a violin under your neck.

You pick up the pieces of your broken heart, put them back together with spit and chewing gum, and rewrite the entire thing for cello because the concerto has a life of its own even though the love it was written to describe is dead.

How do you get to Carnegie Hall? You get famous not playing there and they'll move mountains for you. Then you wait. You practice, and you wait for the show of your life.

What do you expect from her?

She was unavailable. Married. This was about closure. But my heart was in stark disagreement with my mind and fed it vulgar fantasies about separation and divorce. If she was unhappy, I'd rescue her. If she was happy, she'd—

Stop fooling yourself.

I heard her come in. A hundred circumstances had fallen into place, and she was on the other side of a thin paper screen. The hum of her longing pulsed against the skin of my guilt as I played

Ballad of Blades for her, and afterward... when she told me she'd thought I was dead, my skin went cold.

She hadn't rejected me, but she would.

"Do you want to see me?" I asked.

"Yes. And not through a screen."

She demanded my whole self at a low roar. It was too late to change my mind.

"Okay." I placed the cello between my legs and picked up the bow. The instrument was a talisman that gave me strength to be reckless. "I need to do some things, and you need to think about it."

"No, I don't."

"You do." I played a note so she couldn't object just yet. "I'm at the Waldorf. Room 2220. Call me there tonight if you want to see me." I stopped myself. I was creating steps between that moment and the moment she saw my face. "No. We'll meet at the library lions at three, and you'll have one more chance to walk away."

Even as I said it, I didn't want it. If she walked away, I'd be devastated.

My arm moved of its own volition, telling her the truth as the bow ground out a silly pop tune. "I Will Always Love You."

"I won't," she said over the music, speaking as if she knew what that meant.

"Then you'll be mine again. But you'll walk when you see me, Carrie. Anyone would."

She didn't refute it because she hadn't seen me yet.

And how was that fair? How could I ask her to choose when she didn't know what was behind the screen I'd set up?

I pressed the bump on my throat. The wound that had almost killed me had never healed correctly and never would. Touching it tingled. Tucking a violin under my chin was so uncomfortable I'd had to switch to cello.

What if she touched where it hurt?

She wouldn't, but what if she did?

Would I flinch? Push her away? Reject her the way I'd rejected the violin?

No. Never.

That was the trick of her perfect beauty. The way it was grounded in accessibility. I'd been drawn to her but not blinded.

In those early days in the hospital, lying in bed with a face made of pain, I'd feared for her life. Once I knew she was alive, I'd signed away the goddess without considering the woman.

That was my mistake, and I wouldn't make it again.

With my heart pounding and my lower lip shaking with nerves, I called out before she got off the stage. "Wait!"

My feet did what my mind feared, coming from behind the screen, turning my body around.

She bridged the gap between us. Tilted my face up because she didn't know she had something to fear. My memory had made her shorter than she was, but she was five eight, only two inches shorter than me. What else had I forgotten?

"Gabriel?"

Her voice. I'd forgotten its coarse humanness. Its grounding reality. Her beauty lifted the soul to heaven, but her voice fixed it to the earth.

She was and always would be mine. Even if she turned me away.

"Hi, little bird."

I didn't know what to expect. A high five or a hug. A shriek or a mature conversation.

The rest was a blur. I let her see my face. I let her touch my scars.

And when she said she loved me, I believed her.

And when she called my room and told me to meet her at the lions, I ran to her.

And when, under the shadow of the stone lion named Patience, she forgave me with a kiss that reminded me of who I was under the web of scar tissue, I believed in more than her. I believed in me.

She'd kissed me.

I felt like a twelve-year-old standing in shock with his mouth open and half a boner, looking at the girl he'd given his first kiss to with admiration and awe—the whole of his adulthood opening up like a door to a room of treasure. In the back of the limo, my hands shook and my tongue lay still in my mouth with the taste of her disappearing.

I'd kiss her again.

She was going to leave her husband, and she wanted me.

Me.

She'd looked me right in the face and still wanted me.

All I had to do was wait for her to call. Then she was mine again.

I could barely get my head around it.

I killed time playing my cello, pacing, making arrangements with Cherie, and ignoring meals while I waited for her to call to tell me she'd left Peter or changed her mind.

At 6:01, she still hadn't called, and there was a knock at my door.

Was it her?

Had she skipped the phone call and just come to me?

"Come in," I called from a seat across the room. "It's open."

My breath stopped when the door swung open and my lungs squeezed tight, expelling every gram of oxygen when I saw who stood in the doorway.

It was Peter Thorne.

He was pressing a cloth to the side of his face. Spots of blood had soaked through. Before I could say a word, he slammed the door.

I froze.

His coat was open. White shirt half-untucked, wrinkled at the chest, open three buttons.

He was there to tell me to stay away from his wife, and what could I say? I was in the wrong. I had no right to her. No business thinking about her or making arrangements to see her. I was going to have to let him in and take my lumps.

I stayed in the shadows, legs crossed as if I had a muscle in my body that was relaxed.

Peter scanned the room, eyes resting on my cello case for half a moment before falling on me again. "You. You fucker. I knew it was you."

He took the cloth away, exposing a ragged, bleeding injury on his cheek and the bloodstained collar of the white shirt that had been hidden under his jacket.

It was then I realized he hadn't come to warn or threaten me. He hadn't come prepared with a list of ways I'd crossed ethical and moral boundaries.

He'd come with a list of ways he was going to cross them.

"You need a doctor," I said as if I was bored. My anxiety was stuffed deep in my gut. He didn't need to see that or any other sign of weakness.

"Do you know who I am?" He stepped forward, ignoring the blood.

I didn't have or want plausible deniability. I wasn't a coward. I wasn't a liar, but I wasn't a fool either. He'd know what he needed to.

"Yes."

"I'm her husband." He took off his jacket and slung it over the back of the couch as if he was there to stay.

"Congratulations. Is there something I can do for you?"

Peter stopped on the other side of the coffee table. "All this time." He put the cloth back over his wound. "I knew her mind was somewhere else. And you. You were after her the entire time. Waiting behind a mask. Playing that shit for her as if I wasn't sitting right there. Were you trying to humiliate me? Did you think I wouldn't come after you for that? I hired the best, and it took them a damn minute to find you. You're as careless as you are ugly."

"I never sought her out." True enough. I hadn't looked for her until she found me.

"Don't confuse me with someone who gives a shit. I found you. And now I have a choice. Destroy her or destroy you. What do you think I'm going to do?"

Destroy her? How would that even be an option? At that point, it became clear how he'd been wounded and who had done the wounding. If he'd been attacked by a stranger, he'd be talking to the police. He wouldn't have come straight to me with a cheek of ragged skin and open blood vessels.

She'd done it. Carrie. His wife.

Why would she do that unless he'd physically struck her first?

"That's going to scar if you don't get it looked at," I said. "Trust me. I'm an expert on the subject."

Instead of going around the coffee table, he took the straight course, marching onto it, then back onto the carpet. In two steps, he was standing over me.

"Jesus," he said when he saw my face. He laughed, stretching his wound open until it bled fresh. It was a bite. "They really fucked you up."

Who would get close enough to his face to bite him? Who but his wife? How much of the blood on his hands was hers? Was she alone in her sister's apartment?

"Where is she?" I asked. "What did you do to her?"

"She's mine to worry about."

"She was never yours."

I hadn't intended to make an argument like that to the man who had married her, but it was the truth. Carrie and I belonged to each other until the day one of us died. An animal like this would never be worthy of her, ring or no ring.

"If she was yours," he said, "you should've claimed her. But you didn't. You signed her away for money."

The truth spoken through a deceitful mouth cut into me where I'd never healed.

I'd run. I'd been so ashamed that I gave her up. The contract was an excuse. The money only covered a decision I'd already made. I gave her up because I was terrified to see her expression when she saw me. I was afraid she'd leave me, but more than that, I was afraid she'd stay out of guilt.

All the reasons were strings stretched tight over my actions. Peter knew exactly which one to pluck.

The musician was more important than the instrument, and I wouldn't be played.

"Maybe I let her go for money. But you? You married her because she made you look like a king."

He came at me. "I am a king, you freak."

With the peripheral vision on my left side limited, I didn't see the punch coming. My mind shattered into stars and blackness as he threw me to the floor and kicked me in the stomach. A wave of nausea flooded me as he pulled his foot back to nail me again.

Bending my crossed leg toward me slightly, I coiled the tension in my hip and shot it forward with all the leverage I could, kicking him just below the kneecap.

He fell backward with a scream, and I leapt on him, my knees pressing hard on his biceps. He jerked violently. He was heavier. I couldn't hold him for long, and I couldn't let him go. He'd kill me. My body fired a reaction in hot, spinal currents that never found their way to my brain, punching his face so hard a shot of pain went to my elbow. I hit him with my left fist at an angle. I floated above pain, above my body, levitating on the release of two years of impotent rage.

My defensive posture was impossible to maintain while striking him, and he managed to flip me off. I rolled and got into a crouch. He did the same, growling at me with a bloody nose and one eye with busted vessels.

"Now I know who you are," he said. "I came to talk to you, man to man, and you attacked me."

"And Carrie? Did you just try to talk to her before she took half your face off?"

"You bit me." The lie was an illustration of what he'd tell the police. "To make me ugly like you. My blood's all over this room. Your knuckles are bleeding already."

The room phone rang. I didn't look at it until he did.

It could have been Cherie, but it wasn't.

It had to be Carrie, and if Peter answered it, all his suspicions would be proven true. He'd redirect his anger at her.

It rang again. The desk was right beside him. I had no chance of getting there first.

"Stay there," he said. "I'll get this for you."

"Leave it."

He moved his hand six inches to pick up the receiver, put it to his ear, and waited for her voice. "It's you." His attention flicked away from me in a moment of surprise. "He's right here."

I held out my hand. "Give me the phone."

"Was there something you wanted to tell him?"

After crossing the room as fast as I could, I pushed the speakerphone button. "Carrie?"

"Am I on speaker?" another woman's voice came from the desk phone.

"Who is this?" I asked.

"Margie. Carrie's sis—"

"What do you want?" Peter snapped.

"Give Gabriel the phone."

"No. Say what you have to say."

In her silence, Peter and I regarded each other like middle school rivals. My head ached, and the nausea from getting kicked in the stomach was turning into a sick roil.

"What, Margaret?" Peter said through his teeth.

"I'd rather not say this on speakerphone."

"What were you going to tell him that you can't tell her husband?" he asked.

She sighed. "It's Carrie. She's..."

Peter's useless grip on the receiver was so tight his knuckles went pale pink.

"When I got home, she was having a seizure. She was on her back, and... she was suffocating on her own vomit."

"She was breathing when I left."

"She had bruises on her neck. She had blood all over her."

The full-color ugliness of the scene, with the sound of choking and the smell of vomit, her perfect face twisted in a fight to survive.

"What did you do?" I said.

"She was fine!" Peter shouted.

"She wasn't." Margie was near tears.

"What did you do?" I shouted.

"Nothing!"

"She's dead, Peter." Her words were delivered with cold rage. "She's dead, and you killed her."

My heart was already still when he came for me, wielding the phone like a hard, plastic spear. He drove it into my forehead hard enough to move the room sideways, spilling upside down in a thick twirl and bringing the floor against the side of my head with a bang that made my ear ring.

I didn't black out. Not fully. My consciousness was lifted into a gray cloud far above my body, watching Peter yank the phone cord out of the wall as if the connection was the problem. He left my broken body alone behind a closed door, as he'd done with Carrie.

I got on my hands and knees on a seesaw floor. My stomach lurched and gave up lunch.

Carrie.

I had to see her. Be there for her. Sit by her side and tell her everything would be all right. I'd never turn my back on her again.

But there was nothing I could do.

Her body was an empty shell, and the man who had pulled her out of it was running away.

Crawling to the desk, I pulled the phone to me. It rattled along the floor. The cord was frayed. Shot. Maybe that was a sign.

Leveraging my hand on the desk, I pulled myself up, intending to go down to the front desk so they could call the police. Then I'd wait for them and deliver a statement. Then I'd wait some more while Peter used his resources to hide from justice.

Carrie's body would get colder, stiffer, losing its wholeness over time, until all the beauty inside her was digested by dirt.

The Drazens hadn't won.

Drazen was a name for the self-interested. The greedy. It was shorthand for all the ways the powerful impacted the lives of the weak… and never for the better.

Carrie was a Drazen by name, but her heart had another name.

Peter was a Drazen, if not by name, then by the use of his influence.

As my balance steadied, I knew he would try to get away with it, and I knew he might. In the time it took for the wheels of the system to move, it would be harder and harder to bring him to justice. In those months and years, Carrie would still be dead.

Now he was vulnerable.

Now was the crack of time between his panic and his plan.

Fuck the police.

CHAPTER 37

NEW YORK - 1995

*P*eter had left his jacket behind, an oversight that would have gotten a poorer man caught, tried, and sent away for a long time. I found the stub in the breast pocket, printed on letter-sized paper and folded into fours. It wasn't a normal airline stub, but having traveled the world anonymously for two years, I recognized a flight plan when I saw one.

SMO
TEB
N189TS

Santa Monica to Teterboro. It had come in that morning.

He had no plan out. Or maybe he did. But I was sure he hadn't planned to murder Carrie.

It was bitter cold outside. My hat was pulled over the bump on my head where I'd been hit with a phone, but I was otherwise uncovered.

People looked, but I had no time for shame.

Herv was waiting. All I had to do was page him. Just call a number from the desk phone, type in our code for "come around front," and—in one way or another—involve him in Carrie's murder.

The Drazens had ruined enough lives.

"Cab," I said to the doorman in the gold epaulettes.

"Yes, sir," he said without making eye contact. "Where to?"

My destination would be noted in the hotel log. So no. That wouldn't fly.

"Fifty-Second and Third."

"Right this way." He rushed to open the door of the first yellow cab in a long line of them. I got in as he told the cabbie the location I'd given.

The door closed, and the cab moved east.

"Warm enough?" the driver asked, his hand on the climate control. His license said his name was Omar Said, and his picture matched his face. Half of it had the melted look of burn scars.

"Yeah."

"I can turn it up." He looked at me in the rearview, and when our eyes met, he nodded. "How'd you get yours?"

"Knife fight. You should see the other guy. He looks great."

Omar laughed. "Me? Boring way. Grease fire. Now my wife cooks. See how skinny I am?"

He had a wife. I wondered if she was beautiful and loved him anyway. Or if loving him anyway made her beautiful.

Carrie would have loved me anyway. I wished I'd known that sooner.

At a red light, I leaned over the back of the front seat. "I don't really need to go to Fifty-Second and Third." I eyed the clipboard and little pencil in the passenger seat. A trip log. "If you charge me for that on the meter and take me to Teterboro Airport, that would be better."

He turned to face me, one eye half-closed by scar tissue. "That's in New Jersey."

"I have cash." I rooted around my pockets for my wallet and flicked through the bills. "Two hundred cover it?"

"Two-fifty."

"How about three and you say you lost that pencil when you had to log it?"

His good eyebrow went up a quarter inch. "You a spy or something?"

He was going to do it. I could tell. And it wasn't for the money. It was because we were both ugly.

"I have to get there for a woman," I said. "The love of my life."

***

Now what? I asked myself that between the glass-walled terminal and the rock piles of the construction site for the new runway.

I'd spent the trip to Teterboro hardening my resolve to catch Peter and pound him into unconsciousness. Or hold him down until the cops came. Or by some alchemy I didn't understand, turn my cold, quiet anger into justice. But when Omar drove away and I was in the parking lot three hundred dollars poorer, I wasn't quite sure what my plan was.

Except to not think about Carrie being dead.

Not at all.

I had to be furious about it without being sad about it. The fury was more comfortable. It had a direction.

That way.

Toward the terminal for private jets, where I could see Peter through the glass walls and doors, talking on a pay phone.

A security guard stood between the side door of the terminal and plane parking. A couple of passengers flipped through magazines, and agents stood behind the counter to check flight plans, call the porters to move luggage over the tarmac, and route people as necessary. Easy job. Most of the planning was done between pilots and the tower.

But still. Too many people. Too many eyes, and I was easy to identify.

I stood in the parking lot, under a shuttle bus overhang, hands clasped behind my back, and waited. The wind went around me, and the cold was comfortable against the hard ice of my heart.

When Peter hung up the phone, he saw me. But I didn't move.

He'd come for me. I'd lure him someplace we could be alone. He'd offer me a bribe or a deal for my silence. I'd refuse. He'd kill me. I'd join Carrie in death. But maybe Peter wouldn't walk away the way people like him always did.

In the end, even if I was dead, he'd miss his plane.

He left the terminal and came toward me.

Predictable.

"Hey!" he called as I turned and walked away.

I guessed he'd run to catch up, and he did.

"What do you want?" he asked from beside me as I paced to the edge of the parking lot toward the construction site.

I said nothing, walking fast as if I knew where I was going— besides away from eyes and cameras.

"Nothing we do is going to bring her back," he said. "What's the point of going to prison? Look at me. Is this the face of a murderer?"

I didn't answer.

"Look," he said, our feet crunching on salt, then the scree of scattered pebbles. "If it's money—"

"I have money."

"Not like I do."

The construction site was farther away than it looked. I had to keep him close.

"How much?" I asked.

"A million. Cash."

"I have that in my couch cushions."

"Three million, then." He looked at his watch. A private plane wouldn't take off without him, but it would have to change its flight plan, and that meant delay. I ducked under the yellow-and-black-striped construction zone barrier. "Four. I have an account with Credit Suisse I can sign over to you."

I walked, and he followed, catching up at the edge of the reservoir I'd seen on my way into the airport a million years ago. It was frozen over, the size of an auditorium, with a dark-gray splotch in the center.

"When?" I said. "You're getting on a plane. When do I get it?"

"I can call my lawyer. He can—"

"Tell the police? They have to, you know."

"I'll be gone. They won't find me."

"But the money's not going to come."

"It's Switzerland."

Maybe he was right. Swiss banks were so neutral they did what they wanted in defiance of international law.

"Listen," he said, coming in front of me. His feet were on the edge of the frozen lake. It would be slippery. Any move he made could lead to a fall. Good.

"Listening."

"You don't know her."

"Didn't know her."

"She was impossible. So frustrating. I did everything I could for her, but she got in these moods, okay? Nothing was good enough for her, and I was trapped. Her father? That guy's the devil. Never make a deal with him. But you? You're sensible. I'd rather—"

"What kind of deal?"

"I work for him."

"That's a job. You said deal."

"Just come back with me. Get my lawyer on the phone and we can settle this like men."

He thought he was getting the upper hand.

"Talk fast and you'll make your flight." I stepped forward, and he stepped back.

"Look," he said, palms out as if showing me he had nothing in his hands but the truth. "I had some stuff on him, and I was going to use it for a plea bargain. So, he came to me and said, 'I have this daughter.'"

Propelled by a story too insane to be false, I took another step into him. "He gave her to you?"

"It wasn't a gift. Gifts are free."

I took him by the collar, and softened by the prospect of a deal, he didn't have enough adrenaline to react.

"She's not property." I spit the words so close to his face my saliva froze on his chin. "She was too good for you."

I threw him down, and he rolled away, then jumped into a crouch, ready to fight.

Fine. I would rip his throat open. Gouge his eyes out. Rip him to shreds for what he'd done to her life and what he was doing to her memory.

I'd been ready to die to delay him, but I didn't think about death when he lunged for me. We grappled, past gentlemanly punches and kicks, dropping to the ice as if we were lovers in a violent embrace. He bit my ear, and I kneed him in the groin.

We separated, circling around each other.

"The deal's off," he growled, sidestepping to get to the terminal side. He was going to make a run for it.

"Sure it is." I reversed the rotation, getting him close to the center, where the dark patch spread along the reservoir's surface.

"You were never going to marry her. You were a waste of time."

Before he finished the last word, he ran for the terminal, slipping on his second step. He landed on his hip and broke the ice, falling into a growing hole of black water with a splash.

I stood at the edge, watching the black water gurgle. Shards of ice bobbed outward when he came up, gasping for air.

He gripped the edge and started to pull himself out. Without thinking—just knowing—I slammed my heel into the ice in front of him.

He sank and came up again with blue lips and skin as white and translucent as a paper screen.

When he reached for the edge again, I cracked it away.

He gasped, reaching. "He was talking about killing you. Declan."

"Killing me?"

I let him grab the edge.

"The thing," he said, getting his elbows on the ice. "The guys in Italy. It was—"

"A setup."

"You lived because I told him no."

I had to slap my heel on the ice twice to crack it, but it didn't break off completely. "I didn't live." I slammed my heel down a third time. "I died." Still, the ice wouldn't break away, and he was getting his balance. "I died."

I kicked him in the face so hard I slipped and dropped onto my ass. Peter fell back into the water. Getting my feet under me, I crouched by the edge, waiting for him to return.

But he didn't.

The ripples settled, and the bobbing ice went still.

Behind me, the sound of gloved hands slowly clapping.

I spun to find Declan Drazen standing on solid ground between my escape and me.

CHAPTER 38

NEW JERSEY - 1995

*I*t was over.

Carrie was dead, and I was going to prison.

Fair enough, if fair was for other people. Which, when you're Declan Drazen, is the exact meaning of fair.

"You have me," I said with my hands raised. "You win. Again."

"You weren't going to beat me, Mr. Marlowe. That's..." He scoffed. "That's funny."

"He killed Carrie. Your daughter."

He walked away, toward the glowing lights of the terminal.

I ran after him and walked astride. "Did you hear me?"

"Yes."

"She's dead."

He bent his frame under the barrier as if it was nothing and kept walking. I kept up with him, resigned to my fate and yet stunned by his reaction.

"Despite your dramatic imaginings," he said, turning right, deeper into plane parking—the same mistake Peter had made with me—"you aren't dead."

He approached a golf cart. A driver got behind the wheel when Declan sat in the back.

"Where are you going?"

"We're going over there."

"We?"

"Do you want to stay here and wait to be found?" He patted the seat next to him.

I didn't trust him. I'd have to be crazy to do so. But I had nothing to lose, so I sat, and the golf cart sped onto the tarmac.

"You don't seem too upset she's dead," I said.

"There's time for that."

"You're a monster."

"There was a time, not as long ago as you think, when marriage was always a business deal. If it was a bad deal, either party took on a lover and the family stayed together. But now? We prioritize love and break families into smaller and smaller parts. Why? What's the point exactly?"

"So, you would have let him hurt her?"

"If I'd known?" He shrugged as the cart zipped by parked planes and we entered a small runway. "Probably not. I gave him a Drazen, and he abused the privilege. But it's too late for that now and I have a choice. I can kill you—and I would—but it's risky. Better for me to put you on my dead son-in-law's plane."

The cart stopped by a small jet with the airstairs lowered. Declan slid off the seat, but I didn't.

"Why?"

"My oldest daughter is very convincing. She knows I don't like gambling or rushing. And it's better if you run away."

"Two minutes, sir," the cart driver said.

"I'll tell her you said thank you. But you cannot. Ever. If you show your face again, I'll suddenly remember the events of this traumatic night. Behind a mask. Anonymous. Whatever you think you can get away with, don't do it. Not unless you want to die in prison."

"Where is it going?" I asked, indicating the plane.

"The flight plan says Costa Rica, but it doesn't matter. They'll take you as far as the fuel goes. Your choice."

Did I have a choice? Could I stay in the country, shame my mother, end my life in exchange for the life of a man who had killed the only person worth living for?

Did I have a choice to say no to this offer? This trap? This deal with an unforeseen endpoint that could be worse than prison and shame?

I didn't.

I was going to grieve for the rest of my life, and Carrie deserved every minute of it.

Declan got into the front seat of the golf cart, and the driver took his foot off the brake.

"Fuck yourself, Declan Drazen. Really. Fuck you."

"You're welcome," he replied as the cart took off.

Taking one last look around a world without hope of happiness, I climbed the stairs. The doors closed behind me.

CHAPTER 39

VENICE, ITALY - ONE YEAR LATER

*E*very day, I brought my cello to the pillar under the lion in the square of St. Mark's Basilica. Every day, I played something for her. At first, it was *Ballad of Blades*, but that started to seem self-indulgent and a new piece grew inside me.

It had no name, and it never would. It was as anonymous as I was.

Children stopped and pointed at me. Toddlers cried and clutched their mothers' legs. Tourists and natives alike made room for me as if I had a disease they could catch.

Then as the song evolved, so did the response. They stayed and listened to Carrie's song. It wasn't a dirge, though it had notes of loss in the uplifting chords. I didn't give voice to the loss of my name and my choices, but to the death of a perfect beauty in the world. A beauty flawed to perfection with impulsivity, curiosity, and self-doubt.

Sometimes putting the patch on my eye but always leaving the rest of my damage uncovered, I played.

I played for her near St. Mark's Basilica every day it didn't rain. I didn't leave out a jug or case for money. I had plenty of that squirreled away from years of protecting my anonymity. But people found a way to leave lire by slipping it in my closed case or finding a container in the trash.

The pigeons gathered in a cooing gray mass under the winter clouds. The tourists flocked, staring at the grotesque man and staying for his music. The church behind me would stand long after my cello was silent, but I would not be silent as long as I lived.

At least she was free of him. Even if I was an old, ugly man playing on those stones every day as the pigeons pecked at my shoes, she was free.

***

"*Buon giorno*," I said to Calogero. Every third dry morning, he showed up in a beard and long coat to chalk a picture of the *pieta* in the stones.

"*Ciao*," he replied, laying out sticks of blue in the same order as always.

I sat on the folding chair I brought every day.

"How are you today?" he asked in thick English. He liked to practice with me.

"Fine. I think the sun's going to come out."

"Maybe the pigeons will fly instead of shitting on the Virgin."

"Hope so." I got out my cello and left the case open with a sign that said NO DONATIONS in three languages. After a year of playing this square, I'd learned that worked best.

It was almost high noon. I knew from the way the shadows traveled across the bottom of my open case, where a few disobedient tourists always threw loose coins that I'd donate to a children's charity.

I kept playing. When the shade of the pillar behind me moved off the case, it would be time for lunch.

A bill fell into the case and flicked in the breeze. Green American money against the bright-red velvet. It flipped when the draft picked up, revealing Benjamin Franklin's half smile.

It wasn't the first time someone had unwittingly donated a

large sum to the Medici Children's Music Fund. But it was folded and dropped in a way I remembered.

The bow froze in my hand.

"*Ciao,*" a woman said.

The husky, atonal voice flipped a switch of memory that I'd tucked away.

But I didn't look up. I sat there with my bow still on the strings, imagining it was possible my memory and reality matched.

Looking up meant ending that moment with inevitable disappointment.

I wanted it to be true.

"*Ciao,* Adam. Is it still Adam?"

Had I been recognized? The moment of fantasy was cloaked with the potential for a nightmare.

That I understood. I looked up.

The breeze whipped her long, red hair to one side, and her eyes shone like the Virgin Mary's blue robes. She was wearing my coat.

"Carrie?" My voice cracked.

She looked at me as if I was handsome and strong, undamaged and whole. Worthy of her love and alive to receive it.

Was she a miracle?

An apparition?

Some strange twin I'd never met?

"Are you Carrie?"

She wasn't, of course. Carrie was dead, and this woman was as real as the stones under my feet.

"I was. My name is Marie now."

Marie.

Now.

The name meant absolutely nothing to me. It held no connection to a shared past, but now it was the most important word in the world. It was the name of a shared future.

Carrie was Marie now. I bit my lips to hold back the wet sobs threatening to explode from me, but no amount of willpower could keep my cheek dry.

"Nice to meet you, Marie." Her new name was the shape of a shared future, and I said it with measured appreciation. "My name is Gabriel. Gabriel Jefferson."

When she smiled, the sun hit its highest point in the sky.

***

She was radiant. People looked at her. Men, women, children. They looked at me too. Walking with the crowds on Larga San Marco, hand in hand, we were opposite poles of the same magnet.

We stopped for espresso and sat in a dark corner, leaning over the small table.

No one would bother us for hours.

"Margie asked me what I'd do if I could do anything, and I said I wanted to disappear. Change my name. Do what you did."

"I feel aspirational."

"You were. When Margie got home and found me, I was fucked up and crying. I didn't know where Peter had gone. I didn't know he went for you. How did he know where you were?"

"I told him."

"What?"

"I thought he was an old friend. It's a long story. But please. You were the one who was dead. I can't…" I touched her face gingerly, as if she'd disappear. "I can't even believe you're here."

She pressed my palm to her cheek. "I am. I finally figured out where you were."

"Took you long enough."

"Disappearing takes time."

"I know. And being dead."

"I'm not dead." She sipped her espresso. "So, when Margie came home and saw… it was bad, but I wasn't choking on my own vomit. The idea was to tell you where to meet us. Peter was more scared of prison than anything, and he had plans for it, just in case. So, Margie was going to tell Peter he'd killed me so he'd disappear, then you and I would meet up and just kind of lay low until we were sure he was gone. But she couldn't get him on the phone, and when she called you…"

"He was there."

"She had to choose between your story and his."

"His was the right choice."

"Obviously, but then you went off and…" She rolled her finger in a circle.

"I'm… uh." I ran my fingers through my hair as if trying to comb out my embarrassment. I rarely thought about how I'd killed a man.

"Thank you," she said. "Knowing he's gone, I feel safer."

"How did you find out it was me?"

"Deduction. And Margie. Who got it out of Daddy two months ago."

"Does he know where you are?"

"He knows I'm alive but not where. No one knows but Margie. She gets a real kick out of lying to my father. And there's something mothering about her. She's a nurturer. Like she wants to make up for the way our parents are." She bit her lip. "I have to think about that more. But anyway, we figured the best way to do this was slowly. Use their emotional distance to our advantage. So, we—mostly she—moved money in small bits, and I just kept traveling until I used the new passport and I was gone." She slapped her hands together as if getting dust off them. "No more Carrie. She never had a chance." A rueful grin stretched across her face. "But Marie can be anything she wants."

"What does she want to be?"

"Yours."

"That's it?"

"For now, that's enough."

***

My apartment was two blocks from the plaza. I'd paid cash in British pounds for one room with a balcony and private bath.

I carried her over the threshold like a smitten groom and kicked the door closed. She straightened her legs, and I let her get her feet under her. I put her bag on the chair while she smoothed her dress and looked at the bed.

"Little bird?" I stepped back to give her room. "Don't look like that. We're going to take our time."

"I know."

When she looked back at me, I expected to see nerves or doubt. Maybe guilt for the reasonable notion that we weren't going to tumble into bed.

Instead, she smiled and faced the ceiling with her eyes closed and her arms out. "I just want to hug the world!"

Then she leapt forward and hugged me instead, and I forgot I was ugly and scarred. I was made of what I saw, and with her, all I knew was beauty.

EPILOGUE

SIENA, ITALY - 2000

The hardest thing I ever did—harder than disappearing and staying that way, harder than being away from my family, harder than starting my education from scratch as Marie Laramy-Jefferson—was learning Italian. I had no talent for language, and though I could read and write pretty fluently, Gabriel laughed when I spoke it and told me my accent was just left of Chef Boyardee.

After a few weeks in Venice, we'd found the alley where we had been attacked. Gabriel stood on the cobblestones looking down at where he had been cut. He looked up at the flower boxes and balconies under the slash of blue sky. Finally, he put his hands in his pockets and looked at me.

"I should feel something," he said with a shrug.

"There are no shoulds with feelings."

"Good." He nodded with satisfaction. "Little bird?"

"Yes?"

"Do you miss your family?"

"Do you miss your mother?"

"Yes. But I get to call her sometimes."

"I miss them," I said. "But I'm okay."

He put his arm around me, and we left that alley behind us.

After that, we'd felt free to make a plan. We discussed moving to the UK to avoid the language barrier and decided to take the slow route north. Once we landed in Siena, we fell in love with our lives. The slow evening walks. The church bells. The Palio horse race around the Piazza del Campo that blew rich, red dust over everything. The mild winter and blazing-hot summer. The people gave Gabriel a hard time about his scars in a way that was good-humored and out in the open. He wasn't regarded with suspicion or derision, and I felt strongly that that was a luxury he was entitled to.

Before the year was out, we decided to get married. We'd be Gabriel and Marie Jefferson. Married in a tiny ceremony in Chiesa di San Martino. We were named after a boulevard to the east of USC where the groom had almost been mowed down by the bride's Cognitive professor. The six-lane boundary between our prelude and our story.

We both wanted family at the wedding. His mother knew he was somewhere but not where. Some of my family knew where, but only Daddy and Margie knew why.

We weren't dead to anyone, but we were unavailable indefinitely.

On the one hand, that made us free. On the other hand, we had to cling to each other as if we were the only things holding each other steady in a storm of loneliness and isolation.

In the years since I'd found him, he'd become everything to me. I trusted him. He was gentle. He was kind. He made love to me with a reverence that was both honest and restrained.

I remembered his commanding voice when we were together in college. The way he'd told me how to move, where he wanted me, how to please myself in a way that pleased him. When Peter came along, I'd thought surrender was the best part of sex, so my late husband turned it into the worst part. He took what I wanted and perverted it.

Gabriel knew that. He knew I trusted him, but he didn't offer the commanding voice again. I knew what he had in him, so I waited.

His journey to regain the dominance he'd once had was as long as my journey to trust myself enough to submit to it.

We didn't get a fancy hotel for our wedding night. I was a student, and he was a freelance music teacher and musician. We had neither the excuse nor the need to show off.

The ceremony was small. Almost nonexistent. A few neighbors came for the mass. A Scottish couple drifted in. We did all the traditional things, said all the old-fashioned words. I wore an off-white lace dress and pinned a square of lace to my hair. He looked gorgeous in his tux and bow tie. I couldn't believe I'd landed such a beautiful man.

That night, after wine and dinner, we stumbled into our little apartment, laughing about something or other. Probably my accent or his inability to keep his bow tie straight.

But as I was leaning my hand on the wall to balance myself so I could pull off a heel, his voice came from across the room. Four words cut the space between us like a knife.

"Take it all off."

I stood there with a white shoe dangling from my fingers by the heel, and he stood at the foot of the bed, as unequivocal as his tone. As straight as his demand.

"Gabriel?"

"You've asked me to be the way I was, and I wasn't ready because I knew you weren't. But now you're mine, so if there's a reason you can't take your clothes off right now, say it. If you don't want that man back, for any reason, tell me. Otherwise, this is going to be a lot more fun if you obey."

Not petulant or doubting, not even compassionate. He was in charge. I could refuse, but if I didn't, I was his to command.

I tried not to smile. I was happy he was ready to be fully himself. But mostly, I was happy for me.

"Um, I can't…" I turned around, putting my back to him.

He laid his hands on my neck and, with deliberation, quietly pulled down the zipper

"I have plans." He pulled open the back of my dress and ran his thumb down my spine.

"What kind of plans?"

"Something I was going to do our second night in Venice." He stepped away.

I pushed off the shoulders of the dress and let it drop to the wood floor, naked except for white stockings and panties.

"Turn around," he said from behind me in that singular no-nonsense tone.

When I turned on the ball of my foot, my nipples got hard. His jacket was on, but he'd removed the tie and unbuttoned his shirt. He came close, and when I tried to embrace him, he gently moved my arms to my sides.

"Don't move until I tell you to." He undid his belt and pulled it through the loops.

When the belt clanked, I swallowed hard. Fists clenched at my sides.

I didn't know if I was ready for the belt.

No. I was sure I wasn't.

"Gabriel…"

He tossed the belt on the chair. A useless thing he didn't need anymore.

I breathed out all the tension. I could trust him.

"Yes?" he said.

"Nothing."

"You doing okay?" He caressed my cheek. I tilted my head to meet the cup of his palm.

"Very okay."

"Good. Now lie on the bed."

We'd made love almost every night since we were reunited, but he seemed so different. Not a stranger, but someone I didn't

269

know, or had forgotten, and when he stood over me and looked at my naked body as if he wanted to devour it, my skin tingled for his hunger.

"Lie back and open your legs for me."

The insistence wasn't on the command, but on who I was opening my legs for. Him.

I fell back, and as I lifted my legs, he pulled my knees apart, inspecting what I offered before putting my feet apart on the mattress. He opened the top drawer of the dresser and took out two loops of spare cello strings wound into a circle.

Sitting on the corner of the bed, he kissed my ankle, then tied the string around it.

"I've been thinking for months about how I'm going to play you." He tied a knot and strung me to the footboard. "I've planned every moment. But if you're uncomfortable or you don't feel safe, you can tell me." He ran his hand inside my leg, over my core and down the other side, landing at the free ankle. "Even if you don't, I'll know."

"You're not him."

Having tied the other ankle down, he stood above me and took his jacket off.

"No. Because you're going to like this."

He undressed, taking his time while I tingled with arousal. He needed to pick up the pace. My body wanted to be touched so badly that when he kneeled at the foot of the bed, my back arched to get closer to him.

"Patience," he said, kissing the inside of my ankle. "Patience." My calves, the tender insides of my thigh, he kissed up my belly and sucked my nipples one after the other until my legs pulled against the cords that held me.

"Patience." He wove his mouth down me and between my legs, where I was aching for his touch. His tongue gently probed and found where I was sensitive and swollen. Resisting the binds on my legs grounded me as he brought me to an orgasm that lasted longer than I could hold my breath, clutching his hair in my fists.

"You're magnificent," he said, wiping his chin.

"I can barely breathe."

He untied me and rubbed the indents in the skin of my ankles.

"Are you ready to spend your first night as my wife getting bossed around some more?"

"Yes, please."

"You like it?"

"With you."

"Good. Kneel with your feet under you. Hands on your knees, facing the wall."

I did as he asked. Behind me, something creaked, but before I could look around, he came in front and placed the dresser mirror at the head of the bed. At first, I filled the frame, then he adjusted it so I was half cut off by the edge.

In the mirror, he opened the closet door, where a full-length mirror was nailed to the inside.

"What do you see?" he said.

"My back and half my front."

He put his face next to mine and spoke through the reflection. "Perfect."

I brought my arm up and around his neck, but again he put it back down on my thigh. He reached around me, placing his hands between my closed knees.

"Open up for me. Let me see you."

Before I could do it myself, he'd pulled my knees apart, and between the exposure of the mirrors and the force of his hands, a bolt of heat exploded between my legs.

"Not yet." He smiled as his fingertips grazed inside my thighs while his other hand stroked my nipples. "Don't come until I say."

"Okay."

Gently, he slid his finger along my seam, teasing my body with his touch. "You were always a work of art. Today you became my work of art."

He stood. In the mirror, I saw him go to the dresser and pick up a little jar from the drawer. He unscrewed the top and kneeled behind me again, laying his hand on my back.

"I've wanted to do this for so long. It was the only thing I planned to do before the attack that I never stopped wanting." He drew his finger down the length of my back, leaving something cold and viscous behind. "It was unfinished business. But I couldn't." His hand went away and came back on the other side. "I've had this in the drawer for months, and nothing was stopping me. You would have let me do it." He kneeled on the floor so he could get to the lowest part of my back. "But the longer I waited, the bigger it got. More important than a bedroom game." He screwed the cap back on the jar. "I couldn't mark you until you were mine completely."

When he stepped away, I saw my back in the closet mirror. He'd painted two black curves, one on each side of my back. An S and the reverse of the same shape.

He'd made me into a cello.

"The left one's a little too high," he said to my reflection.

"Next time."

He turned away from the mirror to reply. "Next time."

Kneeling before me on the bed, he pulled me to him, lowering me onto his erection.

In one mirror, my body was an instrument for him to play. In the other, my body was wrapped around his, guiding and protecting us.

Both could be true.

***

There, in Siena, we decided to make a life, and I decided what I wanted to do with mine.

We bought an apartment and settled in. My husband composed under a pen name and taught music at Accademia

Musicale Chigiana while I studied undergraduate philosophy at University of Siena.

He didn't cover his appearance with more than a patch, ever, and he rarely wore it when we were alone together. Some mornings, when I got up first, I'd stare at his peaceful face in the Mediterranean light and wonder at the beauty of each scar. How the skin had healed over his wounds and left a mark to remind me of the miracle of his survival.

In the years that passed, I never stopped being grateful for those scars. I couldn't imagine loving him without them.

On the morning of my graduation, I came out of the bathroom, dressed and ready to go. I pulled my blue gown off the hanger and stepped into it.

"Do you have the cap?" he asked, looking around nervously. He was perfect in an ash-gray three-piece suit he'd had tailored in Milan, with the usual patch over his eye. I thought it made him look dashing and dramatic. He thought it made him easier for strangers to talk to. We were both right.

"On the bed." I wrestled with the gown to find the zipper.

"Hang on," he said, getting on one knee before me. He took the zipper head and stood as he pulled it up to my neck, and he kissed me before he let it go.

"Thank you."

"You look..." He stepped back to see me from head to toe. "Brilliant. Wait. You need your *con lode* stole."

"Next to the cap."

He plucked the thin, yellow stole off the bed and draped it over my neck, smoothing the satin flat against me. "Better."

"I feel bad about this." I touched the honorary sash.

Gabriel and I had been over this a hundred times. Because Marie had no educational history, I'd had to build one. I'd taken night classes that didn't require a previous transcript and gotten letters of recommendation from teachers who thought I was some kind of genius. Gabriel said the fact that—as Carrie Drazen—I'd already learned most of the coursework at USC was mitigated by the years I'd have to spend starting over.

"Was your application to grad school dependent on anything you'd learned before?"

"No, but—"

"And are you now totally caught up?" He adjusted the collar under the robe. "You're starting grad studies with the same education as everyone else?"

"I am."

"And did you not have to ace a bunch of exams in a foreign language?"

"I've had advantages."

"You have." He laid his hands on each side of my jaw, resting his thumbs on my cheeks. I felt the callous on his left thumb. "And you're going to use them to help people who don't have those advantages, right?"

"So?"

"So, can you just enjoy your accomplishments?"

"For you." I turned my face to kiss his palm. "Because it makes you happy."

"It does. Seeing you do what you want with your life makes me happy."

"I wish you could too. We should—"

He kissed me before I could suggest all the things I had before. He could go incognito again. Make records. Do shows. Something to fulfill his dreams.

He'd rejected it all so many times. But I thought I could wear him down. At least force him to express some kind of disillusionment. He never did.

"I'm your husband, and I'm making music," he said. "That's what I love doing. In that order."

Maybe I'd already found the place I thought his disappointments were lurking and found contentment instead.

"Are you sure?" I asked.

He took his hands off my face and picked up his cello case. "I'm sure. Playing in the orchestra behind you while you graduate? It's exactly what I want to be doing." He held out his hand. "Grab your cap."

I got my cap off the bed and took his hand. In a blue gown, I walked with him along the streets of Siena to the university. Our neighbors congratulated me on my accomplishments and my husband for supporting me. We were both more than our names. More than our faces. Both more and less than what we represented to those who looked at our faces or heard his music.

With him, I didn't feel pretty.

I felt complete.

THE END

～

What's going on with Margie?

The end of her story is years after the events with Carrie.

If you're curious about her life, her angst, her final trajectory, don't miss **The Sins Duet**.… FREE in Kindle Unlimited.

Strat. A rock god who walked on air.
Indy. A handsome musician smart enough to live through stardom.
Me, a girl with everything to lose and nothing she wanted to keep.

Get THE SINS DUET!
It's FREE in Kindle Unlimited!

～

Get on the mailing list for deals, sales, new releases and bonus content -
JOIN HERE

My Goodreads fan group is called CD Canaries: join the group!

Facebook fan-run group, go here. Most fun, guaranteed.

Facebook fan page is here. I run this, and it's for official news and announcements.

I'm on Pinterest, Tumblr, Twitter and Instagram with varying degrees of frequency.

My email is christine@cdreiss.com.

ACKNOWLEDGMENTS

Here, in no particular order, I acknowledge not only things that are surprisingly true, but all the ways I fell short, got lazy, or knew better and did what I wanted anyway.

1) It's hard to remember a time before 9/11, when airline passengers didn't need to submit to a cavity search two hours before boarding. A time when you could go to the airport thirty minutes before takeoff and buy a ticket with cash. Sure, there was security. No one wanted planes falling out of the sky. But in the 1990s, airlines were happy to accommodate impulsiveness. You even got to keep your shoes on.

2) Teterboro Airport was not under any kind of construction in 1995.

3) The New York Central Library's psychology section is housed in the Mid-Manhattan branch, not the Stephen A. Schwartzman Building. But lions always win. Ask them.

4) It's unlikely Carrie would have been crossing Jefferson from University Village for a host of reasons, not the least of which is that her classes and preferred parking lot would be on the other

side of campus. But I like Jefferson just because. Also, I visited USC recently on a research reconnaissance mission. The Village has been transformed from a dumpy food court into something— shall we say—cleaner.

5) I was two-thirds of the way through this book when the story of rich parents bribing university coaches to recruit their children broke. I feel remiss in not making it a plot point, but when I tried to approach the issue in the context of Carrie's story, it didn't go anywhere unless I wanted her to have an unearned spot. Not only would her family not make that kind of effort to get her into college, I thought it was important to show she was capable of doing it on her own steam. So that was that. If a story device doesn't pay off, it has to go. That's what the profs at USC taught me in the graduate cinema program where I was admitted after two attempts. No bribes required.

6) The concept of quantum entanglement was born in 1934, but the idea wasn't seriously or effectively studied until the 2010s. So, Emerson wouldn't have been talking about them the way he was in 1993, and there's a 98% chance he's misunderstanding it in its entirety. Which means I am. But I figure he'll say whatever he thinks is going to get him in a pretty girl's pants.

7) New York license plates were pretty fucking complex right around the mid-90s. I did my best, but there's a chance that limo wouldn't have had the numbers *Z1C-136*.

8) I believe the delivery entrance to Lincoln Center is on Amsterdam and Sixty-Third. If you know for a fact that it's different, shoot me an email. Also, the position of the traffic light at this corner is past the lot entrance. So, the limo wouldn't have stopped there. Deal with it.

9) Similarly, for Carnegie Hall, I have no clue where the staff or talent entrance is, but I found a discreet doorway in Google Maps and I used it. If you have some kind of personal knowledge of the correct entrance, let me know.

10) I made up the Caruso and Fischer Fellowships because I

couldn't find awards that did what I wanted them to do. Also, I have a weird thing. I feel like by saying a fictional character won a real fellowship in a certain year, I'm taking away from the real people who earned them. I know that's strange, but a girl has to sleep at night.

11) Actual acknowledgements follow: I hereby acknowledge that Alessandra Torre helped me turn an unwieldy story into a blurb, which she does a few times a year with her own magical, genre-bending books. I acknowledge Jenn and Sarah's Herculean contributions to my PR graphics and promotions, including but not limited to communal squeeing over Hang Le's awesome cover. Cassie and her Gentleman. Meghan, who banged this out with me at a Christmas party. Hat tip to Gabri Canova for her help with Italian. Last, my gratitude goes out to the writers I talk shop with and all the goddesses in my group, especially those who love a good *Game of Thrones* chitchat.

12) The last sex scene exists through the generosity of Liz Berry.

ALSO BY CD REISS

Monica insists she's not submissive. Jonathan Drazen's out to prove otherwise.

COMPLETE SUBMISSION

∾

Theresa Drazen is about to accept a proposition from the most dangerous man in Los Angeles.

COMPLETE CORRUPTION

∾

Margie Drazen has a story and it's going to blow your mind.

THE SIN DUET

∾

Her husband came back from the war with a Dominant streak she didn't know he had.

The complete Edge series

EDGE OF DARKNESS

∾

Adam Steinbeck will give his wife a divorce on one condition. She join him in a remote cabin for 30 days, submitting to his sexual dominance.

The *New York Times* bestselling *Games Duet* in one bundle!

HIS DARK GAME

CONTEMPORARY ROMANCES

Hollywood and sports romances for the sweet and sexy romantic.

Shuttergirl | Hardball | Bombshell | Bodyguard | Only Ever You

Made in the USA
San Bernardino, CA
31 July 2020